<u>Book 3</u>

Oy Vey
in a Manger

To Nancy,

Another couple, a
different story, always
with love ... and I
personally love that
you are still an avid
reader at 95 + 96!
Kudos!
Diane
Janelle

Other Books in the Chronicles of Couplehood Series

Sandwiched Hearts: Julie & Mike
(Fall 2024 release, books one and two merged)

Chronicles of
Couplehood Series

Oy Vey
in a Manger

Kelly & Adam

Mary Becker
Diane St.Cyr Janelle

MOUNTAIN ARBOR
PRESS *a Division of BookLogix*
Alpharetta, Georgia

ISBN: 978-1-6653-0711-6 - Paperback
eISBN: 978-1-6653-0712-3 - eBook

Library of Congress Control Number: 2023918292

⊚This paper meets the requirements of ANSI/NISO Z39.48-1992 (Permanence of Paper)

Blessing on page 112, source: Part of a traditional Jewish blessing translated into English. Blessing on page 112, source: Blessing used for Shabbat, with a paraphrasing from the account of Creation in Genesis, translated into English. Blessing on page 166, source: version of a traditional Jewish blessing used often at Shabbat.

100223

For Jenn, Melissa, and Ashley, who bring love, fun, and joy to life, and for the strong in faith who bring the light of God to a world in desperate need. Peace. Shalom.

—Diane

This book is dedicated to love and all its complexities. Whether you experience genuine love through parental concern or unparalleled romance, hold on tight, for there is no greater gift!

—Mary

We can learn to see each other and see ourselves in each other and recognize that human beings are more alike than we are unalike.

—Maya Angelou

Chapter 1

ADAM

Is love at first sight just an infatuation, or is it soul mate real? It sure felt that way the day I met her! She was perfectly adorable, with those short loose curls in her hair proclaiming a fun personality, and her strut interrupted with an occasional bounce in her step. When she entered my world, I turned and took a long look at her walking toward me. Time slowed to a trickle and her confident attitude made me grin. Our eyes locked, our souls were introduced, and I immediately surrendered to the fact that this young lady was going to have her way with me as well.

Adam smiled as his first encounter with his dog played back in his mind. He put on a light jacket and reached for his keys as he recalled Bo being such a charismatic furball of a puppy. Adam had loved just everything about "her" at first sight! It was over two years ago now.

The canine had actually belonged to an elderly client who was recently widowed. Her husband, knowing he had very limited time left on earth, had given the baby goldendoodle to her so she would have a family member to love and be loved by after his passing. The elderly woman, Mrs. Goldstein, had placed the leashed puppy upon the floor once entering the jewelry store where Adam worked. She and her husband had been regulars there. Adam remembered asking for the dog's name that day, and assumed it was a girl when Mrs. Goldstein told him the name was Angel. His recollection drew an image of himself lightheartedly playing with the little tail-wagger until he asked how Mr. Goldstein was doing. He had been shocked to learn that the man had passed even sooner than the doctor's prediction and, for some strange reason, specifically remembered only then noticing the widow's exhausted, bereaved eyes.

Another flash of memory showed him suddenly standing up from petting Angel, and giving the grieving widow a long hug. He remembered shifting to a more somber tone when he asked how he could help her that day, to which she responded that he was frantically needed in the repair of a diamond that had fallen out of the engagement ring her husband had given her. It had been the symbol of their promised future together but was now a heartbreaking reminder to her that the love of her life, like the gem, had fallen away from existence. Adam remembered Mrs. Goldstein's closing words as if he had heard them yesterday: that their kind of love was a rare treasure sought by many but found by few, and that their bond had been pure love from first sight until the fading light of last sight. *Pure love from first sight until the fading light of last sight.* That description of devotion had struck him. Who wouldn't want that?

Adam grabbed the leash hanging on the hook by the door and Bo, now a grown goldendoodle, instantly came running. Adam crouched, hooked his dog to the torso tether, and rubbed him behind the ears. "Till last sight, you and me. Right, buddy?"

Bo barked his excited response before giving his master licks of approval. Adam stood back up and sighed, still lost in the memory. A long moment had passed before Mrs. Goldstein surrendered to her emotions in the jewelry store and released a sigh of loss. The young pup was getting restless and let out a small yip, so Adam had picked up the little ball of fur and rubbed around her neck as he listened to the elderly widow reminisce. He remembered suddenly feeling warm and wet in the area of his suit's breast pocket. He had looked down to see the evidence of the puppy relieving itself.

"Angel Goldstein! Shame on you!" the elderly woman had reprimanded the inexperienced canine. "Honestly, I know Ruben gave you to me just before he passed so that I wouldn't be lonely, but I am at my wit's end! I am so sorry, Adam, and I will pay to have your clothes dry-cleaned. You can count on that! I never had pets before, and the only reason I accepted Angel was because Ruben had a dog when he grew up and told me it would help fill my heart. I can assure you, it does not! This little one has given me nothing but stress. I mean, who knew a pet could piddle so much on anything and everything? And the licks bathe me in saliva. It just all feels so unsanitary. How does that fill my heart? This puppy is a good intention with bad results!"

"I'll take her," Adam blurted while the object of his affection squirmed.

"Excuse me?" the widow had faltered.

"I mean," Adam continued, "why don't I take the puppy off your hands? That way there's no more stress for you at such a difficult time. I've been wanting to get a dog anyway." The last part was not true, but he figured it was a minor lie that could only help the situation for both of them. Mrs. Goldstein clearly didn't want the canine, and he was in love with it. She quickly agreed, and the two years that followed that moment were filled with nothing but happiness, starting the very next morning at an appointment to have the puppy checked by a local vet. Adam had carefully selected the nearby clinic from a group of online listings and reviews. He recalled not wanting a national chain, and Will's Pet Haven seemed to be a quality-above-quantity kind of place. He approved of what he saw when he arrived with his new little friend to the wellness and shots session.

Adam enjoyed that memory as he locked the door to his rented townhouse and headed down the sidewalk with Bo. "Listen, buddy, this has to be a quick one because I still need to stop at my sister's before I head over to pick up Kelly from the airport. That's right. Our girl will be home soon, and I'm sure you're just as eager as I am! She's the only one I know who spoils you more than I do. Well, her and Sully, I suppose, if I'm going to be totally honest. Anyway, let's be quick about taking care of business this afternoon!"

The dog woofed his unconditional consent to Adam. Its yap brought Adam back to Bo's first visit with the vet. Kelly had been the one who walked out to meet Adam and her new client. Adam remembered how he felt when he first saw Kelly. He might as well have been a fish, because he had instantly fallen for her hook, line, and sinker! He couldn't believe feeling this way, not once but twice in two days! He would never forget that double dose of luck. It had definitely been some type of meshuga wonderful.

"Hi, I'm Kelly. This cutie must be Angel, and that must mean you're Adam." Her lively step had announced to Adam that she was happy in her work. They shook hands but he already wanted more. "I know we entered most of the information over the phone, but there's still a bit more I'll need to put in the system."

"Oh, I can definitely give you more," Adam had stumbled over himself. They walked into the next room to a desk, where Kelly entered the rest of the data she needed. They then proceeded to an open exam room where Kelly placed Angel on a small table.

"Right off the bat, I'm going to guess you're new to owning a dog, and that Angel is *not* an Angel."

"I'm sorry. I don't get what you're saying. You're telling me my dog misbehaves? How can you tell something like that? All you did was lift my puppy a bit. And I did own a dog once when I was little. I mean—"

"No, silly! Angel is a boy, so she is a he. You're going to need a new name unless you're good with a boy named Angel! I noticed right away that he has a mini attachment. I figured you never owned a dog because you didn't check under the hood right away, so to speak."

"I . . . I . . . you're right! I never checked. I was just thrilled to have the little bugger. Thanks for that piece of information." Adam remembered the red warmth that had come to his cheeks. "So far, you've proven yourself to be quite a skilled vet!"

"Thanks. I do try to nail down the basics right out of the gate," Kelly had smirked. Her wry but inviting humor continued throughout the preliminary session and her ability to toss quips back and forth had enticed him to flirt with her. It had been one of the first things he liked about her. Adam also remembered thinking she was somehow different than all the others before her. He had studied her attractive body throughout the remainder of the appointment, from the wisps of hair that framed her face to the slight dimple in her cheek and the slender curves of her body.

He had been caught off guard when she abruptly

reached for additional wipes from the counter next to him. She had brushed up against his arm and he remembered reflexively apologizing before she shifted back to her work. Kelly had offered her own mea culpa, explaining that the clumsy sideswipe was a product of her overly swift movement. She then inquired if he always apologized for everything that quickly. He remembered making her laugh with his response. "Well, you see, I'm Jewish. Guilt and I go together like a fiddler and a roof."

Kelly had responded by sharing that she was a Catholic. "I used to feel guilty about everything until I decided to give up guilt for Lent one year. It was so wonderful that I decided to make that Lenten sacrifice a perpetual one."

"Well, look at us laughing at our faiths. You'll have to answer to God for that, and I'll have to answer to my mother!" The banter continued until the puppy's initial exam was completed and his shots were given. Adam jumped at the opportunity to make the appointment for his puppy's next wellness visit. He had left the clinic that day wanting to know more about this vet named Kelly, but he had not been willing to take the bold plunge of asking her out. That's what second visits were for, if well-timed. Or so he had thought. Adam exited his memory and turned his attention to the goldendoodle.

"Woof!" Bo had finished his business and alerted Adam to another walker and dog coming down the street.

"You're a good buddy, Bo, for keeping an eye out like that, but we don't have to worry. We're turning around and heading back home so I can get my errands done and go get our Kelly. Isn't that right, buddy. Huh?" He patted his pet and thought about his parents. "I'll tell you what we have to worry about, boy. My parents! They're not going to do well with a Catholic girl. And I don't think my mom's going to be fair. Poor Kelly is going to be fighting harder than a one-legged man in an ass-kicking contest. That I'm sure of, but I can't tell her that and possibly scare her away." The dog licked Adam's hand as if to console him. "But I'm thinking, maybe, just maybe, Mom will meet her match this time. So we'll just have to wait and see how it goes, you and me! C'mon. Let's go."

The pair made their way back home as Adam morphed himself back into his memories of Kelly and the beginning of their story as a couple. It had been the very next day after Bo's first vet visit when Adam had decided on Bo's name, short for Boaz. It was a great Hebrew name and had scored highly with Adam's parents, the self-ordained Jewish ambassadors to the US. They had stated his choice reflected a great Hebrew wisdom. "You must always be proud of where and who you come from, my *gut zun*! People can take much from you but never your story, your heritage, your soul. Never forget that, or I will have to die that very same day!"

On that fateful day two years ago, Adam was afraid Boaz would destroy the carpets in his townhouse, especially since he kept tinkling whenever he was afraid or nervous. So Adam had brought the puppy to work with him at Dan's Fine Jewelry Store. He had packed his car with a doggy bed, some food, a couple of chew toys, and a water bowl. So far Bo was sticking close to him, so how hard would it be to have him at work for a day or two? Besides, Adam wasn't primarily assigned to the sales floor that day. He had been scheduled as a backup person, doing mostly repair work, starting with Mrs. Goldstein's ring, which he had promised to rush for her.

After arriving at the store, Adam had set up all of Bo's items so he could happily play and nap next to Adam at a large station where his coworker, Sam, was sitting. Once the other employees had enjoyed a few minutes with the adorable puppy, he was placed in his basket and went about the chore of attacking his toys in sporadic order. Adam remembered taking out Mrs. Goldstein's job bag from the store's client vault at that time. As he walked toward the repair station, he manipulated the loupe that was hanging around his neck to inspect the piece more closely.

Fourteen-carat yellow gold three-stone diamond ring. Nicely fashioned. Much older. Okay. Larger center diamond is the one that fell out. He had emptied the remaining contents from the miniature velvet pouch onto the work counter. *And there's the diamond. Other two look fine but need cleaning.*

Adam had then seen a Hebrew inscription of Numbers 6:24. He remembered the commendation: *"May G-d bless you and guard you."* *Okay. So ole Ruben wanted to make sure his bride-to-be was protected with an amulet for an engagement ring, until it became his personal duty. Nice touch, Ruben. A rare treasure does need to be protected! Nice ring, but I don't think we created this one.*

"Hey, Adam. We have a breakout!" Sam alerted him to the basket escapee that was no longer by his master's feet.

"Bo!" Adam placed the loose diamond on its pouch. "I see you're getting comfortable and brave." He scooped up the canine and apologized to his coworker, explaining how he hadn't had enough time to arrange for doggy daycare yet. Adam remembered putting Bo back onto the memory foam bed within the basket and then placing some small jerky sticks to keep him busy chewing. "You stay there while I look up the Goldsteins' customer history with us."

Adam walked over to a laptop and researched his client's long history with the store. Not only had they purchased pieces and had them created, but the couple had also referred many friends and neighbors to the business. Adam had run through the list of pieces twice but had been unable to locate the specific ring he was working on at the moment. He had decided that, even though this piece came from outside the store, this repair was going to be on the house for Mrs. Goldstein. It was the least they could do for her. He had then closed the laptop and turned around to receive a visual jolt. Bo was *on* the counter of the repair station with something in his mouth! Adam rushed toward the puppy.

"Yeah, Adam, little Bo came visiting again and went as far as the showroom, so I placed the little guy on the counter to prevent him from doing that anymore," Sam had explained. "You seemed deeply entrenched in your research so I thought I'd wait to tell you. No place to go on a high counter, right? You should call him something like Marco Polo, though. He's a natural explorer, that one."

Adam had been relieved to see Bo was okay. He picked him up and thanked Sam without sharing his thoughts about the inane and shortsighted idea of placing any type of infant on a high counter.

"What am I going to do with you while I work? You're not making my introduction to parenthood easy at all!" Adam looked down at the puppy's bed and noticed the treats were wet but still sitting on the foam cushion. "Nice treats like that and you didn't like them? At the price I paid, you and I should both like them! So now what am I to do with you? I've got to get this ring and two other pieces repaired!"

Adam had searched his surroundings for an idea that would keep the puppy at bay long enough for him to finish his work. His eyes swept back and forth across the room.

After a few minutes, they rested upon the miniature velvet bag on the counter and took on a new focus. Where was the loose ideal-cut diamond with its beautiful scintillation? It was no longer sitting on the pouch that itself now looked somewhat wet and chewed.

At once it became the new alarming object of Adam's search. He inspected every inch of the counter, the doggy bed, and nearby floor. He extended his search to any reachable destination for a rolling diamond. The centerpiece gemstone for Mrs. Goldstein's antique engagement ring was nowhere to be found! Panic set in as Adam slowly set his gaze upon his newly adopted puppy. They looked at each other in lingering silence. Bo had licked his chops then and let out a soft woof as if to say, "Yeah, good buddy, I did! I did exactly what you're thinking!"

Oh no. No! NO! What should I do? Crap! Tell me this isn't happening! Wait—that's it! I'll get it back when he takes a crap! But how long will that take? I promised Mrs. Goldstein I'd rush it for her. What if she calls? What should I say? You'll get it when crap happens?

Adam remembered letting out a long sigh. His mind had continued racing.

What if the diamond cuts him inside? What if he bleeds to death internally? What do I tell her? Yes, Mrs. Goldstein, your late husband's gift died before crap ever happened! Damnit! Think, THINK! I wish I was an expert on pet emergencies. Wait! I'll call that cute sexy vet we saw yesterday. Not the best impression I want, but I don't care at this point. I need to save myself; I'll worry about everything else later! They accept emergencies and her name's Kelly so I'll ask for her. Adam had called the clinic just as Bo gave him a small lick of support. He shook his head at Bo. "Let's hope Kelly can help us make crap happen quickly, buddy!"

It turned out that Kelly had answered the phone and, after hearing the whole story, generously offered to take care of the issue during her lunch hour, seeing as the clinic was fully booked. Adam had arrived at the designated time and had brought the culprit with him.

"So you're a jeweler, huh?" Kelly asked as she looked over her canine patient. "Well, I know you think Boaz is a real gem of a pet and a diamond in the rough, but I think you need to find something better to feed him."

"Hmm. A vet *and* a comedian. Do you write all your own material?"

"Nope. Sometimes my clients' owners provide the material themselves." Kelly handled the young pup gently as she squeezed eye drops into the center of his eye.

"Looks to me like you're working on the wrong end, doc."

Kelly laughed and shook her head. "When a dog comes in that has eaten something they shouldn't, I first give a medicine that I put directly in the eye that will induce vomiting. It usually happens in about ten minutes. Nothing more I can do for you right now, so I'll be back to check on you and Bo in a few."

After what seemed an eternity to Adam with no productivity on Bo's part, Kelly returned. Seeing there was no progress, she reached for a canine suppository. "This should do the trick."

She inserted the laxative pellet into the goldendoodle while it looked at Adam as if to point out his guilt in the matter. "Now you'll wait until he presents you with a gift, along with the return of your gem. Should happen by tonight. Happy diamond hunting!"

Adam had removed Bo from the table and held him in his arms. "So, doctor and comedian Kelly, seeing as you're saving me professionally and I provided you with your humorous material today, I was hoping I could provide you with dinner as well. Make it a lucky three-pack. May I take you out for dinner tomorrow night, if you're not already attached to someone? It seems like tonight I'll be busy hunting."

"Thanks, I accept the invitation . . . for the dinner date, that is. You can hunt alone, and, um, see how things come out with that event. Time?"

"Seven okay? Would you also like me to call you when 'crap happens' with Bo?" Adam remembered how much he had enjoyed his preliminary flirting with Kelly.

"Tell you what. Call me if it becomes too much crap for you to handle. And seven's good." She had grinned at her own retort before they exchanged numbers and her address. They finished the business end of the appointment and Adam thanked Kelly again for helping him rush his potential problem along, and for agreeing to a first date. He had left Will's Pet Haven thinking that, whether or not crap happened, the outcome was a good one. After all, the following night had become the first of many dates over the last two years.

Adam's moment of happiness returned to the present task at hand so he could leave on time. He carefully removed two exquisite art pieces from the wall of the extra room in his townhouse and wrapped them with sheets before carrying them to the trunk of his Yafah LX. He had purchased both of them on his last trip to Israel. They were an expensive purchase for him but well worth it. His older sister by two years, Sarah, would be waiting for the items this afternoon so she could plan their placement for the upcoming holidays. She adored the two art objects and always borrowed them for important family gatherings.

Sarah made their parents equally proud on the "Hebrew meter," as Adam called it. She was married to a rabbi, Rabbi Joel Weinberg to be exact. She had also blessed his parents with three grandchildren and pleased them by decorating her home with several Judaic pieces. The items he had placed in the trunk needed to be dropped off at Sarah's house that afternoon in order to satisfy her OCD tendencies—and she was not a last-minute person at all. Adam didn't mind because it meant more uninterrupted time with Kelly before his girlfriend met his parents for the first time, and of all places, at his perfectly faith-shining sibling's home. It was going to be interesting, to say the least.

Adam returned one last time to the inside of the townhouse, refreshed his cologne application, checked on Bo, and locked the door. As he entered his car, he thought again of the Goldsteins and their relationship with each other.

Does Kelly think we have the same kind of love? I think we do. Yeah, we have that rare treasure. Especially the way we're crazy about each other, even with our two different religions. I really need to take the next step to keep that treasure. But first we have to get past my parents. Well, Adam, you're a salesman, so you need to sell it. Ha! Biggest sell ever! If only I could know their responses ahead of time, then I could plan my selling strategy around it.

It was not a long drive and Atlanta traffic had cooperated remarkably with his goal of fulfilling his sister's wish before getting to Hartsfield–Jackson Airport on time. Adam touched the mezuzah at the entryway to Sarah's home and kissed his hand before she opened the door and chirped, "Well, hello there, stranger." He carried in the two art pieces. "I thought we would see more of you with

Kelly gone, but I guess you were too busy for your own family."

"Ah. Another line, another day closer to becoming our dear mother. Good for you!" he countered before giving his sister a soft peck on her cheek. They both laughed and Sarah showed him where to place the stained-glass panes. As Adam positioned them, the cell phone in his back pocket buzzed and his sister grabbed it.

"What's the code? I'll answer it so you don't rush and break those beautiful investments of yours," Sarah offered. Adam was never sure if it was a client calling, seeing as he owned a company phone, so he shared his password and his sister answered the ringing. "Hello, Adam's phone . . . Oh! Yes, it's Sarah. I was just answering it for him while he moved a couple of things for me . . . We're at my place. Hold on." Sarah looked at her brother, who had finished carefully placing the glass panes. "It's Mom," she mouthed.

Adam waved his arms and shook his head as he mimed a resounding *NO! NOT NOW!*

"Well, I thought he was still here, Mom. He must be if *his phone* is still here. Maybe he walked into the other room. Hold on while I go get him." Sarah stared at her brother the whole time. She muted the phone before explaining to him, "Okay, Adam, so apparently it's someone from your past who, with great pain, gave birth to you, raised you, and sacrificed totally everything without demanding a single thank-you so you could have whatever you wanted in life. Can you guess who it is and talk to her at all, or am I going to continue being the better one who never broke her heart?"

"You will pay dearly for this." Adam gave Sarah a scolding grin before taking the phone. His sister beamed after sticking out her tongue at him. The conversation, however, was a quick one as he made excuses for not being able to chat with his mother, Freida Cohen. She complained to him that he never seemed to have time for her now that he had this Kelly girl. Adam protested the accusation. "Mom, it's not *now* that I have her. We've been seeing each other for two years! Plus, you know I'm excited you and Dad are going to meet her for Hanukkah this year. She's great. You'll love her. Hey, speaking of Kelly, I have to run to the airport to pick her up right now. We'll talk at Hanukkah, Mom. Say hi to Dad."

"Wait! Is she at least Jewish, Adam, my sweet son who wouldn't even begin to consider breaking his dedicated loving Mame's heart? Tell me she's Jewish. Is she?" his mother inquired as she had done before in the past. There was silence.

Adam didn't know how to answer without starting something. Panic set in. *Think quick!* He looked at Sarah, who threw up her shoulders and gave him an *I'm sorry but I'm glad it's you and not me* look. "Hello. Mame? What did you say? You're — —- up. I can't — — — — stand what — —- saying. Reception doesn't — — — — — here. Hello?"

"Hello, Adam. Hello!" his mother responded. "I'm—"

"Hello! Mame?" Adam faked.

"HELLO ADAM! I'M HERE! OY VEY! I hate these phones!"

He hung up on the conversation knowing he had just postponed the inevitable battle.

"No wonder I'm the good child," Sarah teased.

"You always were," Adam conceded. "I really do have to go, though. Traffic has been good so far today, but you know how that works. The Lord giveth and the Lord can taketh away at any moment."

"Hanukkah is going to be a real showstopper this year.

You and I both know that, my friend. She's either going to kill you or herself before she lets you marry a shiksa. Well, at least you had a good childhood." Sarah patted her brother on the shoulder.

"My childhood was great until I wanted to grow up and our mother wouldn't let me. That's the problem. She'll never be happy with anyone I choose."

"You act like Mom enjoys annoying you and giving you guilt trips."

"Are you kidding me? Our mother doesn't just enjoy giving guilt trips. She runs the entire travel agency that co-ordinates them!"

"At least you grew up with Dad on your side. So that helped," Sarah offered.

"Are you kidding me? He was too busy pricing out our childhood. He's probably going to hand us a bill on his deathbed. And that's okay, because then I'll give it to you, seeing as you're the good child," Adam teased.

"That might be sooner than you think with Hanukkah just around the corner!"

They gave each other a goodbye hug before Adam left for the airport. He easily navigated the Israeli sports car out of her driveway, through the city, and onto the highway. Adam couldn't help but sport a large grin. His other half would soon be in his arms and life would be almost perfect again.

Once he arrived at the airport terminal, he carefully chose a spot to park the Yafah LX, attempting to lessen the chance for any potential dings or scratches. Adam then locked the sports car and rushed to the airport's baggage area to claim his love. Never again, if possible, did he want her to be away from him.

Chapter 2

KELLY

Never again . . . Never again . . . Never again . . . Kelly's thoughts were in sync with the steady rhythm of the train as it raced toward baggage claim. The business trip back to her old California stompin' grounds had held such promise. She'd pictured a perfect seven-day combination of connecting with fellow veterinarians at the convention and then with college buddies. *Never thought seeing old friends would cause such drama! I'd never have stayed the extra time if I'd known what was going to happen. Never again. Nope!*

The train jerked ever so slightly as it came to a stop. People were already jockeying for a position to exit and began to sway in response to the unwelcome syncopation. Kelly was thankful she was seated.

"Welcome aboard the Plane Train. The next stop is for T Gates. T, as in Tango."

I wish it was J Gates. J, as in Joey, the jerk! I'd just toss him off this train and Homeland Security his ass! What an arrogant moron he was at that Christmas Party.

Her teeth gently pinched the left corner of her lower lip. All through high school and college she had thought Joey would be her one and only. Now, even though several years had passed since their brutal breakup, Kelly's soul once again felt the blistering wound created by her very first ex-boyfriend. His final words to her from years ago reappeared like an LED billboard in her cerebrum: "I can't handle this kind of drama. I am out of here and out of this relationship."

Kelly closed her eyes as she thought back to that incident. *What kind of a guy holds your hand while you're recovering from a horrific car accident that kills your parents, then helps you settle their estate, supports you through the manslaughter trial of a drunk-driving teen, and then arranges to go to counseling with you, only to flee five minutes into the first session, saying that he is done with the relationship because he can't handle the drama? It doesn't make sense! Hartsfield-Jackson Airport definitely needs a J Gate!*

Months after that enlightening counseling session, she had done what was necessary and pulled the bandage off their traumatized relationship by moving from Los Angeles to Atlanta. It had been the logical choice, seeing as all her remaining family called Georgia home. It just had not been an easy change for Kelly. Leaving friends and familiarities normally poses the greatest challenge when moving, but surprisingly that was not the case. The biggest drawback was being landlocked in the Atlanta metroplex. Lake Lanier just didn't compare to the Pacific Ocean! Kelly had hoped that by going to the convention in LA she would collect a multitude of coastal experiences and be able to store up enough to last her till she had another opportunity to return. Now she wished she had kept her distance from LA.

Kelly retrieved her cell phone from the outside zippered pocket of her carry-on. She hoped to see a response to the text message she'd sent that her plane had landed, but there was no reply. Sighing, she returned the mobile device to the pocket.

"Welcome aboard the Plane Train. Please hold on. This train is departing."

Kelly was thankful her trip was winding down. The flight from Los Angeles to Atlanta was more than four hours in length. Add the necessary early-airport arrival to ensure getting through security in a timely manner, the unexpected departure delay due to an unusually severe thunderstorm, plus the three-hour time difference, and she was ready to be home.

"The next stop is for domestic baggage claim and ground transportation."

Kelly sensed fatigue taking hold. The last thing she wanted was to be too exhausted to spend time with Adam. This was only the second instance they'd been apart for any length of time since they began dating over two years ago, and she had truly missed him.

"Please hold on. This train is stopping. Please collect your belongings and watch your step as you exit."

Kelly reached down to grasp her carry-on. When the train came to a full stop, she took her place in line with the mob, and together they navigated toward the escalator. It was obvious tonight that any concept of group etiquette was missing. Every individual moved at a frenzied pace as if they were salmon swimming upstream. Kelly turned left toward the south terminal and approached carousel number three, scanning the crowd for Adam's friendly smile. The carousel began to move with luggage cascading down from its chute. *Where's my luggage? I don't see it!* The carousel continued to rotate, with no metallic pink suitcases in sight. Kelly stood there as one traveler after another grabbed his luggage. *Where in the heck are my bags?*

They better not be lost! I don't want to deal with that crap. C'mon! Heaven answered her on cue with the appearance of her pink hardscapes.

As she retrieved her last piece, her phone rang.

"Hi Aunt Julie. How are you?"

"Well, hello, sweetheart. I really thought I was going into your voicemail. Are you already back from your trip? I figured you'd still be on the plane."

"Just got in. I'm at the airport and Adam's not quite here yet."

"Well, I don't want to tie up the line in case he's trying to call you." Kelly suppressed her impulse to laugh. *She still forgets cell phones are totally different from landlines!* "I guess I'll just get straight to the point. I need to ask a favor."

"Everything okay, Aunt Julie?" *She never asks a favor . . .*

"I think so . . . I just got a call from Elizabeth and it looks like that Christmas baby is going to arrive earlier than anyone expected, except me of course!" Kelly could detect her aunt's excitement. "You know I always wanted a Christmas baby, and a Christmas grandbaby is even better! Anyway, Uncle Mike and I are going to be leaving town early and won't be available to be with GG on Christmas Eve. Any chance you could fill in for us?"

Without giving it a thought, "Of course I will" proceeded out of Kelly's mouth.

"Are you sure? I don't want to spoil any of your plans."

"No problem, Aunt Julie. You know I love GG and all her crazy cotton-swab friends." Kelly grimaced. Her nickname for white-haired senior citizen ladies had slipped out before she even realized it was coming. "Sorry, Aunt Julie. I know you don't like that expression."

"That's okay, sweetheart. All those walker-pushing ladies do share a resemblance, if I do say so myself." Kelly could hear an underlying smidgen of laughter. "Anyway, you'll plan on going to midnight mass at six o'clock on Christmas Eve, then?"

Kelly rolled her eyes as she shook her head. *Midnight Mass at six o'clock.* "You've got it, Aunt Julie. I'll be there."

"Thank you, Kelly! Gotta go. Something on my phone just beeped, so I need to see what thingy it is on my screen. Love you, bye!"

"Bye," Kelly replied, even though she knew her aunt had already disconnected. She decided to check for any updates from Adam and was happily surprised by the familiar voice that whispered a favorite verse into her right ear.

"And you're so fair, my lovely lass, and so deep in love am I . . ."

She turned her head to meet the breath that carried the murmured melodic words and joined in completing the next two lines:

"That I will love you still, my dear, till all the seas run dry."

"I was just waiting for you to finish your call." Adam smiled and Kelly threw her arms around him. As Adam drew Kelly closer to his chest, she could feel herself melting into him. *Oh Adam, rescue me from terrible memories. Hold me . . . hold me like this forever.*

Time stood still until Kelly felt Adam's fingertips under her chin. As he lifted her lips to meet his, he shifted his stance to bring about a full-body embrace. He kissed her softly at first, but soon it became an intoxicating connection. As he pulled his face away from hers, she looked into his wistful yet flirtatious eyes and smiled.

Adam was the first to speak. "So you did have some downtime to miss me after all," he teased.

"Unfortunately, yes."

"What does that mean?" He released her with a look of concern. "Do you mean your love of continuing ed was not satiated, or that reuniting with your college buddies flatlined? Or is it something worse?"

"Nothing worse. Actually, the continuing ed classes were outstanding and spending time with my friends was great. I'll explain the 'unfortunate' later, just not now." As Kelly continued to connect with Adam's soulful eyes, she could see a sliver of reassurance. "Believe me, you have nothing to worry about."

"Good to know, doc. Now, let's get outta here!" Adam grinned as he passed her the carry-on and grasped the handles of the two large suitcases in each hand. As they headed toward the hourly parking garage, the twinkle in his eyes put a smile in her heart.

I am so glad to be home!

Chapter 3

ADAM

Adam turned the key and the Yafah LX roared to life while Kelly settled into her seat. He enjoyed driving the powder-blue coupe but only drove it on special occasions. Originally purchased by his parents as an investment and then given to him upon his graduation from business college, it was the only sports car line ever made in Israel. Adam knew his parents had been genuinely proud of his achievement and, as always, a very special and Israeli-made gift had ensued. They believed the chance to possess a rare homeland collectible was somehow a direct blessing bestowed upon a Jewish person from God Himself! Adam was keenly aware what the gift meant to them, so this, in and of itself, was why he cherished the 1964 coupe.

He had shared the insight with Kelly because it was important for her to understand that no one, absolutely no one, was more Jewish American in spirit than his parents. Freida Cohen, especially, was not the average beloved Jewish American mother. She viewed everything with vivid blue-and-white-shaded glasses and lived in the current world with opinions stuck in the nineteen fifties. This would be an important key for Kelly to use in unlocking the pathway to life with the Cohens. His girlfriend clicked the buckle on her seatbelt.

"Ready for my royal ride home in my prince's special carriage, complete with added safety belts. Glad my return made the Yafah LX cut."

Adam had mentioned at one point that the car originally had no seatbelts. These had to be retrofitted so people could legally travel in the vehicle. "My lady deserves the best of what I own. I hope my kindness and servitude shall be repaid later this evening." He wiggled his eyebrows.

"You're lucky your lady is extremely happy to be home, so we shall see what we can do about repayment, although it is in great competition with my royally tired-ass jet lag."

Kelly's quip entertained him as she stepped right into the role of his smart-alecky princess. It was one of the fun things about her that he loved so dearly. Adam's eyes met hers and he smiled. "I missed you like crazy." They kissed, and the touch of their lips made him burn with desire.

Kelly interrupted the tantalizing moment of intimacy. "Look at me already rewarding your duty before you've even started. What kind of seat-belted pushover princess am I?"

"The sexiest and best kind," Adam proclaimed as he navigated the garage lanes and pulled up to an automated machine. Kelly leaned her head back and closed her eyes. Adam placed the receipt in a small tray between the bucket seats because the coupe had no glove compartment. It came from a simpler time and had no place to store anything. *No interior storage . . . nothing to focus on but the here and now. I should take a lesson from this Yafah LX.*

Adam made his way into the mainstream traffic outside the airport. He was glad Kelly was back in Atlanta with him, especially after some terrible ending that supposedly ruined a great time in California. She had somehow crossed paths with her ex, Joey, and some annoying wife of his, JoJo. Kelly had sounded so angry over the phone! *What was it she ranted? Something about this Joey who apparently couldn't commit himself to a life with anyone at all, or even to what type of bagel he wanted in the morning. And how could he ever propose to a ditzy person like that JoJo chick and be engaged after just a year together, with his lengthy track record? Who cares! I'm just glad they split, cuz Kelly's mine now! Wonder how it all went down. If he did something to her . . .*

"Hey, Kell, tell me about your trip. I know you didn't want to talk about whatever happened at that party you ended up going to last night," Adam queried. "You had said something on the phone that you ran into your ex? I say you run into him again and again until he stays down." He looked over at Kelly and, seeing no visible response, added, "Ooh. Good joke. Tough crowd."

"Ha! I'll tell you what a good joke is—Joey!" Kelly retorted. "My ex is married now. Can you believe it? And he's obnoxious about it!"

"If you say it, I believe it," Adam humored her.

"No. Seriously," Kelly insisted. "For years we dated. Then we finally broke up over his inability to commit to any level of anything at all. Now don't get me wrong, I'm glad we did because I wouldn't have met you if we hadn't . . . and you're way better than him any day. But what kills me is that after years of dating, getting through all the issues with my parents' deaths, and then our dramatic breakup, we then run into each other and he makes it all sound like I was the problem."

Adam countered, "Well, maybe you can look at it this way. We're all puzzle pieces. You and Joey didn't create the big picture because your pieces didn't go together.

Now you, my *duvshanit*, you and I are putting ours together to see what beautiful picture we can create. So we'll
let him enjoy his puzzle and we'll enjoy our own. Better to
let it go, right?" He offered her an inquiring smile. "What
do you say?"

"I say amen to that! And I love being your duvshanit."
Kelly smiled. She had worked hard on her Jewish vocab-
ulary since she had entered Adam's life, and her use of the
term, meaning honey, was appealing to him. She took his
extended hand and he caressed the top of hers with his
thumb. Just being together again would hopefully assuage
the bitterness for her ex that had leaked out and exposed
itself all over her injured esteem.

"My little duvshanit puzzle-maker, I missed you!" This
time he gave her hand a gentle squeeze and returned to
driving with both hands on the steering wheel. His analogy
was a wise one he had overheard at a different place and
time, and this was the moment to share it. Adam intuitively
knew how to make his soul mate feel better, as did she, and
this was the essence of the fabric in which their relationship
was clothed. It created that unexplainable, exhilarating
feeling people naturally experience when they are with "the
one." Adam knew they had it. Kelly knew they had it. Now
he needed his parents to know it, but that dreaded task was
for another day.

Kelly responded, "I missed you too, babe, and I am so
psyched to be back in town. The trip was great overall and
so was the convention. Just had a bad ending to the trip,
you know? Anyway, what are we doing for dinner? Eat
out or bring something home?"

They discussed their options and decided to go with
eating takeout at home. Once they were north of Atlanta,
Adam pulled off the highway and stopped at their favorite

Chinese place. It was a hole in the wall, but the food was fast and fantastic. They entered the restaurant and Kelly visited the restroom while Adam placed an order; she had no preference as to what they ate as long as it was hot and entering her stomach soon. Adam waited and then paid for their meal, picking up two large brown bags.

"Did they include double the amount of fortune cookies?" Kelly was back from the restroom.

"Yes, ma'am! Are we ready to head to your place with this lovely feast? Or my place? Your call," Adam offered.

"Hmm. Make it my place. I better text the girls ahead of time to make sure they're not having a bunch of people over to hang. I'm not in a group mood. I just want to eat and go to bed."

"Not even in the mood for me?" Adam pleaded with a silly pout.

"I'm always in the mood for you!" Kelly flirted as she finished a quick text to her roommates. "Okay. That's done. Let's head out and we'll end up at your place or mine once they answer."

They exited the restaurant and returned to the powder-blue coupe. As the motor roared to life once more, Kelly exclaimed, "OMG! It smells so good. I'm tempted to eat it right here and now!"

Adam chided her playfully. "All good things come to she who waits! And *you* need to wait! Besides, my parents will probably drop dead right on the spot if they see any crumbs in this car when they come to visit. Like I said, this graduation gift is a big deal in my family, coming straight from Israel and all."

Kelly grinned. "Yes, I seem to have heard a small rumor to that effect. I actually can't wait to meet them! I know you've told them all about me, too, your wonderful khavera. See? Girlfriend, khavera. I've been learning some basic Hebrew and some Yiddish. I mean, I know I'll be a shiksa, *but* I'm sure they'll realize I'm a wonderful khavera too! Then we'll be fine, especially if you've told them how happy we are together, even with our different faiths. You have told them all about me by now, right?" She poked Adam's side and playfully tugged at his belt.

"I'-m-m-m almost there." Adam defended his body against her short jabs.

Kelly stopped. Her eyes searched his face for visual clues. "Almost there? What is this? A journey of a thousand miles? Just tell them already and get past it. So what if you're Jewish and I'm Catholic?"

Adam began, "You don't understand how hard this will be for them. They're still somewhat old-fashioned. Their son is dating a—"

"No! Don't say it!" Kelly interrupted. "Not a . . . CATHOLIC GIRL! Oh the shame! The horror! The leprosy of living with two faiths! They're breaking out in a religious rash already! Somebody get the Yiddish cream!"

Adam hit the brakes as the frenzy of heavy Atlanta traffic interchanging lanes created hiccups in its movement. A short alert sounded right on time, as if to emphasize Kelly's words and the Yafah LX's sudden stop.

Adam took a deep breath. "I love you, babe. Nothing's going to change that. The only thing I have left to tell them about is your faith. But you have to understand. They're older; they're a different generation and I'm their only son." He jerked the wheel to the right and steered the accelerating LX coupe into a different lane.

"You might be their only son, but you're not alone in this. Remember that. We've got this together, you and me.

Okay? Tell them soon, before I return to ashes and end up floating around in Shiksa Limbo sipping Catholic wine and looking for Yiddish cream." Kelly looked down at her phone. "We're good for my place. Girls are there but they're not expecting anyone tonight."

"Got it." Adam changed lanes once again. "I love you, you know. And I'll find the right time to tell them in person. Be ready, though, because I guarantee you there will be pushback."

Kelly leaned in toward Adam. "I can handle their push."

"But what if you can't?" He followed a line of cars leaving the highway toward the city of Sandy Springs and brought them to the right-turn-only lane.

"I don't know. I'll set my hair on fire and tell them I'm a burning bush. They're Jewish. That should get their attention and respect! Then I'll order them to like me. Heck, they might even take off their shoes for me."

The light turned green and Adam turned onto a multilane main artery of the congested commercial area. "You are incorrigible. You're funny, but you're incorrigible!" He shook his head and laughed.

Adam loved Kelly's red hair that was currently swept up with a large clip in such a way that its slightly loose curls had no choice but to dangle here and there. He felt the style suggested she was a decent person with just a hint of naughty. He loved her laugh, her dimple, her deep blue eyes. They were just going to have to make things work, because he couldn't see himself with anyone else. This woman next to him made his heart beat faster with wild yet calculated abandon, the product of too many tragedies and a cluster of heartbreaking moments. Adam knew he had planted a seed of hope at the very center of her soul, and he could tell how it was growing by leaps and bounds from their first months together. He loved their story, the relationship they had nurtured for each other, the couple they wanted to be instead of what the world dictated.

Kelly interrupted his thoughts. "I'm not incorrigible. I'm hungry! What did we get? Damn, it smells so good."

Adam declared, "You, my dear, are going to be dining on some mighty fine crab rangoon . . . some fried rice . . . spring rolls . . . shrimp stir fry—"

"Of course shrimp is included! What is with shrimp in my universe lately?"

Adam was lost. "What's up with shrimp? We've had it before."

"That's right! I didn't share the whole Smidgee fiasco with you yet. Well, let me fill you in," Kelly declared. "Okay, when I was invited to the crazy party at the end of my trip, it was with some of the people that I hung out with while I was with Joey. I didn't want to risk running into him, and I even asked my old roommate, Brittany, ahead of time if Joey was going to be at that Christmas party. She said that he wasn't. So I'm at the party, and who shows up but the jerk himself with this bimbo JoJo and he brags to me that they're newlyweds. She's all giggly and saying things like, 'He's Joe and I'm JoJo. See? It was fate all along. Even our names are the same!'

"They both went on and on as if they were the original creators of fate and love. I should have insisted on leaving right away when my gag reflex went into overtime but I was kind of trapped. At one point, when I was able to break away for a bathroom run, I found out that Brittany's sister Brooke decided to play cupid and match them up. When I asked Brooke why she would hook up a known ex with a different friend, she said, 'Hey. He's good-looking, so why waste a good-looking guy? Besides, it had a great ending.' Talk about shallow and trashy!"

"Shallow for sure," Adam agreed. "Wanna be good-looking and trashy with me tonight? You've got the good-looking part down already." He smirked.

"Hold on, hold on!" Kelly interjected, ignoring the invitation. "There's more! So I'm getting my jacket and purse, but I run into Joey and JoJo again. This time he made a dig about our relationship. I was looking down at some snack bowls and candies when he said it and I decided to be the one to take the high road. I coolly looked up from the treats, handed Joey a couple of chocolate taffies and said, 'Maybe you should just fill your mouth with some Smidgees and enjoy the party.' I turned to leave and he blocked my path saying, 'Is that supposed to be a shot at my wife? I won't allow you to get away with that without an apology!'"

"Get away with what?" Adam was intrigued by the turn of events.

"That's what I asked!" Kelly exclaimed. "Apparently JoJo, his wife-o, suffers severely from achondroplasiaphobia."

"What's that?" asked Adam.

"Again, that's what I asked," Kelly explained. "Apparently she has a fear of midgets, according to Joey."

"Midgets? That's an offensive word."

"Midgets. I know. His term. Not mine. That's not what I call them."

"Like in little people?"

"Like in little people. Better term."

"Wow. That's an unusual phobia. I've never heard of that."

"I know. Neither have I," replied Kelly. "Anyway, Joey thought I was making a dig at his wife when I offered the Smidgees. That's when she got upset because she thought that somehow I knew about it and was making fun of her. I just watched in disbelief as the whole crazy situation got even crazier. So Joey piped up after he saw how apparently *hurt* she was and lectured me on how to treat people facing posttraumatic stress disorders. POSTTRAUMATIC STRESS DISORDERS! All I kept thinking was, *Are you kidding me?* The man who couldn't support me one bit, not one bit, when my world came crashing down, is now reacting with overkill to support his wife who's afraid of little people?"

"What happened next?" Adam asked.

"I shot back at him with my own question. I asked him if that would be the same type of apology as the one he refused to give when he was so mean and tormented my cat, Mr. Shrimp! That's when JoJo the bimbo, whose elevator doesn't go all the way to the top, pipes up and whines, 'She did it again, Joey, she said *shrimp*! Make her stop! She's so abusive to me!' He looked at her, then back at me, and growled, 'Apologize to JoJo!'

"Oh, dude, if I had been there, he would've been put in his place," Adam offered in support. "So then?"

"Well," Kelley answered, "I was trying to control my rage, but somehow, I ended up saying, 'I'm *so* sorry. It was very, um, *little* of me to do that.'" Then I walked past them and out the door to dropped jaws. Pretty sure I left them both in shock."

"Well done, my love!" Adam applauded his duvshanit.

"Yeah, it felt good to get in those jabs in the heat of the moment, but at the same time, I hated being part of a scene at the party." Kelly reached for the bags of Chinese food and placed them on her lap as Adam turned onto her street. "I'm sure the apartment was buzzing after I left and that Tweedle Dum and Dumber gave everyone their spin on it without me there to defend myself. Well, at least I went out with a bang with that crowd."

"That you did, my love! I'm proud of you." Adam slowed down as he reached the apartment complex.

"Let's park this car so we can get up to my place and eat." Kelly handled the two bags and opened her door once the Yafah LX was parked. "You know, it's good to be home with my people."

Adam got out of the coupe and opened the trunk to remove her luggage. "Well, one of your people, who happens to be the craziest about you, loves that you're back! The earth is finally spinning once again and I'm no longer lost. My north star has returned."

"That's laying it on a bit thick, but I do appreciate your adoring words. And you know what? I think we're part of the same star." Kelly spread her arms and leaned in to kiss Adam in between the bags of Chinese food. He put the luggage down and wrapped his arms around her waist, his hands finding the hollows of her back. A rush of pink painted her cheeks as Adam squeezed her in closer. He moved his mouth over hers, devouring its softness. His demanding kiss compelled her to respond and she did so with urgent desire. Then, as quickly as it had started, it subsided as Kelly pulled away. "Okay. Kissing while holding two big bags of Chinese takeout is, in my opinion, a great way to work out, but we don't need to be some horn toad's peep show. C'mon. Let's head in and continue the show privately for dessert."

"But what if there's little people visiting your condo?" Adam teased. "I might have achondro-blah-blah-phobia. Maybe kissing here for a little longer might help me."

"The only thing that's going to help you is to let me eat. Then I'll be able to help you with whatever phobia you want. And don't worry. I won't be short with you either! Ha! See? Two can play that game!" Kelly grinned smugly as she started walking away from the car. Adam grinned as well. He appreciated the swing on his girlfriend's porch.

The two made their way through the parking lot and a neighbor exited the building just as Kelly was about to stop and enter the passcode to gain entrance. They exchanged hellos and the young man held the door open while the two juggled their belongings through the doorway. With a little more maneuvering, they made their way to the elevator and got out on the third floor. Adam rolled his girlfriend's suitcases down the long corridor while carrying her overnight bag. They arrived at Kelly's apartment and she knocked on the door while juggling the packed brown bags.

"Hope they're still here. I don't want to have to put the bags down to get my k—." The door opened and the two were greeted by Jenn, the oldest of Kelly's roommates. She grabbed one of the food parcels and gave Kelly a quick hug. "Glad you're back, girl. Hey, Adam. Ooh. There's a light out down the hallway. I'll have to call management tomorrow and have them change it right away." The couple exchanged looks as they followed Jenn into the apartment.

"Why does it have to be changed right away? There's other lights in the rest of the hallway, so it's not quite an emergency." Adam wanted to understand the short brunette's statement.

"Nope. Sorry. Has to be right away," Jenn insisted. "There are lots of stories about bad things happening to people in dimly lit hallways of apartment buildings. As a matter of fact, there was this one Korean lady . . . what city was that again? Oh yeah—"

Kelly interjected, "Lay off the cyber stuff, Jenn! Those are all urban legends. You know that."

"Yeah, I know. But it made it onto the internet so it might be true. Maybe the gangs or killers call that stuff urban legends to keep us off guard, know what I mean? Hey, this bag smells amazing. Any extra you're willing to share?" Jenn placed the takeout on the kitchen counter.

"Hey there, everybody." Ashley came out of her room. "Welcome back to the princess palace." Ashley was the youngest of the four roommates and the three sisters. Adam remembered Kelly sharing with him that she had been a bit apprehensive when she moved into the unit with the three women after graduating from vet school. She had been afraid to feel like an outsider, seeing as they were family and she was an add-on.

At least her Uncle Mike and Aunt Julie were not far away from the large four-bedroom unit and it was a secured building, which was another plus. Everyone had their own private space, and Kelly had promised herself to move out at the end of her first lease period if it hadn't panned out. It was already more than two years now since her move-in day, and Kelly had called it the best decision she ever made, besides agreeing to date Adam, of course. During this same period of time, they had grown to be a close and constantly evolving, almost exhilarating, couple. They wanted to be better because of the other and were not afraid to hand out challenges when they differed. Adam and Kelly were ahead of their years in wisdom as to the ways of the world. And all this developed and converged from two different viewpoints and pathways.

For instance, Adam would have invited Kelly to live with him, but she had already stated that she wanted to stay committed to her theology and save her chastity for her wedding night. He loved her enough to respect her religious wishes. Though there were indeed times he yearned for their physical union, he had to remind himself that anyone worth loving at the highest level was worth the self-sacrifice. His respect for her faith was his gift to her soul. He knew they would both carry that same gift through the course of each other's different faiths in order to find their common heart, and treasure that gift together. Love always did find a way, and theirs would too. It already had in his opinion.

Adam found Kelly to be an intriguing and complicated person who would, at one moment, be a free spirit willing to ride life with wild, fierce-feeling abandon, boldness, and laughter. At other times she would contradict these with quiet, unsure moments of self-doubt that were met with sobs and the need for his comfort. Adam somehow knew their life together would be anything but boring, but in the end very rewarding, having made the journey together. He did naturally always prefer peace of mind for Kelly, especially after what life had served her in the past, so anything that made her happy became an extension of his contentment. They were both in a great place for now, despite the looming challenge of his parents' approval, and his girlfriend was happy with her living arrangements. Her roomies, Jenn, Melissa, and Ashley Harty had their quirks and quarrels as sisters, but overall, their growing friendship with Kelly was better than she could have ever imagined.

"Is that groceries or takeout?" Ashley remarked. "Cuz if someone lost their appetite, I found it and I'm ready to use it."

"Chinese," Jenn replied. "Not sure if they're sharing yet."

Adam delivered Kelly's luggage to her room. He could hear her fending off the hungry natives. "Boy! I live in a shark tank now? Let Adam and I take what we want and you can have whatever's left. I'm warning you, though, we're pretty hungry ourselves. Didn't you guys eat dinner?"

"Who lives in a shark tank?" Melissa entered the kitchen behind Adam as he returned to claim his meal.

"We do, apparently," Jenn replied while getting a drink from the fridge.

Ashley continued, "Can't you see we're circling the food now? Hope they don't feed us by hand. Fingers will be lost. Just sayin'."

"Feed your own fingers to yourself, *if* there's anything left, and there may not be. Just sayin'," Kelly returned the sarcasm. The two bumped.

"Glad you're back, girl," Ashley added as she took utensils out for no one in particular. Melissa came closer. Kelly handed Adam a plate heaped with food.

He hesitated. "Wow. That's a lot."

"Gotta take it while you can. There'll be no seconds with these three here," Kelly advised. The couple sat to eat and let the ladies move in on the leftovers.

"Well. I'm not sure I'm even having any," Melissa stated. "It looks so good, but we just ate a couple hours ago. Should I? You know what, maybe I will. Although I'm trying to be good with working out and eating and all. But maybe a little won't kill me. Is there even enough left for the three of us? Ah! Decisions! They kill me." The other sisters did not wait patiently for her decision.

"If they don't kill you, I will!" Ashley declared. "And, in my opinion, I don't think you should have any."

"Why? You think I should be good then?" Melissa asked.

"No," Ashley countered. "I just think it means more for us." The group burst out laughing.

"You know, I read on the internet that there's dog and cat meat mixed into Chinese food sometimes. Are you sure this takeout is good? You know the place, right?" Jenn gave her usual PSA.

Kelly spoke up first. "We do, but Jennifer, you have got to stop being so Goo-gullible."

Melissa echoed the word at a higher pitch. "Goo-gullible!"

"What's that?" Jenn asked, giving her sister a chiding look.

Kelly answered, "Goo-gullible. That's how you describe a person who believes everything she reads online, whether or not it's true."

There was a moment of silence. Ashley piped up, "Except, of course, for the people eating fingers like sharks. That might be true." The group offered another round of laughter, except for Jenn, who was considering the thought.

"I'd like to feed my ex to those sharks! Ran into him at a party in LA," Kelly sneered.

Ashley jumped on the information. "Spill, girl! What happened?"

"Yeah," Jenn added. "Inquiring minds want to know."

"Inquiring minds," Melissa echoed with a chuckle. Kelly glanced around the group, relishing the chance to give someone her side of the contentious encounter. She repeated the whole narrative, complete with every whine, dig, and editorial remark. Upon finishing, she launched a group check to see if the girls agreed with her handling of the unplanned confrontation.

"I probably would have reacted the same way. Your exit was awesome. That's what I think, anyway," reassured Ashley.

"I will say you've got more guts than me," Melissa declared. "Like, I would think it, but probably not say it. Well, maybe I'd say just some of it. Actually, I'm not sure how I would have handled the whole thing. I don't know. What do you guys think?"

"I think I'm certain you can't make up your mind about anything, is what I think!" Jenn replied before addressing Kelly. "I think you're good. They attacked you and you just defended yourself. You might have some of their bad karma left, though, so you'll have to perform actions to nourish your spirit and invoke well-being on every level, including your aura. If you want, I can send you the URL with that information."

"Ahh! Goo-gullible!" Kelly objected. "You need to stop working from home and get a job where you're not online all the time." She shook her head.

"Gotta love me," Jenn defended herself. "And do let me know if you change your mind about the link."

Melissa interjected, "I'm pretty sure she doesn't want it, Jenn." She hesitated. "Unless you do, Kelly. Do you?" Kelly, Adam, and Ashley busted out in laughter at the traits of the two girls showing themselves yet again.

Choosing to move on, Jenn suggested, "I think we should head out to top off tonight with a couple of drinks. Nothing major. Just grab a couple somewhere close and casual. Who's in the mood?" Her sisters announced their decision to join her while Kelly and Adam declined the idea.

"I'm beat from traveling, and I have to head into the clinic midmorning tomorrow to meet with Sully. I'm going to share info about the new items on the market for vets that I saw at the Going Animal Expo and bring the fliers and samples I brought back. So I want to hit bed as soon as I can," Kelly explained.

"And I just want to grab the last few minutes that I can with my very missed girlfriend before I say good night. Sorry, ladies!" Adam leaned toward his love and gave her a quick squeeze. The girls took a few minutes to refresh their looks while Kelly and Adam finished their food. Each sister said her good night to the two lovebirds before heading out for nightcaps.

The last words Kelly and Adam heard belonged to Jenn. "Guys, wait for me! That hallway light hasn't been changed yet, and you know what the internet says about being alone in dim hallways!"

Kelly smiled at the words while gazing into Adam's seductive, deep brown eyes. He leaned in and embraced her with a long kiss that he hoped would radiate throughout her entire being and penetrate her heart. He wanted her willpower to fade away into a strong desire that urgently craved him. Their kisses became longer and deeper.

Adam drew Kelly even closer and placed his hand on her cheek so she would feel like she was the most precious thing he had ever experienced. He felt her passion build, but then, it left as quickly as it came. He knew her brain had just fought and won a short battle with her heart. He knew it would become their discussion about her need for abstinence until the one day when they would wed, if that day ever did come.

He also knew what questions would resurface. *Would my old-fashioned Jewish parents accept her being a faithful Catholic? How would we raise any children?* Then there were the unspoken but loud innuendos they experienced with some friends as well as strangers when certain situations occurred. He knew they were committed to each other strongly enough to face anything together, but were the odds stronger than them? That was the question.

Kelly stopped. "Adam, honey, I missed you so much while I was away, and I love being with you, but I have to get some sleep now. I really do."

"I understand, my duvshanit." He released her with

subtle but definite disappointment and she walked him to the door. "To be continued tomorrow?"

"Yes," she replied.

"And the day after that? And the one after that?" he flirted.

She smiled with a nod. "Absolutely."

Adam exited the apartment after one last kiss and waited for Kelly to lock the door. He walked away until he heard her reopen the door momentarily while calling after him, "Watch out for the dim hallway! You know what they say."

He turned and replied, "Only tonight. They're changing the light tomorrow!" He watched Kelly smile and then shut her door before he left the building.

He loved that they got each other's humor. He also absolutely loved having her in his life. Sometimes the universe throws some extraordinary blessings into an otherwise plain and ordinary life. Kelly was that blessing. She was that second bonus rainbow that catches a person's breath when they discover it. How could he ever thank Kelly for the gift of her in his life? Perhaps he could show his gratitude by traveling with her back to California so he and his duvshanit could enjoy scaring the wits out of Team JoJo by offering Joey's new wife Mr. Shrimp and a bowlful of Smidgees.

Chapter 4

KELLY

Kelly blindly searched her nightstand in hopes of shutting off her cell phone's alarm. Normally the melodic strains of smooth jazz would soften her transition to a conscious state, but that wasn't happening. *Should never have invested in those blackout drapes. What was I thinking?* With the alarm now silenced, she remembered exactly why she'd impulsively purchased the extravagantly priced item that succeeded in enveloping her room in darkness. Performing two back-to-back emergency surgeries in the middle of the night earlier that month had necessitated her bedroom to be a place where she could truly rest and recharge when the night duty of on-call rotation came her way. She needed her sleep!

Kelly commanded her cell phone to turn on its flashlight. She carefully found her way past the strewn luggage, ignoring the multiple dust bunnies that floated in the cell phone's beam, and opened the drapes. The morning sunshine spilled into the room, casting a perfect spotlight on Mr. Shrimp, who had now taken a forbidden pounce up onto her bed. "Hey there, buddy. You know you aren't supposed to do that!"

Kelly lovingly picked up the exotic shorthair and softly scolded him. "You're lucky this alcove is so small there's hardly enough room to swing a cat, or you just might be flyin'." Of course she didn't mean it. She'd been in love with every creature, critter, mutt, stray, and varmint that she'd ever met. In high school Kelly had even picked up a dead cat on the side of the road, hoping by some miracle she could nurse him back to health. Those failures did not dissuade her dream. She knew she wanted to be a veterinarian.

Slipping into her Turkish cotton bathrobe and fleece-lined slippers, Kelly made her way to the kitchen with Mr. Shrimp right behind. "I know you're hungry. The usual?" She winked at him as she lined up her favorite mug, inserted the coffee pod, and pressed brew.

"Meow," he replied. Yes, Mr. Shrimp knew the routine well. Kelly measured his allowed portion and placed it in his designated dining spot. Tilting his head toward her, he appeared to smile. "You do love breakfast, don't you?" By the time she had washed his water bowl and refilled it for the day, coffee was waiting for her to enjoy.

Kelly sauntered back to her bedroom to cozy up in her barrel chair and sip the hot beverage. She had never been a morning person, but after a lot of conscious effort, she now appreciated the slower-paced routine she'd developed, especially when her roommates were still in bed and the aura of silence blanketed their place. Glancing at her phone screen, Kelly saw she had two hours till her meeting with Sully at Will's Pet Haven, the family-owned veterinary, where it really did feel more like family than business.

Sully's grandfather had first opened the establishment following WWII, immediately after he completed serving in the Army Veterinary Corps. Now well into his nineties, he was a rare visitor to the animal office, but when he was feeling up to it, nothing could keep him from venturing out to the business. He loved telling a story or two about examining the pups used as war dogs or providing care for the birds of the signal corps. His son, Will Jr., had taken the reins in the mid-1980s, serving the community. When Junior's daughter Sully graduated from the University of Georgia College of Veterinary Medicine, she made the logical choice to carry on the family business. Kelly considered herself very lucky to have landed her job. More than two years had passed since she walked through the front doors, and every day she was thankful to be a part of the family's staff.

Kelly shifted in the chair as Mr. Shrimp began kneading her leg. "And you, my beloved Mr. Shrimp, are thankful I am home!" Placing her hand under his extensive belly, she gently lifted him to her lap. He responded by extending his front paws up onto her chest, headbutting her chin, and then staring into her eyes. "Ahh, you are in the zone of complete comfort, aren't you!" Kelly smiled. "I'm totally taken with you too. Now if we could just teach that rascally Bo to be more like you." She laughed. After all, if it hadn't been for that mischievous pup, she would have never met Adam.

Completing her morning routine in record time, Kelly surveyed the few remaining professional clothes hanging in her closet. *Ugh, nothing matches!* She was now faced with the task of finding a suitable outfit in one of her travel bags. After rummaging through her luggage, she found her favorite pair of jeans and narrowed her choice of tops down to a subtly stained blouse or a rumpled silk sweater. *Hmmm. A new consequence of overpacking! No choice to be made here. Scrubs it is.* She tossed the jeans onto an over-flowing heap and headed back to her closet. It actually felt good to be getting back into scrubs. The breathable material made Kelly feel like she was still in her pajamas, not that she ever had the opportunity to spend much time in them, but it also meant returning to a normal routine. She was actually looking forward to getting back to seeing patients again and problem-solving for her clients.

Kelly bent to stroke Mr. Shrimp and said goodbye. "I'm off to see Sully, your second most favorite vet. You be good." He twitched his tail and looked away. She closed her bedroom door as quietly as possible and did her best to sneak out without waking her roomies. A last-minute conversation with any one of the three siblings would more than likely turn into a long monologue about last night's pub visit.

A southerly breeze greeted Kelly as she stepped into the sunlight. *Hardly feels like December, but that's all right with me.* Kelly still preferred the Southern California climate to the risks of snow and ice that happened from time to time. Any December day in Georgia that felt even remotely like sixty-some degrees brought a smile to her face. Driving toward the clinic, her mind swirled with so many celebratory holiday options. How could she possibly fit them all into a short time frame? Shopping, wrapping, tree trimming, cookie baking, Charlotte's yearly Christmas soiree, plus Hanukkah. *I'll make it happen—even Midnight Mass at six o'clock!*

Kelly made the sharp left into Will's Pet Haven. The parking lot was bursting with activity as the county animal shelter was holding a free adoption event. The compassionate volunteers were pressed on all sides by the furriest and most lovable four-legged bachelors and bachelorettes as potential owners moved from table to table. The occasion, advertised as a pet speed-dating event, appeared to be a huge success. Kelly smiled. *There's nothing better than finding forever homes!* Making her way past the barking, the meowing, and the chattering, she walked into the empty lobby and laughed out loud.

"Hey, Sully, this is not a normal Saturday!"

"I know. Isn't it wonderful? There's a lot more to having a successful business than just bringing in the bucks."

Kelly agreed. "But then again, you are a very smart businesswoman and know full well more than half of those new pet parents will be calling Monday to make appointments."

"I know that, but it still does my heart good to be the Humane Society's matchmaker assistant. So, how was the conference? Learn anything new? Anything we should be implementing here?"

Kelly walked over to the hospitality counter and grasped a chilled mini bottle of sparkling water before taking a seat. "Let's see. There was the usual debate about vet consolidation. The belief that independent practices will be swallowed up by larger corporations is running rampant. Predictions are it could be anywhere between thirty and fifty percent within five years."

"Yeah, we know about that, but I still believe there is a genuine niche for us little guys. It's definitely something we need to pay attention to, though. Any new ideas on how to battle it?"

"Actually, there is, and I found that to be pretty interesting. Do you know who the new king and queen of veterinary needs are?" Sully furrowed her brow but did not reply. "It's us Millennials. We're taking our dogs everywhere, and it looks like this trend is here to stay." Sully nodded. Kelly continued, "What do you think about branching out to offer classes on properly socializing your dog? Participants would first need to complete a basic obedience class, but once they pass that, we could offer advanced training. I mean, who wants to just blindly take their precious pup to the local dog park and run the risk of having a super bad experience with an ill-mannered attack dog? We've already got that huge fenced-in area out back. Plus, I bet if you tap into your wonderful partnership with the Humane Society, you could work out a deal to use their small indoor arena for after-hour classes."

"Interesting," Sully remarked. "It certainly wouldn't require any additional capital investment. Let me mull it over before I decide."

"Mull away, Sully. Just don't simmer the idea for too long. Santa is going to be bringing lots of new puppies very soon, and this idea might be just what's needed to increase our clientele."

"Well, look who's thinking like a business owner," joked Sully. "There might be hope for you yet!"

Both women grinned as the phone rang. "Will's Pet Haven. Sully speaking. How may I help you?" Kelly studied her cohort's face as Sully answered a myriad of questions. *She looks tired, really tired.* And why wouldn't she? Sully had been widowed for almost a year, and the wrenching months since Brad died had definitely taken their toll. *A widow at thirty-six . . . Two little kids to parent alone. I wonder what . . .*

"Earth to Kelly! Hello?"

"Sorry, Sully. Just tuned out for a minute."

"Daydreaming of that good-looking guy of yours, I suppose. You have a hot date tonight?"

"Is there any other kind?" Kelly laughed.

"Not for you!" Sully volleyed back. "So, what are your plans? Are your roomies going to give you two some personal space so you can attempt to prepare a romantic dinner for your honey?"

Kelly rolled her eyes. "You need to stop reminding me of that awful incident! Remember, that was my very *first* attempt to fry chicken."

"Is that two years ago already?" Sully questioned, and then in her most liquid imitation Southern drawl added, "Why, you were just doin' what any good, Southern-by-choice girlfriend would do, right? You little Georgia Peach!"

She knew Sully was only mocking her, and yet Kelly was always mortified whenever she was teased about her lack of culinary expertise. She tried to curb her answer to one emphatic *No!* but true to form, it was quickly followed with a string of expletives as she tried to defend her ignorance. "How was I supposed to know that if the oil overheats, you don't cool it down by tossing in ice cubes?" Kelly could still picture the oil mushrooming like Mount Vesuvius. "At least neither of us got hurt." Kelly detected her friend's raised eyebrow, challenging her to complete the rest of the story, admitting defeat. "And yes, I have not tried to cook anything for Adam since."

Sully stood and patted Kelly on her shoulder. "Good thing Adam was so understanding or that one incident could have ended any chance of a relationship."

Kelly nodded in agreement. "Good thing he thinks I'm a keeper anyway."

"Ah, so things are progressing. 'Tis the season for proposals, you know! Christmas Eve, Christmas Day, New Year's Eve, New Year's Day. What do you think?"

"I don't know. What do you think?" retorted Kelly.

"I think the date won't matter because you will be

wowed by whatever ring Adam gives you. There definitely should be a huge advantage to marrying a jeweler!"

Kelly laughed politely and changed the subject. "So how does this week's schedule look?"

"Pretty light actually. Four spays, two neuters, three dentals, and one declaw. So, I'll see you Monday morning at six?"

"Absolutely."

"Well, don't exhaust yourself with your loverboy tonight and come in here Monday dragging your ass. Which reminds me, you never answered me when I asked what you two are doing tonight."

"That's right. I didn't," and Kelly winked at her as she shut the door.

In fact, she had not told anyone about tonight's plans. Kelly knew all too well that if she had shared the details with Sully, an hour-long guesstimation would follow, and Kelly just didn't have that time to spare. Besides, it was fun to have some plans with Adam that would not be dissected by Sully or her well-meaning roommates. *There will be plenty enough questions after tonight. Better make mental notes too, cuz they will definitely want to know who and what about everything!* Kelly chuckled. She felt like Cinderella attending the ball.

After stopping at the salon to replenish her favorite products, she headed across town for her manicure appointment. *Thank God my shoes for tonight are closed-toe, certainly no time for a pedicure.*

Kelly loved The Speedy Nail Hut when a special occasion was on her calendar. There was no chitchat, no small talk, no assessing the latest and greatest news. It was always the same process, starting with clipping, buffing, and filing, then ending with applying the topcoat. That was why Kelly was there; she did not want any unnecessary fluff.

Once inside the small salon, she found her reserved seat with the "Welcome Kelly" sign. *The sign. Oh no! I never said anything to the roomies and I didn't put a sign on the shared bathroom to reserve it for me. Aaargh!*

When the topcoat was dry, Kelly quickly handled her bill and flew out the door. *Three o'clock. Right on schedule. Adam's arriving at six. Plenty of time . . . Just need to get one of the bathrooms for myself . . . Calm down . . . There's plenty of time!*

Kelly thought about texting one of the sisters regarding bathroom occupancy but decided against it. Her roommates were considerate, and the chances of anybody leaving as early as six o'clock were minimal. Certainly two-plus hours would allow ample time to primp and polish her appearance, and if necessary, part of her routine could be accomplished in her bedroom. Kelly reached for the dial to find some music that would induce an alpha state of mind. Deep-breathing exercises with closed eyes might not help her while driving, but she could find melodies to soothe her concerns.

As Kelly pulled up in front of the apartment complex, she could see a silhouette in the front window. *Is that Jenn in front of the computer? She's gotta be the most Goo-gullible compuholic I know!* Balancing her purchases on one arm, she successfully closed the car door and made it all the way to the apartment entrance before the packages became a cascading waterfall. *Damn! I broke a nail!* Kelly collected them and fumbled for her keys as the door mysteriously opened on its own. She decided to ignore the mystery, instead of investigating it, and headed to the elevator. Once on her floor, Kelly made her way down the hallway and was greeted again by the door being opened. Her roomie must have spotted her as well.

"Need an extra hand?" asked Jenn.

"Thanks, but it's a bit late for that. What I need is a new nail."

"Oh, I just hate it when that happens." Jenn took a firm hold of Kelly's injury. "Red hot, right?"

"What?" Kelly pulled her hand back.

"The nail color is called Red Hot. Right? I've got that color in my stash and can help you out."

"Thanks. I can do it myself, but I appreciate you letting me borrow."

"Kelly, you're right-handed and the damaged nail is on your right hand. You're telling me you're gonna be left-handed for polishing? No way, girl, that ain't happening."

Kelly shrugged and gave in to Jenn's admonition. "Whatcha been doing all day?" she called toward Jenn, who was heading to retrieve the polish. "Still working on that blog post?"

"Yep," Jenn hollered back. Kelly could hear the shuffling of bottles in her overstuffed nail caddy.

I hope she finds it!

"You know, sometimes the words just come easy as pie, but today, it's a hard row to hoe. Know what I mean?" Jenn motioned for Kelly to sit down at the kitchen counter as she continued. "Writing about the best holiday party ever is not an easy stunt. I mean, unless I write about that Christmas party you and Adam went to last year." Kelly pursed her lips. This was not a topic she wanted to discuss, but Jenn was obviously more focused on the damaged nail. "What was the name of that lady who gave the party? I forget."

"Charlotte Buchanan."

"That's right. That famous actress. And I believe the

Christmas party was at her Buckhead mansion? Wait a minute. It wasn't a Christmas party; it was a masquerade, right? Cuz you and Adam wore Roaring Twenties outfits, right? Why can't I remember anything!"

Kelly took a deep breath. She really hadn't wanted this topic to come up, and here it was just because she broke a nail. "You're right on both accounts, Jenn. It was a Christmas Masquerade Party that benefitted the Humane Society. Because Charlotte was going to be out of town filming over New Year's, she couldn't host her traditional Masquerade Ball, so she moved the benefit up and combined the costumed event with a Christmas celebration."

"That's right." Jenn paused as she finished applying the first coat of polish. "Those stories you shared were incredible. The food was scrumptious. And the people you met? Wow! Those stars were the crème de la crème. Now that would make a great blog!" Jenn hesitated, and with one look, Kelly could tell she was waiting for permission.

"You can't write about that, Jenn."

"Why not? You going back this year?"

There it was. Kelly's secret was about to be leaked before the event even occurred. Her plan would be common knowledge before Adam ever arrived.

"You are! I can read it on your face! It's tonight, isn't it? No wonder your nails are painted red. You never wear polish because of surgeries unless it's a special occasion. Wow! You need to tell me everything! What's your costume?"

"No costume this year, Jenn. It's strictly a Christmas Party."

"You excited?"

"Of course."

"What are you wearing?"

"My little black dress."

"Oooh, formal. Nice!" Jenn had finished applying the topcoat but was not releasing Kelly's hand. "Do you think that hot guy from the Atlanta hospital TV series will be there again? I'd love to meet him! Could you help me with that if he shows up?"

Kelly just shook her head as she retrieved her hand from Jenn's firm clasp. "I doubt it, Jenn. Right now I need to get a small snack so I'm not starving when I get to the party. Then I really need to start getting ready. Is all the chicken salad gone?" She headed to the refrigerator.

"It's in there. What time's Adam picking you up?"

"Six," Kelly answered as she retrieved the small bowl and pulled a fork from the drawer.

"Oh! I need to call Melissa and Ashley. They aren't gonna want to miss this send-off!"

"No need to overreact. It's just a special evening with fancy clothes—"

"And fancy food and fancy folks, Kelly. And maybe a fancy ring? If a guy wanted a perfectly magical setting to pop the question, this could be it. What d'ya think?"

Kelly almost choked. That thought hadn't crossed her mind. "I haven't even met his parents yet, Jenn," she mumbled as she tried to swallow at the same time. "I'm sure he's not going to ask me before I meet his family."

"Why not? He's a grown man. Might make your concern regarding his parents' reaction to this Jew-Cath combo easier if their son's already made a commitment to buy the cow." Kelly's face contorted. "You know what I mean, Kelly. No personal reference intended!"

"Well, I doubt that is going to happen tonight, and right now I just need to get ready. Thanks for the touch-up."

"Sure. Just remember your substitute esthetician when you see an eligible movie star tonight!"

Kelly shook her head as she closed the bedroom door. She placed her snack on the nightstand while resisting the urge to scoop her pet up into her arms.

"Sorry, my boy. My personal esthetician's handiwork needs protecting."

She fluffed her pillow, took another bite of salad, and lay down on the bed to contemplate Jenn's comments. *Could tonight be the night? It's a fairytale setting. Could be very romantic . . . Last year certainly was.* Kelly rolled onto her other side and Mr. Shrimp insisted on joining her by jumping almost to the top of her mattress, and then clawing the rest of his way up the blanket. After his success, he spent a quick moment grooming himself and then waltzed to Kelly's side before plopping himself down in expectation of some affection. Kelly continued her contemplations.

But his family is so important to him. Would Adam really propose before they even met me?

She rolled back onto her other side to check the time and whispered to her four-legged companion, "Sorry, buddy, no time or chance for some love right now. I need to start getting ready."

By the time she finished showering, blow-drying her hair, styling it, and applying her makeup and newly purchased fragrance, she was ready to shed the bath wrap for tonight's special outfit. Her roommates believed the sole purpose of a little black dress was to seduce men. Kelly had a different opinion. She believed its purpose was to help her feel exceptional, and when she slipped into it, that is exactly how she felt. Yes, the dress was a bit snug and did embrace curves that were seldom seen while wearing scrubs. She did have to admit that the bodice was kind of low-cut and the slit over her right leg did go a bit high, but from the very first time she tried it on, Kelly felt like it had been made specifically for her.

Now for the frosting on the cake! She opened her jewelry armoire and chose the chandelier earrings she'd been waiting to wear with her LBD. The elaborate layers of dangles added a touch of classy glamor. The shimmering finery gave a sensuous look to the ensemble.

Hearing the doorbell chime, Kelly slipped on her shoes and took one last look in the mirror. Her smile reflected the beauty within while her outward appearance made her look elegant and classy with a hint of sensuality.

Girl, there's gonna be a lot of celebrities and hot people at that event tonight, so you need to bring your A game. Annnd, Kelly tugged on her dress here and there, *if you fail the A game, then you always have the A man. Hope Adam thinks I'm a knockout!*

Chapter 5

ADAM

Man, you need to knock it out of the park tonight. I mean, Adam Cohen, you're going to do this once again! Same as last year! Adam checked himself out in the mirror as he took turns holding up three different shirts. He decided on the white long-sleeve silk shirt and pulled out a luxurious hand-pleated silk medallion bow tie with thin red, white, and hunter-green stripes. He finished dressing and checked the mirror once again. "What do you think, Bo? Am I dashing or am I dashing?"

"Woof!" the goldendoodle replied with enthusiasm. He jumped off his bed and headed straight to his master to give a lick of approval, though he would have done the same if Adam had stayed in just his boxer briefs. It was an obvious unconditional love.

"Whoa there, Mr. Boaz! Easy, boy! I can't get messy." Adam smiled. "But you are right. I am indeed dashing, and it certainly helps that I invested in a couple of tuxes that work for these Christmas events. Before Kelly, I was dressed in nothing but blue, white, and yellow for the holidays! Feels good to broaden my festive horizons." Adam grabbed his select cologne that he used for special occasions and slathered it on all the right spots. The fragrance had set his wallet back three figures and would have given his dad a financial coronary on the spot.

He could even hear his father's ranting voice. "You could have gotten yourself that same fancy smell for half the price with a backstreet knockoff. No one but the designers and cologne makers themselves would have known the difference. You're telling me you don't have better ways to spend your hard-earned money?" This would be followed by a Jewish rant that Adam knew meant *Everyone complains about a lack of money, but none complain about a lack of brains!* And his mother would have shaken her head, in agreement with his dad.

Adam did not hold his parents' opinion in high regard in this matter, though, because they were too old school in all things dating, relationships, and marriage. If he let them have their way, his future would have been decided by a professional matchmaker! Adam wasn't going to let that happen in any universe. He was also confident that anything he did to improve himself for Kelly was well worth the investment.

His phone rang and he checked the screen. The incoming call displayed *Tate & Mame*. "Well, just think of Dad and Mom and look what happens, Bo!" Adam was ready early, so he decided to take the call, especially seeing he had three missed calls from his mother since they had spoken at his sister's house.

"Adam, honey! What a relief to hear your voice! Your phone kept breaking up and I didn't know if you were okay. I called Sarah later that day because my health was barely holding on with all that worrying about you and she said you were fine. For this, Adam, my beautiful son, I gave a humble prayer of thanksgiving. Then, after that, I had your father go and speak with Moshe, our neighbor's son-in-law who works at the mobile phone kiosk. It took almost two hours, but your dad can get you a great deal on a new smarter phone that will work when we talk. Of course, we'll get it without all the needless frills and—"

"Mame! Stop! I don't need a new phone. It was, uh, the reception, not the phone. It would have cut out no matter what phone I was using." Adam knew he was fibbing about that past call but the present statement was true.

"No wonder it didn't work! I don't think your phone is supposed to cut anything out. I'll have your dad do the deal with Moshe and we'll bring the new phone for you. We should talk when we want to talk! Here's your father."

"Nope. No phone, Mame. This one is fine."

"Adam. Listen. The new one doesn't have all the fancy stuff I know you like, but it's a good one. And I'm not bragging, but I'm pretty sure I ran circles around Moshe. I'll go back and seal the deal." Morty Cohen tittered with pride.

"Tate. No. Mame was mistaken. My phone is fine," Adam insisted.

"The two of you should make up my mind! *Di tsayt iz tayerer fun gelt!*" Morty protested.

"Thanks. I know time is more precious than money. It was a misunderstanding. Forgive us. And, please, no phone." Adam knew this was all he had to say to his dad.

"Okay, okay! Forgiven! Flying out to see you at Hanukkah still? Or were we mistaken about that too?"

"Yes, that is for sure. You'll finally meet Kelly too! Isn't that great?" Adam had already begun his sales pitch.

"Yes. Knowing you she's probably very pretty."

"Yes she is, inside and out."

"Well, good. That's fine. As long as this Kelly is not a

kolboynick like the last one, or a shiksa! Then I'm good. Of course, pretty helps, but the other two are most important. Here's your mother."

"Dad! She's not a know-it-all and neither was my last girlfriend," Adam objected.

"No. It's your mother, Adam." Freida Cohen took over the conversation. "So? She's not a shiksa, right? Kolboynick I can fix. But a stubborn shiksa is almost impossible, even for me!"

"Mame, Kelly is *not* a kolboynick. She's a smart, beautiful, witty woman, whom I happen to love very much!"

"Of course you do. You wouldn't date someone you hated for two years! But what is love at your age? Do you even know?"

"It's the same love you and Tate had when you were my age. Actually, you were a little younger," Adam defended himself.

"That was different," Freida explained.

"No. Places change, times can change. Who or what you love can change. But passion, desire, and love . . . those are the same for all people. It's the same for me and Kelly as it was for you and Tate." Adam was knee-deep in his defensive sales pitch.

"So now you're a philosopher?" his mother asked. "Well, philosopher shmilosopher. We'll work it out. I'm glad she's at least Jewish. It's good to stay with your kind, my love. Jewish, right? Adam? She's Jewish, right?"

Adam wanted to take the plunge and go through the first round of the great debate with his mother but knew the timing was just not good. The rebuttals swirled through the same familiar thought process that had haunted him the last two years as he witnessed the entire argument take its course in his mind. What could he possibly say to postpone the discussion just a bit longer? He automatically leaned against the same enticing crutch he had used as an earlier exit.

"Mame . . . you there? Hello? You're . . . up. I can't . . . stand what . . . saying. Hello?"

"Adam! Not again! Hello? . . . Oy! That phone! Nothing but shlok! Morty! I know Adam said no to the Moshe deal, but I think we should get it for him anyway. What? Because his phone cut something out again just when I was asking him if Kelly is Jewish or not. What? You're afraid the problem is with the girlfriend and not the phone? I don't understand! Hold on. Adam? Are you there? Hello? Oy!"

Adam panicked and hung up. He knew he was going to have to handle this issue before the holidays, but tonight was not the time for it. Plus, he had to get going if he was going to pick up Kelly on time. He switched his phone to airplane mode in order to ascertain his mother's usual follow-up calls would not be answered until he was ready to continue their conversation.

Adam was confident of his desire to continue his life with Kelly, despite anything or anyone, including his parents. However, he was also well acquainted with the guilt of not wanting to lead his life without his parents' approval. Their blessing felt like a necessary spiritual attachment with a nonessential function. What does one do with that? Lately Adam felt like he was already struggling between his happiness and theirs, without his parents having even met his girlfriend yet, as if one was a committed black and the other white! Surely there could be a consensual gray that could work for all of them.

Kosher Contentment Gray. Adam liked the sound of that color choice. *Maybe I'll design a jewelry collection for specific interfaith couples and I'll aim for a Kosher Contentment Gray as the signature color. And I could intertwine Jewish and Catholic symbols. Create solid pieces with the theme of merged commonality rather than differences, that it's meant to be as if there could never be any other choice.*

It then occurred to Adam that his approach to his parents should be exactly that—as if there will never be any other choice but to accept his and Kelly's love. *Ah! But it's going to be all uphill no matter what direction I take.* He let out a sigh and nod of determination. *I'll just have to be firm no matter what.* Adam checked on his goldendoodle's water and brought a few chew toys, along with a bone, close to Bo's doggy bed.

"Woof!" Bo knew these actions meant his master was leaving for a while. He followed his sentiment with a whimper, picked up one of the placed toys, and returned it to Adam.

"Not now, buddy! We'll play tomorrow. Right now I have a date with a lady we both know, and we're heading to a hot party with lots of celebrities. I'll let you know if I rub elbows with any canine ones, okay?"

Adam patted Bo before commanding him to go lie down. Once the dog obeyed, Adam set the security system, gave one last look around, and closed the door before heading out to his sports car. *Hmm. Busy time for the Yafah LX, that's for sure!* A whistled tune emerged from his lips. He was a perfectly happy man, at least for this evening.

Adam exited his driveway and drove toward the boulevard that would take him closer to Kelly. He envisioned putting his arms around her in some new sleek gorgeous holiday dress, kibitzing with all the other party guests. He closed his eyes for a short moment and sniffed the air. He could smell her hair and perfume in his mind. After the party, they would enjoy some private intimate time and his longing, his need for her grew. He opened his eyes and was rushed to reality as he slammed on the brakes. Adam had almost crashed into the BMW stopped at the light in front of him.

Oh wow! That was close! Well, this proves I love Kelly even more than my Yafah LX. I definitely need to pay more attention so I have a future with both of them. The light turned green and Adam accelerated forward, completing the rest of his trip to Kelly's without any additional close calls.

He parked the sports car and looked in the rearview mirror, confiding in the well-groomed reflection that faced him. A black limo pulled into the parking lot and Adam secured the Yafah LX for the evening, grateful that there were active video cameras monitoring the property. He signaled the limo driver as he approached the long vehicle. "I'll go see if the princess is ready. As soon as she is, we'll be right out for our ride to the ball." The driver smiled and confirmed with a double-finger salute from his cap.

Adam entered the building, using the passcode Kelly had given him, took the elevator, and knocked at the door. He was blown away when his girlfriend answered in a snug black dress that showed off her body in all the right places and in all the right ways. "I am in love with the most perfect woman in the world! I knew you would look amazing, but you've shown me once again that no matter what I expect, you always find a way to exceed it."

"But do I look good enough for Charlotte's event of the year?" Kelly asked.

"You, my duvshanit, are a knockout!" Adam stepped forward and kissed her.

"Good! Because that's what I was aiming for tonight. That's why I answered the door myself, to see your initial face and reaction," she explained while he held her in his arms. "Nailed it!"

"That you did." Adam's last words were smothered on her lips as he kissed her once again. Her response was eager, and this yearning pulsated back to him and made Adam feel vibrant.

"Get a room!" Ashley shouted as she greeted the couple and brought the pair back to reality.

"Actually, we're getting a limo and it happens to be here already," Adam replied.

"Oh! Okay." Kelly broke away from their embrace. "Just let me make one last mirror check and we can leave for Charlotte's party."

"Party? That's no party!" Ashley commented. "That's a soiree, a gala, an event of the year! And y'all better have some good dirt for us when you get back."

The other two sisters joined Adam while Kelly exited to the bathroom.

"Are you two staying for the whole thing or just part of it?" Melissa threw her question into the ring.

"Not sure. Depends how it goes. Probably the better it is, the longer we'll stay. We don't have any definite plans," Adam responded.

"Well, make sure you give us all the juicy details, and don't leave anything out about any celebrity!" Melissa instructed.

"Yes, I've already been told that by your younger sister." Adam grinned. "Doesn't matter who will be there, though, I'll still have the best woman in the place."

Jenn put her hand up for a high five. "Triple score on that one!"

Adam obliged the hand gesture. "I really mean it."

The sisters gushed at his heartfelt honesty. The group

continued their small chatter and Adam was overly complimented on his tux and cologne until Kelly reentered the room, announcing she was ready for the limo. Adam put his arm out and bent his elbow to signal his companion to join him. The two giggled all the way down the floor's hallway as the sisters threw comments out to them.

"Stay for the whole party so you don't miss anything!"

"Try to snag some photos for us!"

"Yeah, especially with celebrities!"

"And you can see the hallway light that was out has been replaced! I read somewhere online that lights can symbolize things in our lives."

"Just stop it with that nonsense!"

"Why would they write it if it didn't have some truth to it?"

"I didn't think of that. Well, maybe it's true. Nah. It can't be. I don't know!"

"Great. I'm stuck at home with Wishy-washy and Goo-gullible."

Kelly and Adam exited the building and Adam helped Kelly into the back of the limo. Together they smiled at the luxurious moment and their luck in being able to enjoy it. Adam broke open the chilled champagne that sat in an ice bucket. They cheered to the evening and their love as the limo headed to its destination. Adam knew it was going to be a great night.

Chapter 6

KELLY

As the limo entered the private drive, a reminiscent sigh escaped Kelly's lips. With cocktails on the loggia, dancing in the music room, and the opportunity to mingle with Atlanta's upper crust, she already knew this would be a fascinating evening.

Adam leaned toward her. "Even in this dim light, I can see you're beaming."

"I am. I just love that we got invited back this year!"

"Why would you think otherwise? Despite me shooting my toy tommy gun a bit much last year, of course," he snickered.

Kelly laughed. "Thank goodness this year's theme is Black Tie for Tails. I don't think I could take a redo of the incessant firing of that weapon!"

"I mean, we did behave ourselves last year, and re-member, this is also a Humane Society fundraiser. It never hurts to invite a jeweler who will donate an expensive, sparkling bauble."

"I know. It's just that I've only seen Charlotte twice since then. I wasn't sure there'd be an invitation coming in the mail. It's not like we run in the same social circle."

"True. Perhaps you're the only middle-class individual she invited so she could undermine anyone's attempt at social elitism. There's a lot to be said for being a respectable vet with no internet sensationalism." Adam chuckled. "What's that look? Are you disappointed you're not included with the nasty hearsay of Atlanta's upper crust? Don't feel like you're missing out. I'm confident that if you lend Charlotte your ear, she'll fill it with more scuttlebutt than you care to hear."

Kelly interrupted, "That isn't what I was insinuating."

Ignoring her comment, Adam continued. "She'll probably share enough juicy tidbits to satisfy even your roommates."

"That's preposterous, and you know it!" she quipped. "My roomies' quota of steamy scandals is never met. No matter how many interesting details I share after the party tonight, they'll wish for more."

"Of course. Can you blame 'em? Those girls would love to be in your shoes tonight—attending a soiree that's sure to be featured in some Atlanta society paper, and probably plastered all over social media, to Jenn's delight specifically. Plus, you've got a good-looking guy on your arm."

"I know." Kelly smiled and kissed Adam on the cheek. "We're going to have a wonderful time."

"Not a doubt in my mind. Nobody throws a better bash than Charlotte."

"Absolutely."

Charlotte Buchanan was a living illustration of Southern hospitality. Her charm was more than her dialect of extended vowels with the slower pace in which she spoke, and Kelly enjoyed their conversations. They had first met at the Fulton County Humane Society's Party for Pets fundraiser. Kelly remembered how Charlotte had drawled when they were introduced. "Why, hello. I didn't know I'd have the pleasure of a personally guided tour by a doctor, as I can see by your badge."

Kelly had been surprised by the request but happy to accommodate one of the shelter's best-known philanthropists. Together they had slowly walked numerous aisles, frequently pausing to assess a caged canine. The dogs' verbal pandemonium did not affect Charlotte as she repeatedly stooped to lock eyes with potential pups. Large or small, young or old, hairy or hairless, it did not seem to matter. Kelly wondered if Charlotte had something specific in mind that she was not discovering. After evaluating the very last kennel's occupant, Charlotte wiggled her index finger and beckoned Kelly to follow her into a quieter hallway.

Charlotte had been first to speak. "I do declare that was quite a heart-wrenching experience."

Kelly nodded. "Totally agree. It's sad to see so many animals in need. I'm so sorry you didn't find someone who interests you."

"On the contrary, my dear. My purpose in coming here today was to liberate the most rejected resident. Instead," she paused, "I am rescuing three."

"Three?" Kelly could hardly believe what she heard.

"That's right. At first, I was just going to take that German shepherd with the facial scars."

Kelly's heart skipped a beat. For weeks she had been working with that abused fellow, desperately trying to coax him from hiding in the corner of his kennel. It had only taken one hello from Charlotte and his long tail began to thump, but when Charlotte had moved on to look at others, Kelly had lost hope for his adoption.

"I am going to name him Bosley, after my daddy who died last year."

"I'm so sorry for your loss, Charlotte. Your father must have been quite a man."

"Indeed he was, my dear. That man held my heart till he walked me down the aisle on the day I made the biggest mistake of my life. Fortunately, he was still alive to help me pick up the pieces of my broken heart after I found out about my husband's affair. I guess you could say Daddy rescued me just like I'm rescuing these creatures."

Kelly smiled. "Which additional two stole your heart?"

"Why, those yippy little chihuahuas in the kennel next to Bosley's. They were bundles of energy when I spoke to them," Charlotte laughed. "They will definitely keep Bosley in line."

"Would you like me to bring them to the training room so you can see how they interact?"

"No. I know they'll be just fine together." Kelly had offered a pessimistic shrug. "Really, Kelly. I could tell just by watching those three there's a bond among them. Deciding on a pet is a lot like selecting a spouse. It's all about compatibility. Remember that."

Kelly's thoughts returned to her present task of admiring the Italian Renaissance Revival architecture looming before them. The massive home had been built by the great-great-grandfather of Charlotte's ex-husband. The patriarch had gained notoriety and considerable wealth by investing in one of the South's first ice factories, a detail that would later come to light as Charlotte stated her ex turned out to be "as cold as ice." The sophisticated house certainly was in stark contrast to the pillared Southern mansions. This elaborate abode, crowned with central cupolas, gleamed in holiday extravagance. It was the perfect venue for this evening's celebration.

The limo slowed as the chauffeur spoke. "Sir, I will be

waiting here on the circular drive when you are ready to depart."

"Thanks," replied Adam as the limo came to a stop.

The chauffeur exited, opened Adam's door, and came to the passenger side. Once the chauffeur had opened that door, Adam offered his hand to Kelly. As she looked up into her date's eyes, excitement rippled through her heart.

Kelly pivoted her legs, took Adam's extended hand, and carefully stood.

"This home seems like a palace," Kelly whispered to Adam as they began ascending the steps to the poinsettia-lined porch. "It's absolutely breathtaking."

"As are you, I might add. That dress shows curves I appreciate. You're definitely the belle of the ball, my sweet."

Once they reached the oversized veranda, the doorman stepped forward and extended a warm, welcoming smile. "Merry Christmas! Welcome to Buchanan Manor." He opened the door, and the couple entered the grand foyer showcased with detailed moldings, columns, and a sweetheart staircase boasting graceful banisters.

"Well, look who's here, two of my favorite guests! Merry Christmas!" Charlotte embraced Kelly as she gave a wink to Adam.

"Yes, Merry Christmas!" Kelly echoed. "How are your fur babies?"

"They are absolutely wonderful and anxiously waiting for Santa. Bosley is getting a new bone the size of a dinosaur leg, and Itty and Bitty are getting new wardrobes."

"Kelly is always showing me their outfits on social media," Adam shared. "How long before you capture them wearing stilettos?"

"What a wonderful suggestion, Adam," Charlotte gushed. "Such a great idea! I need to remember that! Happy Hanukkah, by the way. I just love holidays, don't you?"

"Absolutely," Adam agreed. "It's Chrismukkah for Kelly and me!"

Charlotte grinned. "We can call it whatever we want, but it's definitely the season of overindulgence, whether you're eating or shopping. And speaking of gifts, Adam, thank you for the generous donation to this evening's silent auction. That diamond and sapphire love-knot ring is absolutely stunning! I'll be tickled pink if my bid wins."

"Glad you like it, Charlotte. Can't think of anyone I'd rather see wearing it," Adam replied. "Sure hope it brings in a tidy sum."

"I'm sure it will, dear," Charlotte concurred. "Well, I do need to mingle a bit, so I am setting you two lovebirds free to enjoy the evening. Lots of interesting people to meet. On the veranda you'll find the best hors d'oeuvres from that new little bistro on East Paces Ferry, but first grab a libation in the library or the parlor. And Kelly, I do believe you'll recognize Maggie, my personal assistant who's one of the bartenders. I think you've worked together at the Humane Society several times. Make sure you ask her for my personal favorite, the candy cane martini. Y'all gotta be careful though, cuz it does pack a punch! Oh, and the silent auction items are in the library, too, so be sure to check them out. I'll catch up again with you two at some point."

"Thank you, Charlotte, I—" But before Kelly could finish her sentence, Charlotte moved on to greet additional guests. "She's one bustling lady."

"Yep. Let's go get that drink."

The library was the first room off the grand hallway, and immediately upon entering, the evocative fragrance of the twenty-foot Douglas fir embraced the couple. The red-and-gold tree trimmings added to the warmth of the dark mahogany walls rising behind the deep, brown leather chairs and brass floor lamps.

"This is definitely a special place. Might be my favorite room," Adam acknowledged as he surveyed the library. "I know it would definitely be my dad's favorite, especially if there was a humidor hidden somewhere."

Kelly cringed. "Your dad smokes cigars?"

"Not routinely, and definitely not on Shabbat. He does consider it to be one of the little joys in his life though." Adam paused and then added, "Yes. My dad would relish sitting here with friends and schmoozing, just socializing without any women present."

"No women?"

"Umm, specifically not my mother," Adam noted. "She would never approve of him smoking a cigar in the house."

"I'd take your mom's side in that situation. If I had a room like this, it would have one purpose only and that would be for reading. I'd snuggle up in that well-worn leather wingback over there and devour books."

"Well, mosey on over. Save me the seat next to your wingback while I grab us a couple of drinks. Cabernet or merlot?"

"Neither. I'll try one of those candy cane martinis."

"Ooh. My girl's living on the wild side tonight. I won't be held responsible for any type of bad behavior, will I?"

"You'll just have to wait and see."

Kelly cozied into the comfortable spot and placed her arm on the adjacent chair to save a seat. She watched as Adam patiently waited in line for one of the two bartenders. When Adam stepped forward to order, the previous client turned, and Kelly just happened to link eyes with the man. There, in all his studly glory, was Jenn's fantasy, the well-built actor who left her roommate breathless every

Monday night. Holding her gaze, he changed direction and appeared to be walking straight toward her. Kelly immediately lowered her face in an attempt to disengage any potential interaction. As she began to fidget with the slit of her dress, all the while hoping to maintain its full control and become invisible to the approaching star, she detected advancing footsteps. Holding her breath, she looked up—it was Adam with their drinks. "What do you say we check out the auction items? Might want to bid on something."

"Okay," Kelly exhaled as she emptied her offered glass in one long quaff.

"Downed that a little fast, didn't you?"

Kelly shrugged. "Probably." She saw a question mark spread across Adam's face. "I'm fine. Guess what?" she continued. "Jenn's heartthrob TV doctor was just standing right in front of you when you were waiting in line."

"Really . . . any chance we can meet him and make Jenn's dream come true?"

Kelly replied, "Not sure, but I'll keep an eye out for him, just in case. Wouldn't that be crazy?"

As they strolled past the auction items, Kelly was impressed with the vast array of signed memorabilia, custom artwork, travel packages, and more. As she compared the bids listed to items that caught her eye, it was evident that one of two things was true. Either the attendees were quite generous, or they were in desperate need of sizable tax deductions. In the center of the display was the love-knot ring Adam had donated.

"That is one pretty ring, Adam. Sure hope Charlotte gets it."

"So far it looks like it's hers. According to the bid sheet anyway," Adam stated as he surveyed the paper. "Believe me, Kelly, that lady can afford to get anything her little heart desires." He pulled her closer to him. "How about you? Any desires?"

Without hesitation she replied, "Yes, another candy cane martini!"

Adam laughed. "How about some food? Probably a good idea before you down another glass or two."

"I'm fine, just thirsty. You know how I love peppermint. And besides, I'd like to say hi to Maggie. The few times we worked together she was so nice."

The two headed over to pick up more drinks. Their conversation with Maggie was a happy one, though it was cut short due to an influx of guests. Kelly volunteered, "Hope we meet up again soon," as Adam grasped her hand and headed back to the grand hallway with its tall, heavy wooden doors opening into various rooms. The parlor was almost empty in contrast to the massive dining room overflowing with guests vying for a seat at the sumptuous table.

Kelly would have loved to dash to the adjoining pantry, the scene of their romantic interlude a year ago. The storeroom, lined with cupboards and shelving, had been an unusually romantic location, and she would have appreciated a replay of the moments they'd shared before being discovered by a sous chef. Unfortunately, Adam kept walking down the grand hallway and continued to weave through the ever-increasing crowd. All the while, Kelly never stopped keeping her eye out for someone famous . . . the governor, an owner of an Atlanta sports team, a rapper, or that TV doctor, of course.

Once they reached where the orchestra was performing, they paused. The bass-heavy number was indeed working its magic and bringing guests onto the dance floor. It was quite a sight to behold. The grandeur of the elegant room with faux marble walls was in stark contrast to the unsophisticated twisting and turning of the black-tie participants. Some of the dancers might have even been double left-footers, but no one seemed to notice, except Adam.

He pulled Kelly closer to him and loudly whispered, "We will definitely have to lay down some moves before we leave tonight. I think I can blend in with this group of bad dancers and not cause you any embarrassment. Some of them might even make me look really good."

"Don't be silly. You're a better dancer than you think."

"Even without lessons?"

"Absolutely. But first, I still want to get some food!"

"That's my girl. Let's go nosh!"

Ooh. Nosh. Need to remember to use that term when I meet his parents.

The closer they got to the veranda, the quieter and less congested the hallway became. Once they reached the oversized French doors, an attendant keeping watch over Charlotte's beloved German shepherd welcomed them to enjoy the fresh air.

"Hello Bosley, my old friend!" Kelly cooed as she stooped to pet the tender-hearted watchdog. "How have you been? Remember me?" She stared into his expressive eyes and smiled. "I'll take that thumping tail as a yes!"

Adam stooped alongside his date. "I see you're in good hands, or 'paws,' with Bosley, so I'm going to fetch us some more drinks. Be right back."

Kelly nodded and stood back up. "Great to see you, buddy. I know Charlotte loves those two little dress-up chihuahuas, but you are the king of the castle."

"That he is," acknowledged the caretaker as he opened the door.

Kelly responded with a smile and stepped onto the veranda. The starry sky lent an aerial elegance to the simple outdoor decor. Towering Green Giant Arborvitae and a multitude of outdoor patio heaters dressed with fairy lights shone lustrously amidst the high-top tables covered in red Christmas fabric. Mini boxwood tree centerpieces graced both the buffet tables and the antique bar. A southern breeze carried a nostalgic aromatic blend of roast beef, chocolate, and pine.

Mmm . . . That must be the mini beef wellingtons I smell. Yum!

Kelly turned and began walking past a row of high tops toward the buffet table when "Bosley, no!" rang trouble through the air. Mayhem ensued as the door attendant made a gallant, but unsuccessful, effort to apprehend the quick-moving canine. Kelly pivoted toward the ruckus just in time to meet the full force of Bosley's forward motion, slowing his progression enough for the doorman to apprehend his fugitive. Unfortunately, the collision caused Kelly to take three precarious steps backward, forcefully banging her head against a patio heater before stumbling back and making uncontrollable contact with an individual.

Gathering what little composure she could muster through her watering eyes, Kelly turned to apologize, but what escaped from her lips was not what she had intended. "Madame President!" Kelly could feel her face becoming the color of the table coverings. There she stood, somewhat disoriented. *What just happened? OMG! I just called her Madame President! She's not the president, she just plays the president. What is her name? I KNOW I know it! What's her damn name?*

The actress responded, "I'm fine, no harm done. That dog is quite a force to be reckoned with, but are you all right?"

Kelly just stood there, dumbfounded. *She's one of my favorite actresses . . . Don't blow this once-in-a-lifetime opportunity. Don't say something stupid. And for heaven's sake, stop the tears! This isn't how to act when you meet someone famous! Pull yourself together; what IS her name?*

"Are you hurt? Are you all right?"

"I think so."

The leading lady responded, "Why don't you just join me over there at the booth in the corner where we can both recover. I see by that empty martini glass you're a fan of Charlotte's holiday concoction. I've got an extra one there along with a plate of hors d'oeuvres. My date is inside. No need for the food or that sinfully tasteful beverage to go to waste, right?"

Kelly nodded. *Ayanna! It's Ayanna!* "Yes, President Ayanna!"

The celebrity was amused. "Well, that has a nice ring to it, but I assure you I only *play* the president."

Kelly was embarrassed. "Of course you do. I apologize for the fact that I seem to be starstruck! You are an absolutely amazing actress."

"Why, thank you," Ayanna replied graciously before turning and walking toward her destination. Kelly followed her new acquaintance to the corner booth.

As they sat down and the conversation ensued, Kelly found herself being asked all sorts of questions. Rather than talking about herself, she wanted this opportunity to be about movie stardom. The moment the actress stopped asking questions to chew a morsel of food, Kelly jumped at the opportunity to gain control.

Thinking she would start off with a simple, noninvasive question, Kelly asked, "Is this the first time you've attended a Humane Society benefit?"

"Yes, and it's my last."

Oh, no! Wrong question! "May I ask why?"

"Number of reasons, but basically, despite what you read online or in the tabloids, I'm a very private person. When I have free time, I like to stay home. My agent thought it would be great publicity for my date and me to attend tonight. It's been wonderful for my escort, but I could have done equally as much good by writing a check." The actress smiled. "I can see my date is finally coming back." Kelly turned to see a throng of people making their way toward the booth where they were seated. "It's been a pleasure speaking with you."

At the realization that their time was ending, Kelly sputtered, "Wait! Before you go, could I please get a photo?"

"Sure." Ayanna stood and smoothed the wrinkles from her dress.

Kelly grasped her phone and began to click a series of shots.

"Don't you want to be in the picture, Kelly? Let me ask Jim, my favorite press photographer, to snap a photo of us. He's right over there with Charlotte." She waved toward Jim, beckoning them both to come join her. No longer needing her phone, Kelly set it on the table in exchange for her martini glass and took another sip.

"Are we taking a picture?" a deep voice rose above the chatter of the group that was now standing feet from their booth.

Sweet peppermint-flavored mixture sprayed from Kelly's mouth. "Omigosh! It's you!" She teetered with the knowledge of who was standing before her. She took one more sip as she tried to calm her nerves and drink in the man's stunning appearance as well. *No wonder he's a model:*

perfect face with high cheekbones, deep-set eyes behind intellec-
tually styled horn-rimmed glasses, full lips, and just the right
amount of designer stubble to make me want to ask Adam for a
hallway pass . . . The girls would just die!

"Yes, it's me," he divulged with a playfully sincere grin. "I guess you could say that tonight, with this lady on my arm, I'm the First Man," he joked, showcasing his irresistible dimples before planting a kiss on his date's cheek. "Would you like a shot of us three?"

"Jim and Charlotte are headed this way, Josh. He'll shoot the photo for us."

Kelly stood motionless and speechless. There she was, for real, with Madame President and her date, the new number-one male underwear model of America, who had to be half Ayanna's age. *Wow! Josh is Ayanna's date!* She was totally enveloped in the surprise.

"You do want to be in the picture, don't you, Kelly?" Ayanna repeated.

"Oh. Uh . . . yes, of course," Kelly stammered.

"Might as well get the whole group. I always say, 'The more, the merrier.'" Josh turned away from the actress, bent forward, and lowered his glasses toward the tip of his nose. Peering over the rims, he whispered to Kelly, "Aren't you a sexy distraction."

Kelly's eyes widened. "Uh, thanks." She took another long sip of her beverage, desperately trying to steady herself and not scream like a fan. *Does he think I'm hot?*

As the photographer took command of the entourage to be captured, Kelly noticed her drinks were taking effect and her head was still sore from the earlier mishap. The group was growing in size and the more Jim directed folks on Ayanna's side to squeeze in closer, the more difficult it was for Kelly to remain surefooted. Sensing something was amiss, Charlotte slipped between Kelly and Ayanna, whispering, "Where's Adam? It's a shame for him not to be in the photo."

"I'm sure he'll be back shortly. He's been gone a while."

"Jim?" Charlotte barked. "Jim? Can we wait for just one more to join us?" The photographer reluctantly nodded as he encouraged the crowd to now turn sideways toward the middle of the group.

"Look here, Kelly. Timing is everything," Charlotte announced. "We're over here, Adam. Come join us!" she hollered and raised her right arm, hoping to get Adam's attention. She not only got his attention but everyone else's as her arm made contact with Kelly's shoulder, causing Kelly to lurch forward, losing her grip on the stemmed glass and bathing the supermodel's trousers with the peppermint liquid. Instinctively Kelly made a frantic attempt to end the glass's downward spiral only to be stopped midreach because her chandelier earring became caught on Josh's cummerbund. Her head then jerked to the right and came to a stop with a view she had never anticipated. She was so close to the newly crowned mega celeb, she could count the teeth of his trousers' zipper.

"Oh my gosh! I'm so sorry. I have my napkin here and I'll just kinda-sorta wipe . . ." *Oh! No I won't!* "I just mean . . . ah jeez! I'd move but my earring is caught in your cummerbund. I can't believe this. I'm so sorry!"

Josh played it cool. "Yeah, we caught the sorry part. Tell me. Have I lit up your chandeliers yet?"

Chapter 7

ADAM

Adam stepped out onto the veranda and surveyed the crowd for a few moments. "We're over here, Adam. Come join us!" Turning, he saw Charlotte waving, beckoning him to join the large group gathered in front of a high-reaching Christmas tree. Adam set the drinks down at an empty high-top table, laying claim to the vacant seats, and strode toward Charlotte. There appeared to be a small-scale stadium wave in progress. He was not prepared to see Kelly outlandishly stooped in an extremely embarrassing position.

"What . . . in the world?"

"It's all my fault," acknowledged Charlotte as she knelt by Kelly and tried to undo the mishap. "My waving caused Kelly to fall forward and . . ."

Kelly interrupted, "No, it's my fault for losing my grip on the martini glass and trying to catch it."

"Or for wearing chandelier earrings that catch in a cummerbund," Josh joked. "Didn't that jewelry come with a disclaimer?"

"See, Kelly? That's what you get for shopping at some little boutique and not at my store," Adam quipped as he helped the now disconnected Kelly stand erect.

"Now that I'm thoroughly embarrassed . . . Josh, this is my boyfriend, Adam, and Adam, this is, uh, Josh, America's underwear model extraordinaire." Kelly swept away imaginary wrinkles from her dress to distract from her embarrassment.

"You okay, Kelly? Josh, nice to meet you." Adam shook Josh's outstretched hand.

"The pleasure's all mine. Kelly here was bending over backward to have her picture taken with me, or should I say bending over forward? Which would you say, Kelly?" The celebrity grinned and winked at Kelly.

"I would say I was delighted to meet you and have our picture taken but that I was also the victim of circumstance!"

"It certainly was a different way of 'hooking up,' wasn't it?" Josh bantered, seeming to test the waters.

"That it was. And now you're just 'joshing' with me," Kelly returned a taste of their wordplay and waited for her volley to land.

"Ooh! Well played. I'm impressed with your quickness, not to mention your beauty. I would love to 'josh' with you again sometime." Josh tipped his glass toward her in salute and then sipped its contents while maintaining eye contact.

Adam watched Kelly's slightly delayed and slurring speechlessness. "I . . . I mean . . . I'm flattered. I think—" Her hand touched her cheek to perhaps check its redness.

Adam intervened and contained the moment that may have been driven by their holiday consumption. He himself was feeling some of its effect. "It's one of her qualities that I adore too. I'm a lucky guy to call her mine." He took Kelly's hand to claim his girlfriend in a macho moment of the everyday, matching its worth versus celebrity. The male model gave a slight congratulatory bow to Adam for defending his heart's prize.

Both waited for the other to speak, but the hostess intervened. "Let's just get this photo taken before any more foolishness can happen," encouraged Charlotte. "Adam, you stand between Kelly and me so I don't make another drastic mistake. And Jim, please hurry and snap this photo!"

Several hours later, after an abundance of Adam's rhythmless dancing and Kelly's peppermint indulgence, the couple decided it was time to call it a night. The silent auction had surpassed last year's record, which not only put a smile on Charlotte's face but also the love-knot ring on her pinky finger.

"Ya know," Kelly slurred as she grabbed Adam's arm, desperately trying to steady herself while navigating the steps to the waiting limo, "I'd say I feel like Cinderella, but I'm afraid I'd lose my glass slipper."

"I wouldn't focus on losing a slipper," Adam responded as he wobbled. "We need to focus on not losing our footing. Walking down these steps is another story. I'd hate to take a tumble and roll into the driveway. Think we might have indulged a bit too much?"

"Not a doubt in my mind. Sure glad you hired a limo." Kelly flashed a contagious smile to their chauffeur, already standing by the open door.

"May I assist you?" he asked.

"I think I might be beyond help," Kelly spluttered as she toppled into the seat. "Those candy cane martinis went down waaay too easy! We had a ball, though, right babe?"

Adam slid onto the seat next to his girlfriend. "Absolutely correct, my shuvdanit." He had to admit it was fun meeting celebrities and mingling with Atlanta's elite, but this moment, riding in the back seat of the limo with his arms around Kelly, would forever be the memory he truly savored. Her face was so close to his that he could smell the cocktail's distinctive, minty-fresh scent. After he requested the chauffeur raise the privacy barrier, he closed his eyes and pulled Kelly's mouth to his, kissing her softly at first but then more fiercely until she returned his kiss with reckless abandon. Their two bodies coalesced into one silhouette as the limo cruised toward Kelly's apartment. At that moment, Adam knew Kelly wanted him as much as he desired her. They were alone in their own world, one where he wanted to stay.

"Ahem." Neither one acknowledged the chauffeur's interjection. "Here we are."

Raising his mouth from hers, Adam gazed into her eyes. They had arrived at Kelly's. His princess was home.

Once again, the chauffeur broke the silence. "Here we are." He had already circled the vehicle and opened the door. "Thank you for the opportunity to serve you this evening." It was an awkward exit for both as they tried to bring their wits about them and regain their balance. Adam was just thankful he had prepaid and did not have to deal with anything else.

As the limo drove off, Kelly leaned into Adam and loudly whispered, "Maybe you should call that man back and have him take you home. If you can't walk steady, my mind warns me you shouldn't drive."

"I'm fine, and my mind says he's already gone," Adam murmured.

"Well, *my* mind doesn't mind then," Kelly garbled.

"Good," Adam declared, "because I don't want to leave you. How about a nightcap before I kiss my Cinderella good night?"

"That is an offer I just can't refuse . . . And you should know I'm not talkin' about that nightcap," Kelly flirted.

Adam wrapped his arm around Kelly's lower back and

together they steadied each other and made their way to the apartment building. Once inside the multistory residence, Adam eyed the elevator and blurted out, "You know what I have always, always wanted to do?" Kelly shrugged. "Kiss a girl in an elevator. And now's my chance." Before she could respond to his verbal fantasy, the doors began to part and Adam forged ahead, pushing her against the back wall.

The enclosed space offered an even greater sense of privacy than the limo, and Adam followed his impulse to make full use of the moment. He felt his heart pounding out of his chest as he pressed his entire body against hers. Eventually, when their lips parted, Kelly breathed, "Do you think we should push the button for that floor I live on before someone else wants to get in here?"

"Hmm, probably . . . Three, right? I always do three," and he chose that floor. "Whew, that was even better than the thought of it."

"Glad I didn't disappoint and burst your elevator bubble," Kelly slurred. As the door opened to the third floor's hallway, she added, "Thank goodness that burned-out bulb's been replaced. Heaven only knows what could be done in a dim-lit space. Or is that dimwit? No! Dim-lit!"

They both laughed as they walked the short distance to Kelly's place. Adam studied her as she attempted to insert her key and unlock the apartment door. After a minute of her fumbling, alcohol-induced attempts, he advised, "Why don't you just let me handle this, my hottie honey babe."

"Much appreciated, hottie hero guy. Don't want you, sir, to think I won't make you that coffee, Sir Hottie."

Once inside, both signaled the other to be quiet, with Kelly adding a loud whisper of "Shh!" They had presumed her roommates were sleeping by now. As they settled onto the couch, Adam asked, "You sure you don't want me to spend the night? I promise I'd be a well-behaved bed buddy. I could warm up those sheets for you."

"What I want and what I'm doing are two different things, baby honey." Kelly smiled. "Maybe someday, though."

"Oh! How I love someday!" Adam prodded. After a pause, he added, "Can someday be tonight?"

"So very sorry, my love. It's so very hard for me, too, but it'll be so very worth the wait. You'll see. It'll be the veriest." She defended her stance the best she could in her condition.

Adam watched his girlfriend stumble to the kitchen to brew coffee. *Man, I want her!* He sighed and closed his eyes, leaning back against the headrest. His mind wandered through all the sensual things they would do that "someday" and every day after it. He dreamed of the pleasure they would explore together, from head to foot, over and over again. He wanted to be with every inch of her, to touch her, feel her, smell her . . . and in the morning there would come the mishmash aroma of coffee and bacon, along with incessant whispering. *Coffee and bacon? Loud whispering?* Adam transitioned from temporary confusion to the awakening vision of Kelly's three roommates.

"What? Where's Kelly? When's the coffee going to be ready? I don't—oh, wow. I must have fallen asleep and dreamed it all."

The volume of Ashley's voice rose. "Hey, girls. I think Adam's awake, and he's mumbling about Kelly and a dream. Let's find out what he dreamed before he realizes he's awake! This could be good!"

"I'm awake," Adam informed whoever was listening.

"Never mind." Ashley was disappointed.

"Any ibuprofen in the house?"

"Sure. I'll get it, but it'll cost you," Ashley teased.

"Oh, wow. Look what I found on the net. Can you believe it?" Jenn gasped.

"Oh my word! What is she doing?" Melissa joined her sister in studying the photo on the screen.

"Great question . . . obviously a whole lot more when compared to the group photo." Jenn zoomed in on the image.

"I know what you mean! Must have been a really wild night." Melissa shook her head in disbelief.

"Couldn't have been too wild if her prince slept on the couch, if you catch my drift," Ashley commented as she joined her sisters.

"Well, there's only one way to find out. Which of you two is nervy enough to wake her?" Melissa popped the million-dollar question.

Both Ashley and Jenn looked at her in disbelief. "You're thinking we should wake her up? Is today National Make-a-Dumb-Move Day?"

"I'm just being practical," Melissa defended herself. "She deserves to get ahead of this, right? You should apologize for the dumb remark."

"True, I guess. And I'm sorry that you're dumb," Ashley ribbed.

"Ha ha. You're so funny. I'll take one for the team and do the dirty work. You both owe me." Melissa disappeared to rouse the sleeping subject of the tabloid's viral piece.

Adam had heard enough to put together what was now common internet knowledge. Someone had captured last night's cataclysm and posted it for the world to see. As Kelly walked into the kitchen, he rose from the couch and tried desperately to wake up and focus on the conversation. "What's happening with the computer?" she asked.

"Well, first of all, you'll need to sit down," Jenn announced as she pulled the chair out from the table. "Then you're going to want to brace yourself."

Kelly's reaction pinned itself to the last portion of the eldest sister's recommendation. "Oh no! No, no, *no!*"

"Spill the tea, girl! What happened?" Ashley interjected. Adam picked up the ibuprofen as he made his way to the coffeemaker and Kelly recounted the previous night's events to the mesmerized trio. After filling two cups with the strong ink-like liquid, he placed one in front of Kelly as he kissed her on the cheek and pulled out the chair next to hers to join the foursome.

When Kelly finished recounting every detail of the evening, Jenn was the first to speak. "I can't believe you were in the same room with my favorite actor and you didn't try to meet him. What were you thinking?"

"Jenn, come on! What are *you* thinking?" Melissa countered. "Kelly just experienced crazy at a whole different level!" She swayed her head from side to side as if weighing options. "If that happened to me, I think I would have just ripped that blasted earring out and let the blood squirt where it may . . . Although having a bloody stain in the groin area of America's number-one underwear model is not the best scenario I'd shoot for, per se, so maybe I would have done the same as you, Kelly. But then again . . ." Her head swayed once more.

"Really, Melissa?" Ashley quipped. "Everyone has the right to be indecisive at times, but you are abusing the privilege." Turning toward Kelly, the youngest sister continued her commentary. "Don't worry what people think, kiddo, because most do it without doing it at all."

"Sure hope you're right, Ashley." Kelly put her palm to her forehead. "Pass me that ibuprofen, please."

"Sure." Adam offered the bottle and then reached for his vibrating cell phone. "It's my sister. This might take a minute." He retreated to the couch, hoping to conceal himself with a false sense of privacy. "Don't want to bore you ladies with a family conversation."

"Ooh, that means sibling drama," Jenn thought out loud.

"Good morning, Sarah. Everything okay?... What? Questionable photo? What are you talking about, Sarah?... No... If you do, my dear sister, your jewelry shopping privileges will certainly be revoked... No... No, you will *not* let anything slip, Sarah... *Sarah*. Sarah?" A roar of nothingness filled the terminated call. With lightning speed, Adam tried to reconnect with his sister. *Of course it's going straight to voicemail. It's too late!*

"Well, I'm guessing that conversation did not go the way you wanted," Kelly murmured as she cozied up to Adam.

"You have that right. Prepare yourself for an onslaught of questions when you meet my family. This viral photo has already been seen by my sister, and I would bet that if my mother sees it, you'll be grilled like a charred steak."

Kelly laughed. "At times I admit I am a smidge concerned about meeting your family, but it really can't be that bad. I'm picturing it like interviewing for a job. I'll be sweet, kind, complimentary, and hide my psychotic side."

"When you meet them, just don't withhold the 'I'm in love with your son' aspect. That, my duvshanit, is our secret weapon." Adam pulled Kelly closer to him and whispered in her ear.

"Really?" questioned Kelly.

"Do tell!" urged Ashley as she plopped down on the oversized ottoman.

"We have no secrets in this house! Especially right now," added Melissa, to which everyone started laughing.

"That's true," agreed Jenn as she nudged her way next to Ashley. "Because by the time Melissa has weighed the pros and cons of keeping someone's secret, we've all heard her analysis and the secret's been exposed. So you might as well spill the info. It certainly can't be worse than what we've seen and heard this morning."

"Ladies, you have no idea! As my great-uncle used to say, 'Some days you're the dog. Other days you're the hydrant.'"

"Well, in my mind, you will always be the dog." Kelly wrapped her arm around him.

"And speaking of tail-waggers, I need to go rescue Bo so he can get to a fire hydrant! Want to come with me now or should I circle back for you?"

"I want to come with you." Adam nodded and Kelly continued. "Just give me a minute to feed Mr. Shrimp and get ready. I promise not to take long."

As Kelly scurried out of the room, Jenn called after her, "Remember what I told you last week, girl. Make it happen!"

Adam raised an eyebrow. "What'd ya tell her?"

"Well, according to the latest survey, women on average take fifty-five minutes to get ready every morning. By reading this research on the internet, I learned that you only need to spend five minutes showering, not fifteen, and less than twenty minutes on hair and makeup. That saves at least thirty minutes a day, which means you get an extra three and a half hours a week, fifteen hours a month, and one hundred eighty-two hours a year. With twenty-four hours in a day, that's like seven and a half days of free time in a year. That's like a whole week's vacation." Jenn paused to ponder. "Ya know, even better, if you don't count the hours you sleep each night, you're freeing up twelve days from your bathroom time. With most people on average getting two weeks paid vacation, actual vacation time is doubled. Isn't that amazing?"

Adam furrowed his brow. "No, Jenn, that's just the internet. But I do have to ask, how's it working for you?"

"It's not." Embarrassed, Jenn quickly passed Kelly as she reentered the room.

"Might not be working for Jenn, but it's absolutely working for you. Ready?" Adam asked.

"In record time, thanks to Jenn sharing some online info with me last week. Did you know—"

"Yes, I do. She shared already." Adam smirked and started toward the door. "Have a great rest of your day, ladies, but please, do *not* share that photo!"

"Understood," they replied in unison.

"I mean it," Adam threatened. As he shut the apartment door behind them, he commented, "Much easier navigating this hallway today than last night."

"I know, right? A little sleep, some ibuprofen, and black coffee make all the difference."

"Add a shower for me and fresh clothes to that list. This tux needs a trip to the cleaners. Do you mind putting that on your list of errands we're doing?"

"Gotcha," Kelly agreed. "I already listed breakfast in my mind as well. I'm starving."

"Me too. How about the classic 'everything plate' at the deli?"

"Sounds perfect."

As they stepped out into the sunshine, both picked up their pace as they walked to the Yafah LX. There was no time to waste in getting to Adam's place to take care of Bo, and Adam knew their other tasks would be short, easy ones. The work week following that day went surprisingly well, with only a few mentions of the infamous paparazzi photo. It was nothing Adam couldn't handle, and Kelly reported the same to him. The only ones obsessed with the photo seemed to be the three sisters and a handful of internet trolls. This struck Adam as odd. Why weren't they collecting more flack? Why didn't Sarah call back? Why wasn't she teasing him more, like she usually did?

It was probably his sister's reaction that he questioned the most, especially after her first phone call. When discussing it with Kelly, they both agreed that if the week was so easy, then why did it feel like the calm before the storm? Perhaps they were bracing themselves for what they knew would be the real storm. They had been able to take care of their issues as a couple so far, but only God knew how they would take care of his parents and the phone call that was coming.

Chapter 8

KELLY

It was Friday and Kelly was proud of herself for being beyond punctual. She hopped into her car twenty minutes ahead of time and drove to Adam's place. "Wow. You're early," Adam noticed. "I'm not quite ready."

"Go ahead and finish while I visit with my other favorite guy." Kelly was enjoying her early arrival playing tug-of-war with Bo. Adam's cell rang and Kelly spotted it on the entryway table. "I'll answer it for you, honey." She picked up the phone while reading the caller ID.

"NO!" Adam yowled. "That's the ringtone for my parents!"

"I know! It'll be quick and easy. Then I'll pass it to you!" Kelly pressed the button and answered the phone.

"NOTHING WITH MY PARENTS IS QUICK OR EASY!" Adam dashed to retrieve his phone. "DON'T ANS—"

"Hello. Adam's phone. Kelly speaking." After a moment she continued in front of her boyfriend's shaking head while he repeatedly mimed for her to end the call. "Yes, I am indeed Adam's girlfriend. It is so nice to meet you, Mrs. Cohen, at least by phone anyway."

Kelly was thrilled that any type of introduction was

finally taking place. She would show her partner that his worrying was for nothing. Her smile grew. "I have been looking forward to—" Her expression was gradually replaced with one of confusion. "Oh . . . well, no, I'm Catholic. However, I have learned a great deal about Judaism and some Yiddish too . . . What's that? Of course. He's right here. First, I just want to say—excuse me? Sure. Here he is." Rather than pass the phone, she put it on speaker and tightened her grip so Adam could not grab it from her. This conversation, good or bad, was going to be postponed no longer.

"Adam? Hello, Adam?" Freida Cohen spoke while her son closed his eyes and reopened them with a heavy sigh. Kelly offered him a nod of encouragement but continued to grasp the device.

"Hi, Mom."

"Adam. Oy vey! My heart is broken. I feel like a shlimazel right now. She's not Jewish, my son, my son for whom we made countless sacrifices every step of the way so you could have the best in life. Were you aware of this?" his mother lamented more than she asked.

"Mame, we've dated for two years. Of course I knew. And that does not mean you're an unlucky person." It was obvious to Kelly that Adam had been avoiding the task of telling his parents what her faith was because he knew it would be the worst news possible in his mother's mind.

"She is clearly not the one Adonai has intended for you. You must accept this right away," Freida Cohen replied matter-of-factly. Kelly's heart sank. Her sullied past feelings of not being good enough washed over her, seeping into the fast-growing stain that had almost disappeared from the cracks in her heart. Adam reached out and squeezed her idle hand.

"Mame, listen. The Lord, I mean Adonai, also intends for me to be happy. Two faiths woven together can be a good thing in life. Is a bridge not stronger when built with more than one vine?" Adam winked at Kelly.

"And if a bird and a fish should marry, what baby will they have that can swim *and* fly? Tell me this quickly because you are giving me shpilkes. Oy! I may even faint soon." Kelly rolled her eyes at the comment and Adam agreed with a nod.

"You're just upset, but I'm telling you there's no need for this."

"—A puffin! Puffins swim *and* they fly!" Kelly interjected.

"Is this Miss Kelly again? Where did my son go? I was talking with Adam just now!" The elderly woman was thrown.

"I'm here too, Mame. Don't worry," Adam tried to calm his mother. "We put you on speaker so we can both listen and talk."

Freida was silent for a moment. "Well, your father is here and I will put us on the phone speaker too. Now we are equal in number!"

"Mame, this is not a two-on-two match," Adam countered.

"Two on two? No one is on anyone! Please! Stop this nonsense and don't try to do the fast talk with me. And what are these puffins? Don't drop off the call either. We must discuss this issue! Morty, say hello so these two can know I meant what I said," Freida demanded.

"Hello, Adam. It's your father. So your girlfriend is a shiksa, huh? Good for you on a girlfriend, but enough playing with life, right? You must get a serious wife. Now I spoke with our friend Moishe and, for a few more transactions thrown his way, I can get you a few dates with some nice Jewish wife material instead and—"

"Stop! I'm happy with Kelly. I'm very happy," Adam asserted.

"Hello, Mr. Cohen. This is Kelly and I'm joining Adam in this conversation as well."

"Hello, Miss Kelly. It is a joy to be able to speak with you, a real pleasure, yaddah, yaddah, yaddah. Now could you please shut off the speaker and give Adam his phone so we may speak privately with our son? Thank you. Oh! But tell Adam to send us a picture of you," Morty requested. His words were followed by a jostling noise. "What? Slap your own arm! I just asked to see what she looks like is all I did! That is *not* encouraging a relationship! Fine! Fine already!" The father redirected his conversation back to the young couple. "Uh, so a picture is not necessary. May we please speak privately with my son now? Again, it's been a pleasure and so forth."

"Adam? Are you there? It's your mother, the one who is getting older every day, and who knows how many days your father and I have left." Adam pursed his lips and mouthed *Sorry* to Kelly before speaking.

"I'm still here, Mame," he reassured her.

"Adam. Listen. I have excellent news for you. At my ladies' weekly chavurah a couple weeks ago, I found out from my cousin's friend's daughter, Rachel, who married well with my cousin's other friend's son, and is already expecting the blessing of a baby, that your ex-girlfriend, Golda, has broken up with her boyfriend. They say she is single and searching again. I think it's a sign from above that you should be reunited with her. I always liked Golda, and she would be a baleboste. She would sail a tight ship for sure! And just think—"

"It's run. She would run a tight ship, Mame," Adam corrected his mother.

"So you agree. See? Already we're making progress in the dimming time of my final years. This is good, Adam! Keely can be a friend, but of course not too close, and you can reconnect with Golda, and it will all be good again. Let fish swim with fish already!" Freida pushed. "And, if not Golda—but I think it should be Golda—but if not, I can ask my cousin to ask her friend to see what she has left for available Jewish girls, at this late marrying age."

Morty intervened. "Probably not Golda, though. She's too much like your mother, so let's go with something different." Another jostling sound came through. "What? Stop with my arm already! What? It's uh, because you should shine alone, my sweet, in control no matter what I say or do, love of my very long marriage in this life, yaddah, yaddah, yaddah already. You should shine alone. Very much alone. No other woman should ever add to your light, my shefela . . . ever."

"Guys! I'm not going back to Golda and I'm all set. And it's Kelly, not Keely," Adam protested. "After two years, you should know this. I also suggest you focus on what we have in common instead of our differences. Okay? Now Kelly and I need to head out for Shabbat tonight with Sarah, Joel, and the kids."

"Sarah, she married so well, a rabbi even. We're so proud of her." Kelly recognized this as a dig at Adam and tried to add a positive tone to the conversation.

"Sarah and her husband seem so nice," she offered. "I'm looking forward to meeting them tonight, and I'm excited about taking part in the Shabbat. Like I said earlier, I've been studying and learning a lot about Judaism. And I'm looking forward to meeting you and Mr. Cohen in person as well."

"Yes. Yes, of course. I'm sure you're a nice person. Is

Adam there?" the elderly woman efficiently tucked away Kelly's attempt at connecting. Her heart sank at the quick and undeserved dismissal. She now understood why he dragged out any meeting with his parents.

"Still here, Mame. On speaker. Remember? So let me ask you this. Do you both still love me?" he inquired as if presenting a case before a judge.

"Do we love you? At your age, you should still have to ask that? Does a bird first ask its mother if she will share the worm she brings back to the nest before opening its beak?" Freida chastised her son.

He protested but was reminded of the strength in his couplehood with Kelly by her gentle stroking of his arm. "If you want me to soar across the sky, then first you must allow me to fly in my own way."

"All birds fly the same way, with their wings, but eagles fly with eagles and pigeons stay with pigeons!"

Morty interjected, "Speaking of wings, I brought in a large half-priced order of designer wingtip shoes because Moishe told me they're making a comeback to the business world. So, Adam, if you know anyone who would like—"

"Not now!" Mother and son clamored in unison.

"If not now, then when? You mentioned wings!" the older man defended himself. An unidentified noise escaped through the speaker. "Enough with the arm already!"

Adam offered a simple proposal. "Look. At least meet Kelly first and then we'll talk. Let's at least agree to that. You might be surprised."

"Okay. So we'll meet. We'll come and we'll meet. And, of course, we love you. No need to ever ask that question, my son." Freida Cohen had finally voiced her agreement to include Kelly at the occasion. Kelly, however, realized that connecting with the Cohens, mostly Adam's mom, would be more daunting than she had first anticipated.

"Looking forward to celebrating Hanukkah with you, Mr. and Mrs. Cohen!" she professed, feigning confidence.

"Thank you, Mame and Tate. I'm excited for all of us to get together," Adam added.

"For you, Adam, so you can first fly, and then we'll sort the birds," Freida stated with resolve. "Goodbye for now. See you next week!"

"Send me a text, Adam, if I should bring some wingtips with me," his father called out. "Keely, nice to talk to you, looking forward to meeting you, always a pleasure, yada, yada, yada. Bye, Adam."

Before ending the call the couple could hear a muffled sound followed by the older man's voice. "Stop that! It hurts! Enough with the arm already! She might be a shiksa, but that's not *my* fault!"

Kelly let out a sigh after Adam pressed the End Call button. "Okay. I'll admit it. I understand why you kept postponing this."

"Mmhmm," Adam replied.

"Your dad is a riot, but I think I'll do okay with him. Your mom's support, however, is going to be a real uphill battle. There doesn't seem to be any thinking outside of the box for her." The young couple hugged.

"Yes, my mom is going to make it a tough climb, but I think you have the turbo power to make it to the top, babe." Adam leaned in to kiss his girlfriend while softly holding her face. Kelly welcomed his advance and became powerless to resist. He moved his mouth over hers and let his tongue trace the fullness of her lips. They pulled each other in closer with desperate need and the musky scent of his cologne sent a wave of deeper desire crashing over her. Kelly wanted him more than ever, right here and right now. They slowly stepped together toward Adam's bedroom without interrupting their growing passion. They could no longer deny the urge to express their deeply connected love.

Adam gently lifted Kelly in order to carry her to his bed. Time stood still and the world disappeared as they entered into a different existence created for just the two of them. He placed her on the bed, kissing her mouth, then her chin, and moved on to her neck. Kelly's breathing became heavier.

"I love you," she whispered. He responded with words she couldn't make out but she understood them by their tone. Adam began to undo the top button of her shirt. Kelly bolted up into a sitting position, causing him to lose his grip and fall facedown onto the bed. "We can't do this. Not now, and for many reasons."

"Sure we can do this, and for many good reasons!" Adam insisted, pulling himself up to address yet another twist in events.

"No. I'm sorry, Adam. I just can't. We *have* to take care of your work and then head over to my church and then your sister's for Shabbat, and we have to go because there's too much happening today. And, if we don't leave now, I'm afraid that I won't be able to save myself for my wedding night. I need to keep that commitment I made. It's really important to me! Okay?" Kelly could see the disappointment hidden behind the love in her boyfriend's eyes. Their long, somber gaze spoke volumes.

Adam sighed. "Sure. I get it. I don't like it, but I get it." They both stood up and adjusted their clothing and hair. He quickly finished getting ready while Kelly took care of Bo. They headed out to Dan's Fine Jewelry so Adam could finish a few tasks before leaving for their volunteer duties at Kelly's parish, St. Anthony of Padua Church. Her church was presenting a live Christmas nativity event for families. Once at the store, Adam completed his projects quickly with his girlfriend's assistance. "Ready to check nativity animals at St. Anthony's with your handsome helper?"

"Absolutely! And thanks, Adam, for defending me earlier." She kissed him. "And I still can't believe your mother thinks I'm a pigeon without even meeting me in person!" She shook her head and started the engine to her car while Adam admired her.

"You're an eagle all the way in my book, babe."

It was not a long trip to the church. Kelly pulled into the temporary parking area for workers created for the special event. It took only a few short minutes to grab her black bag from the trunk and set herself up at her designated area, while Adam was escorted by a parishioner to the section he would be working. She found a clipboard of forms that would certify the health of the animals participating in the evening's live nativity display. Kelly was glad she would only have to take care of the prescreening and placement of the animals, thanks to Sully coming to help with the event itself.

A short stream of animal trailers began pulling in near her station. She gave a quick glance over to Adam, who was filling buckets with water and attending to other small tasks. During the next ninety minutes, Kelly examined sheep, goats, a small cow, and a couple of donkeys. Instead of cantankerous camels, a trio of fairly calm alpacas had arrived for their check-in as well. Kelly next checked each one's location, ensuring that the appropriate food and water had been placed according to need. Anything that helped the animals remain tranquil was very important. Once satisfied with the results and quite happy that her task was accomplished without incident and well ahead of time, Kelly walked back through the church grounds to locate Adam, but to no avail. She inquired about him with a few committee members but they all stated that they had seen him, just not within the past half hour. No one had a clue as to his whereabouts until she asked the chairperson, who informed her that he did great until he stepped in some donkey dung.

"Donkey dung?" she exclaimed.

"Unfortunately, that's correct," the older parishioner replied. "He was backing up to turn around and his foot went right in the treasure mound. Lost his balance, too, when he panicked and slipped in his reaction to it. Good thing he put his hands forward as he fell, even though that meant his hands caught some of the dung too. Otherwise, he would have landed face flat in it. Better the hands than the face, right? Anyway, he went inside to the restrooms in the church basement. He's going to clean it up the best he can. Said something about going home to change again, if possible, before something else you two have going on tonight."

"Oh my goodness! Thanks." Kelly rushed toward the church building in search of Adam. She entered the rear side entrance and made her way down the basement stairs toward the restrooms. The custodian was mopping the hallway floor with what her nose detected to be a lemon cleaner.

"Careful there, Miss. We had someone here earlier with donkey manure on himself. Stinks to be him! Get it?" The custodian chuckled at his own pun.

"I do get it. He's also the guy I'm looking for right now," she added and continued past the worker.

"You won't find him down here," the man informed

her. "He tried to wash in the men's room, but left just as I arrived. Told me it was from a donkey. Guess you could say he made an ass of himself." The custodian laughed alone as Kelly gave a polite grin. "Probably headed home by now and—"

"Sorry! I'm in a time crunch here."

Kelly hurried up a set of stairs. She assumed he didn't go home because she knew he would never leave without telling her. Once on the next level, Kelly turned and looked. There were about a dozen scattered praying parishioners sitting or kneeling in the pews. She returned her eyes to the very front and noticed something strange about the Christmas season baptismal pool positioned to the far right of the altar. There were soiled white linens hanging around it. As she approached, she could see telltale splashes of water between the streaked, disheveled pieces of cloth on the rim of the pool, and the surrounding carpet was marked with dark splotches.

No. No. No. Kelly climbed the two short steps into the sanctuary area. The stench, along with the brown-streaked linens, told her everything she needed to know. *I can't believe this! Adam used some of the purificators the altar servers give the priest to wipe the chalice during mass! I will never be able to drink from the chalice again without thinking of this whole mess. Oh God, please help me right now. Help us! Where—is—Adam?*

She renewed her search as she carefully placed the linens in one small pile. Then she spotted the tall Paschal candle and held her breath for what seemed like an eternity. It was lit, which was very odd, seeing as it was only used during the Easter season and very special occasions, like the receiving of sacraments. *Oh, Adam. Why do I have the sinking feeling that you're connected to this as well? Ugh! What else have you done?*

Kelly grabbed the long handle of the nearby snuffer and extinguished the tall candle. She was growing more worried. A few arriving parishioners exchanged whispered greetings with her as she descended from the sanctuary area and crossed paths with them on their way to their chosen pews. She decided to finish scanning the inside before heading back out to the nativity event.

Why are all the votive candles on the stand in front of the Mother Mary statue lit? She remembered once counting forty-eight of them, and the whole stand was ablaze. *Like, all four dozen of them! The whole damn stand! Adam, are you connected to this too?*

She shook her head as her Catholic guilt envisioned all possible repercussions and then turned her gaze toward the back of the church. If Adam had done these things, Kelly was certain he had a reason, and it was nothing maliciously or even jokingly intended. They would fix whatever needed fixing, and if the people of her parish couldn't be understanding of a clueless Jewish guy within their church, then she and Adam would find a parish that lived a better definition of Christianity. She also almost certainly knew that would not be the case. Here they were helping at an event at her church, and then tonight they would be celebrating Shabbat. Both respecting and cherishing the other. Now if she could only find him!

Kelly headed to the small rooms in the back of the church. *Hmm. Maybe Adam thought there was some place better to wash back here.* She came to an abrupt stop. Adam was sitting in one of the rooms, where confessions were sometimes heard, and he was nonchalantly chatting with Father Charles.

Why is he sitting with my pastor of all people? It can't be for confession. He's not Catholic. Oh. This can't be good. Wait!

They're sharing some kind of laugh together! Okay, laughter is good. But what could they be laughing about? Kelly couldn't hear what was being said behind the room's large glass pane. She hurried to the small room in a panic. "Um. Hi there, Father Charles. You've met my boyfriend Adam before, but I think this private meeting is a first for all of us. And Adam, I've been looking for you everywhere! I heard about the donkey dung." She hesitated. "Ooh! And I can smell it too! We're sorry, Father. Am I rambling? Sorry."

Father Charles reassured her, "Hi, Kelly! You're fine. Adam and I have been getting to know each other somewhat more, like the fact that he's Jewish. The fact that he smells like a donkey's behind was the very first thing I noticed when he came in for a, uh, chat session."

The last line made Kelly even more nervous. "Oh? A chat session? So he didn't walk into someone's confession or anything like that?"

"Well, as a matter of fact," Adam chimed in, "it was indeed the time allotted for confessions, but Father actually called me in because he wanted to know why I lit all the small votive candles as well as the really big one, the Paschal candle, I believe. That one's really important. Right, Father? And I knew it was important, but not *that* important."

"Yes, those are the correct names I mentioned to you. And, no, there's a lot you didn't know, but it turns out there are some things that you *do* know." The priest turned toward Kelly. "So, we've been chatting and getting to understand things more, while correcting what needs to be rectified." Kelly looked down, totally embarrassed.

"Honey, I know that look. Don't worry. It's okay. Father Charles knows I didn't do anything on purpose, and I told him we'd totally wash those purifiers. Well, I did do that on purpose, technically, but he knows it wasn't with bad intentions."

"Purificators is the correct name, as long as you're being technical," the pastor offered.

"Right. Purificators. Thanks, Father. Anyway, honey, they have time to treat the water and I told Father I'd pay for anything involved with that. I was going to do that all along. Then he's going to bless it again, and that's the part I didn't realize. I guess it's blessed water. I was just trying to wash off the dung quickly and I saw the tub and all."

"Baptismal pool," Kelly and Father Charles corrected in unison.

"Baptismal pool. I tried the sink in the men's room but it was too small and I was making a mess."

"Got it. So you were aiming for many small messes instead of one big mess," Kelly replied with sarcasm.

"Kelly," her pastor interrupted, "Adam meant well and this can be fixed before masses this weekend. I already have Gaetan mopping the floors to clean them and, uh, get rid of the problematic scent. Then he'll take care of the purificators by putting them in the washer at the rectory and I'll have the housekeeper run the load. So, no worries there either. I can tell you feel embarrassed, but there's no need. Okay?"

"Okay, Father, thanks for understanding. I would have been with Adam but I was still outside finishing up with the animals." Kelly offered a smile.

"Yes, and thank you for doing that for our parish."

"I used the snuffer and took care of the Paschal candle. What do you want to do about the votives?" Kelly inquired next.

"I knew enough to put money in the box as a donation for the votives. So that's all set too," Adam explained.

"Okay. About those votives, why *did* you light all of them? I mean you, like, lit *all* of them!" Kelly yearned to know.

"Yes. Why *did* you light all of them?" Father joined in the question. "Did you have that many intentions?"

"No. Just one." Adam explained further, "But it's a *huge* one, so I figured Kelly and I needed them all."

"How's that?" Father Charles was puzzled.

"Oh, I get it!" Kelly's face lit up and the couple gazed at each other for a moment with unified smiles. They reached out to hold hands and faced the priest.

"You see, Father, I lit all those votives because our relationship is going to need all the help in the world in getting my Jewish mother to accept Kelly as my very serious but very Catholic girlfriend."

"And I agree with Adam that it's going to be a huge challenge," Kelly acknowledged.

"Adam, I understand your reasoning, but please, no Paschal candle in the future and only one votive is needed per intention. No matter the size, big or small, God answers all. And your mother's acceptance of your relationship may be huge, but God gladly accepts the challenge."

"One candle for each intention and no Paschal candle. Got it," Adam replied. "And God may have just met his match, but we're hoping He wins the contest. Thanks for your total understanding of a Jewish man trying to fit in at a Catholic church."

Kelly chuckled. "Yeah, trying to fit in like a husky man trying to fit into a junior-petite-extra-large-sized pair of pants."

Adam was unsure of her comment. "What size is that even, junior-petite-extra-large?

"Exactly," Kelly quipped. "You need someone else to tell you whether you're fitting in or not. But it's still fun to watch!"

Father intervened. "Kelly, be gentle now. One day you

or I may need Adam's understanding should either of us ever make a mistake while visiting his temple."

"Good point," she agreed. "Well, we have to run now. We're heading over to Adam's sister's house for Shabbat, and I'm pretty sure Adam is going to need to do a quick wash and change so our evening isn't filled with a bouquet of donkey dung!"

"Ooh. That's right," Adam agreed. "Nice chatting, Father Charles."

"Let's do it again sometime, hopefully under better circumstances," the priest offered.

"Definitely," Adam agreed and shook hands with him. "And please do let me know if I need to reimburse you for any cleaning expenses."

"I'm sure we'll be fine. Always nice to see you, Kelly," her pastor added.

She returned his pleasantry as the couple turned and exited the room. Once outside, Adam whispered to Kelly, "If your pastor spent one day with my mom, I bet he'd personally light all the votives *and* the Paschal candle too!"

Chapter 9

ADAM

After turning into his sister's driveway, Adam brought the car to a stop and faced Kelly. "Well, I'm changed and smelling better, so I'm ready for this. How about you?" Total silence. "Hey, you. Don't freak out. It's going to be fine. It's not like my parents are here tonight!" Kelly grimaced. Adam reached for her hand. "Sarah and her family are gonna love you! Don't be nervous. Just be yourself. Now, let's get out of this car and not keep them waiting. I guarantee my niece has been peering through the plantation shutters, broadcasting that we're here."

Before they could even reach the porch, the unofficial welcoming committee burst through the front door cheering, "Uncle Adam! Uncle Adam!"

Adam braced himself for the onslaught as his nine-year-old niece ran full speed to jump into his arms. "Gut Shabbos, Esther. You look very pretty tonight."

"Thanks. It's my new dress for Shabbat. Mommy says I can only wear it for special occasions."

Adam smiled. *So far, so good. Esther is being unusually sweet, and Kelly doesn't look nervous. Might get through this just fine after all.* "Esther, I want you to meet my friend Kelly. She's going to celebrate Shabbat with us tonight."

"Hi, Kelly. Shabbat shalom!" blurted Esther. "I know all about you! You're a doctor for pets, you have a cat, and this is your first Shabbat because you're *not—*"

"—Hungry?" Adam had instinctively covered the little diva's mouth to muffle her words. Turning away from the little rascal in his arms, he asked, "You are hungry, aren't you, Kelly?" She nodded. Adam lowered his niece, took her hand, and said, "Let's go inside. We're hungry!"

"I'm hungry, too!" Esther chirped. "Come on, Kelly, let's go!" Grabbing her guest's hand, Esther placed herself between the couple. "I'm so glad you came to my house!"

"Me too," answered Kelly as they stepped into the foyer. "What's for dinner?"

"Really good stuff! My mom made all my favorites just so I wouldn't complain!"

"She's a good cook, all right," acknowledged Adam as Esther ran off to entertain herself. He touched another mezuzah, followed by Kelly. "My sister is also super smart to make that little one's favorite food to ensure a happy and peaceful dinner."

"Who's super smart?" questioned Sarah as she rounded the corner. "Someone must be describing his favorite sister."

"My favorite and only!" Adam gave his sister a soft peck on her cheek. "Thanks for the invite."

"Nothing like a dry run before the Morty and Freida show rolls into town . . . Well, enough said about that! You must be the lovely doctor who monopolizes all my brother's free time. Welcome to our home. I'm so happy to finally meet you, Kelly."

"Thank you. I'm very happy to be here."

"And probably unnecessarily nervous. Please don't be uneasy; we welcome all types here!" quipped Sarah's husband as he entered the foyer.

"Now stop that, Joel Weinberg!" scolded Sarah. "Can you make it through Shabbat without the jokes and horsing around?"

"No, I can't. You know what they say, Sarah: 'With horses you check the teeth; with a human you check the brain.' This girl understands. She's checked horses' teeth and tonight I am going to check her brain. I'm sure she'll pass." The rabbi impishly grinned before giving Kelly a hug. "Welcome to our home, Kelly . . . Oh, and hello to you too, Adam."

"Yes," Adam sarcastically replied. "Hello to you as well, Joel. So nice of you to lose the habitual flannel shirt and dress for this special occasion. And you're wearing wingtips?"

"Yeah, I heard they're coming back, so your dad said."

Adam shook his head. "Interesting."

Joel shrugged. "It's not easy for this Jewish mountain man to part with his nappy plaid shirts, but I try."

"You're a mountain man?"

"My brother-in-law likes to envision himself as an explorer of the wilderness."

"Like Moses," commented Kelly.

"That's quite a compliment." Joel grinned. "I always equate it more to my love of the outdoors and the history of the wild, wild west though."

"Oh, no. Don't get him started," interjected Sarah. "He'll tell you all about the Jewish mayor at the O.K. Corral and then move on to the Jewish mayors of Deadwood, Dodge City, and Tombstone." Sarah laughed and continued, "By the time he finishes, our dinner will be burned, or worse yet, Esther will have tied her brothers to the banister, pretending to have captured the nastiest outlaws. We really can't wait any longer to begin, Joel. Please go get the children. I know you'll encourage them to behave. We'll wait for you in the dining room."

Adam appreciated exactly what his sister was privately conveying. *Go read our three anklebiters the riot act!* No one communicated the Fifth Commandment better than Joel. Both Sarah and he fully believed in teaching their youngsters to honor their parents, respect rules, and have good table manners. Dead air filled the hallway as Sarah led the way. It was Kelly who broke the silence once they entered the dimly lit dining room. "What a beautiful table. This is lovely!"

"They eat like this all the time," Adam deadpanned.

"Oh really?" Kelly laughed.

"Only every Friday, Kelly," Sarah corrected her brother. "Shabbat is an important time for our family and I really enjoy setting a festive table and using fancy dishes."

"No plastic tableware for this dish queen," Adam snickered as he surveyed the perfection his sister had created. The rich blue tablecloth provided a striking contrast to the golden charger plates layered with white china, the numerous white rose centerpieces, and the antique candlesticks. "Where's the traditional white tablecloth with the Shabbat designs? You know Mom is going to expect to see that when she's here."

"Precisely why it's not on the table tonight."

The room became wrapped in silence as Joel marched the children to their assigned seats. Even two-year-old Noah understood the importance of standing quietly next to his mother. After Sarah put coins in her charity box, she struck the long-handled match, placed her hand over

Esther's to help her light her smaller candle, and then lit the remaining ones. She placed the matchstick on a fire-safe plate to extinguish on its own, waved her hands around the candles three times, covered her eyes, and prayed. "Blessed are you, Lord our God, King of the universe, who has sanctified us with His commandments, and commanded us to kindle the light of the Holy Shabbat."

"Amen," everyone responded in unison.

Sarah continued with the blessing for the children. "Jacob and Noah, may you be like Ephraim and Menashe. Esther, may you be like Sarah, Rebecca, Rachel, and Leah. For our children: May God bless you and protect you. May God show you favor and be gracious to you. May God show you kindness and grant you peace."

Almost immediately the family began singing, and once finished, Sarah's husband held a beautiful sterling-silver cup in the palm of his right hand and filled it with wine. He then began very quietly, "There was an evening, there was a morning. The sixth day: And the Heavens and the Earth and all they contained were completed, and on the seventh day God desisted from all the work that he had done. And God rested on the seventh day from all the work that he had done. And God blessed the seventh day and sanctified it, for on that day he rested from all the work which he had done in creating the world. By your leave, rabbis, masters, teachers!"

The family responded, "L'chaim!", and the rabbi continued to chant. Once Joel had completed the blessing, everyone raised their individual wineglass to take a sip. Adam's mind wandered. *Glad some of tonight's menu is not totally foreign to her.* He was sure their two religions had enough in common to make it work. He had already spent time with Kelly's Uncle Mike and Aunt Julie and thought they did not have any big objections to him being with Kelly. After the foursome's initial meeting, her Aunt Julie apparently confided to Kelly that even when a couple shares the same religion, there is sometimes negotiation. Aunt Julie would fast on Ash Wednesday and Good Friday and abstain from meat every Friday during their Lenten period, but Uncle Mike could never pass up a double cheeseburger any day of the week. That left his family as the wild card. *No doubt differences will be a discussion topic later tonight, a warm-up to the upcoming saga. "Morty and Freida Meet an Alien: Close Encounters of the Worst Kind." Oy vey!*

The beautifully embroidered cloth covering the challahs on the cutting board was now in front of Joel. He removed the cloth and placed it to the side. Placing one of the challahs on top of the other, the rabbi held the loaves in both hands, raised them, and spoke the traditional blessing, to which everyone responded with an amen. Joel then cut the bread, sprinkled the piece with salt, and ate a small bite before cutting additional slices. He sprinkled more salt over the cut portions and passed the cutting board first to Sarah, who would assist Noah in his high chair, then to Jacob, Adam, Kelly, and lastly Esther, who set it back down in front of her dad and let out a dramatic sigh. "Well, that sure took long enough! Let's eat!"

Joel chuckled and tried to deflect his wife's reprimanding stare. "Yes, let's eat," he affirmed, and then added, "Esther, why don't you help Mommy bring the meal to the table?" Once the mother-daughter team had exited, he continued, "The rituals did take a bit longer than normal. Usually we streamline the length of the prayers so the kids don't get too fidgety, but with Morty and Freida coming for Hanukkah, we know they would not appreciate any shortcuts."

"Aaahhhh, tradition," laughed Adam. "You're right. Much easier to rationalize impatient children to my parents than to justify abbreviated worship."

"Well, I thought the kids were great," offered Kelly as she gave a thumbs-up to Jacob and Noah. "I know when I was a kid I probably would have not been so well-behaved."

"Really?" questioned Joel.

Adam laughed. "Let that red hair of hers be a warning, brother-in-law. This woman is feisty and has been known to speak her mind. One of her many best qualities, in my opinion, and just another reason why I love her."

"Who do you love, Uncle Adam?" pried Esther as she carried a towering platter of artichokes into the room and set it on the table. "Don't you forget I asked that, but first, I still have to bring out more food. You remind him about my question, okay, Kelly?"

"Absolutely. I'll be glad to do that for you. But Esther, do you need some more help bringing the food to the table? I'd be happy to lend a hand."

"Oh no, that's okay. Uncle Adam usually helps, though." Esther grabbed her uncle's hand attempting to pull him out of his seat, and with a shrug, Adam headed into the butler's pantry with her.

A more intense aroma greeted Adam as he stepped into the kitchen. "So? What do you think?"

Esther didn't hesitate to answer the question that was not meant for her. "Well, I think it smells yummy. Thanks, Mom, for making my favorites! Can I bring the soup to the table?"

"*May* I bring it to the table," corrected Sarah. "Remember, Esther, use *may* when you are asking permission."

"Yes, ma'am. *May* I bring it to the table," reiterated the pint-size life of the party.

"Yes, you may." Sarah's eyes remained focused on the white-glazed soup tureen as she wiped a miniscule drip from the rim and secured both the ladle and the lid. "Take your time, Esther, and be careful. That soup is hot!"

"I'll get the door for you," offered Adam.

As the proud soup-bearer strode out of the kitchen, Adam turned toward his sister and repeated, "Well, what do you think?"

"I think you can start slicing the roast while I get the potato kugel out of the oven."

"Come on, sis, that isn't what I was asking."

"I know that, but how can I have an accurate opinion when we haven't even had a real chance to chat yet?"

"You mean interrogate."

"No, that's our mother's job."

"Sad . . . but true," Adam conceded as he steadied the long-handled meat fork and began slicing.

"What's true?" asked Esther as she bounded back into the kitchen.

Always trying to stay one step ahead of her daughter, Sarah quickly answered, "Your favorite vegetable salad has all the colors of the rainbow."

"Mmhmm. It's so much fun to eat colors other than just green. I don't know why my brothers only like peas."

"You should ask your brothers," suggested Adam.

"I think I will," agreed Esther as she grasped the handles of the white bowl heaped with vibrant vegetables. "I'll be back!"

Adam earnestly stared at his sister as she removed the last remaining side dish from the oven. "Look, it's a big deal to me to finally have you meeting Kelly. I've waited a long time to bring someone home to meet the family. Can't you just give me a first impression?"

Sarah placed the last roasted carrot on the platter. "She's pretty, Adam, and seems very sweet. Right now the only problem is that I can't get that horrible photo of her with the underwear model out of my head!"

Neither of the siblings had noticed Esther's return. "Well, you know what I can't get out of my head?"

"What?" Sarah and Adam replied in unison.

"Asking about green vegetables. Jacob said he likes eating green peas cuz it reminds him of eating boogies! Mom, I can't carry the peas. Can we leave them here?"

Sarah suppressed the urge to laugh. "Uncle Adam will carry the platter and I will carry the kugel. How about if you lead the way and announce that dinner is served."

"I can do that!"

Once the final dishes were delivered, the trio of servers sat down and surveyed the mouth-watering spread. Sarah was the first to speak. "Hope it's okay that we brought everything to the table at once."

"Of course," replied Joel.

Sarah turned toward Kelly and continued, "It's just easier doing it that way with the kids rather than eating in courses."

Kelly nodded in agreement. "This is just wonderful, Sarah. Everything looks so tempting and smells so good! And boy, that bread is delicious! Did you make it?"

Adam smiled as he passed the platter of artichokes. *Score a bonus point for Kelly the baker!*

"Yes, I did. Our grandmother lived with us when we were growing up. She claimed to have been born making challah, and for a long while I actually believed her! Every

Friday when we'd be kneading the dough, she would reminisce how, as a child, she would start making it before leaving for school, always making her dad promise to punch it down while she was gone so it would be ready to bake when she got home. Before she would shape it, Grandma would always tear off a small piece, say a blessing over the bread, and then put it in the oven."

Esther chimed in, "We do that, too, Mommy. You say that's because it reminds us how a long time ago a loaf was given to the priest at the temple."

"That's interesting, Esther. Did you help your mom make this loaf?"

"Yes, I did! I'm proud of that."

"My dear, sweet daughter, you must not be proud; that is a sin," Joel gently admonished. "I think what you meant to say is that you are confident you can do a good job because Mommy has taught you well."

Adam smiled at Esther. "Being confident is a good thing, sweetie," and then added, "We're all gonna have to watch our words when Mame and Tate are here—especially Mame, she can be so critical. You should have heard our conversation on the phone earlier today, and that was just about *meeting* Kelly!"

Bzzt . . . Bzzt . . . *What is that sound?*

Kelly shrugged. "I think you're being too hard on them, Adam. All things considered, I thought our conversation with them went pretty well."

"So, you've already had a conversation and are not running away?" Sarah jested in between bites of the rainbow salad.

"Kelly *is* an optimist."

"Yes, I am, Adam. It's all about perception."

"You forget that perception and reality are two different things and that your perception of my parents is not my reality." Adam gently poked Kelly under the table. *Must be her phone again. Doesn't she hear that buzzing?* "Your reality can change, ya know. Just wait and see."

"And how will you accomplish that?"

"I'm working on my plan, starting with buying a perfect little present for each of them. Just need to go shopping and figure it out."

"I have some shopping that needs to get done as well. If you want to go together, I can help you," offered Sarah.

Ignoring another nudge, Kelly wondered out loud, "Would you really? That would be great! I have Sunday off and was planning to go then. Does that work for you?"

"Absolutely. My friend Becca has the perfect little shop on Canton Street in Roswell. I've always found ideal gifts for my parents there. I'll text you the address. Does two o'clock work for you?"

"That's perfect. I can't thank you enough, Sarah!"

"Kelly, don't you hear that? It's the third time your phone is buzzing," complained Adam. "You should answer it. It's driving me crazy."

Sarah added, "No harm done, Kelly. It's okay if you need to take the call."

Once she had retrieved the phone from the depths of her purse and saw the caller ID, Kelly knew she had to answer it. "I am so sorry, guys. It's Sully. Please excuse me."

"But I thought you weren't on call tonight," Adam protested.

"I'm not, but I'm sure it's something serious if Sully is calling me. She wouldn't unless it's important. Hello, Sully . . ."

Esther whispered to her uncle. "Who is Sully?"

"She's the lady who owns the clinic where Kelly works," Adam explained.

"Oh, okay." Her curiosity satisfied, Esther took another sizable bite of her favorite salad.

"Please chew with your mouth closed," coached Sarah, "and Noah, do not blow bubbles in your cup or you will have to give it to me."

"NO!" demanded Noah as he repeatedly puffed into the sippy cup.

"Yes," responded the determined mother, reaching for the small fist clutching the blue handle.

"Mine!"

"No, sir," Sarah calmly replied. "Not when you blow bubbles after Mommy asks you not to do that." The warm, nostalgic scene of a family enjoying dinner together was now under attack, thanks to the two-year-old pitching a fit. His plate of chopped-up food and cup filled with milk went flying in every direction. "I know what you're thinking, Adam. Don't even say it." Her cheeks were transitioning to a deeper pink. "Joel, could you please take our fallen cherub while I clean up this mess?"

"Certainly." Joel reached for Noah, who howled in protest.

"Oh! What happened?"

The already embarrassed Sarah turned to see Kelly standing in the butler's pantry.

"The usual," intruded Esther, as she blotted the puddle of milk on her plate. "My brother just likes to get his way, and when he doesn't, my mom says we hit a bump in the road. Tonight it's a big bump."

Kelly nodded in agreement. "I hit a bump in the road, too, Esther. I'm sorry to say that I have to leave." She turned to Adam. "Sully needs me to come to the office.

There's been an explosion at the Humane Society and they're bringing in some seriously injured animals."

"How awful. Do you want me to drive you?"

"I already called for a ride and they're just two minutes out." Turning from Adam, she continued. "Sarah, thank you for the lovely evening. I'm so sorry I have to leave."

"Me too, especially considering this awful situation. We'll just have to make up for lost time when we go shopping Sunday."

"Agreed." Kelly's phone began to vibrate. "My transportation must be here. Please say goodbye to Joel for me. Nice meeting you, Esther and Jacob."

Adam stood. "I'll see you to the door."

There was no time for any lingering goodbyes and he quickly returned to find Sarah sitting alone in the quiet, empty dining room. "Must admit this is an unfamiliar sight. Where are the kids, and where did my constantly busy and productive sister go? I thought you'd already have the table cleared, dishes washed, and be scrubbing the floor," he jested.

Sarah laughed. "The kids have gone off to play and I am savoring the quiet. It rarely happens around here."

Adam sat down at the table across from his sister and after a few minutes broke the silence. "It's said that quiet can help you calm down and contemplate. How's that working for you?" He grinned. "Are you envisioning the looming lack of tranquility that will be arriving in a few days?"

"No. I am purposefully trying to avoid any vision of our parents' arrival and the problems that will come when they meet Kelly in person."

"Problems? What problems?" boasted Joel as he joined the siblings at the table.

"Dating someone outside of our faith is a serious subject for my parents," answered Sarah. "You know what I'm talking about, Joel."

"Ah, yes." He contemplated his wife's remark. "Perhaps when it comes up for discussion with them, I should offer some insight into what scientists conclude."

"And exactly what do they claim?" asked Sarah.

"They say," Joel paused for dramatic effect, "that if we Jews continue to marry outside of our race, in less than one century, we will be diminished to a nation of sumptuous blondes and ravishing redheads—just like your Kelly, I might add!"

Adam responded with a concurring laugh, but Sarah pounded the table with an outstretched fist. "Joel! Have you no shame? Stop with the wisecracks already. This is serious. There is no doubt in my mind that my parents will have an issue. They don't share our more tolerant beliefs for dating, let alone marriage. This is a *big* problem for them."

Joel reached across the table, tenderly wrapping her tightly clenched fist within his large hand, and spoke softly. "Yes, my dear, it is controversial for your parents. No one sitting at this table has the illusion that your parents' visit next week will be smooth. We must remember that they are the ones who must decide what they can live with and what they cannot. If necessary, may I remind them that Adam and Kelly are just dating? They are not engaged."

"But isn't marriage the point of dating?" she countered. Adam knew Sarah had advanced to a point where she desperately wanted to win this verbal battle.

"Yes, of course, but that decision is for Adam and Kelly," responded Joel.

"Well?" interrogated Sarah, turning her attention to her silent sibling. "What *are* your intentions?"

Adam held her gaze. He knew Sarah well enough not to divulge his thoughts to the one person on this earth who could never keep a secret. "My intentions are mine alone, but I will share one thing I believe." She leaned forward, just waiting for the juicy tidbit she could report to their mother, or Kelly, or just about anyone. That was her nature. "I believe, well, I believe it's time for me to go before you pry anything out of me."

Sarah stormed out of the room. "Men! Can *any* of you be serious when it comes to love and relationships?"

"I'm sorry, Joel. I think I just left you with a mess to clean up, and I don't mean the kitchen."

"No harm done, Adam. She'll get over it." As the men stood and began walking back to the front door, he continued, "She just wants the best for you, ya know. She really loves you and wants you to be happy."

Adam nodded in agreement. Once they reached the front door, he asked, "Got any advice for me?"

"Sure. I always give the same advice to couples who are thinking of getting married."

"What do you tell them?"

Joel placed his hand on Adam's shoulder. "I tell them that once you have made the decision to marry, you need to hang in there. Remember, the first ten years are always the hardest."

"And how many years have you been married?" asked Adam.

"Ten years," Joel replied. "Ask me next year and the answer will be the first eleven."

Chapter 10

KELLY

"Well, look who's finally awake." Ashley was surprised to see her fellow roommate shuffling into the kitchen.

"Didn't think we'd see you till happy hour," Jenn remarked as her eyes remained fixed on the laptop screen. "I've been reading about the fire at the Humane Society. According to what I'm learning, Will's Pet Haven is a real hero."

Melissa nodded. "Looks like our resident vet had quite the weekend! Grab a cup of coffee and join us, Kelly. Spending time with the sisterhood is a great way to fill the minutes between waking up and happy hour."

Kelly brushed crimson curls from her baby blues. "Right now, my definition of happy hour is a nap."

Ashley laughed. "Sundays *are* my happy hour. No work obligations, no commitments—total freedom for this girl to do whatever she wants, including putting Irish cream in my coffee." She extended the brown-bottled cordial to Kelly.

"Thanks, but I'll pass."

"All the more for me." Ashley smiled as she set the bottle next to her mug.

"On second thought, Ashley, maybe I will have just a touch." Kelly poured the caramel-colored liquid into her steamy mug and stirred the libation. "It's been quite a weekend."

"Yeah, how was Friday's dinner? Everything go okay?"

Kelly frowned. "If you don't count having to leave in the middle of dinner, I'd say it was a smashing success."

Always the sympathetic one, Melissa tried to reassure her. "Look on the bright side. At least you got one 'meet the family' out of the way. Next one should be easier."

"I hope so. We'll see."

"And what about that awful fire at the Humane Society?" Jenn questioned. "The internet article said it was like a scene out of the movies."

"Worse than a horror flick, no doubt," added Melissa. "Sure am thankful Ashley and I were at the cinema instead. What else does it say?"

Jenn opened her laptop and scanned the column as she shared some of the hair-raising details. "It says here, 'It was an agonizing evening. . . . The high-rising flames could be seen miles away,' and that 'there was an eerie glow to the sky . . . almost an out-of-this-world look.' Were you at the fire, Kelly?"

"No, I went straight to our clinic. Another vet office down the road had their staff set up a triage to evaluate those poor creatures and treat any that were not in immediate danger. The EMTs rushed the ones with serious injuries to us."

"How many were there?"

"Sully and I treated about fifteen. The majority had severe burns. We also had three surgeries. Two dogs had fractures from part of a wall collapsing on them and one disoriented cat was hit by a car and had a broken pelvis. Plus we have a homeless litter of kittens."

"That's absolutely awful!" lamented Melissa. "No wonder you didn't get home till really late last night."

Kelly paused. "Ya know . . . It's incredibly sad to think about, but it could have been so much worse."

"How so?" Ashley asked as she refilled her roomie's coffee cup.

"If that fire had happened at a different time of year, there would have been more animals at the shelter, and probably a lot more fatalities. With it being so close to Christmas, many had already been adopted."

"Plus," Jenn interrupted, "you and Sully just did that pet speed-dating event. That was mentioned in the article too. You know what else I saw at the end of the feature?"

Kelly took a long sip of her coffee. "Haven't a clue."

"A photo of you and a great-looking guy," teased Jenn. Both Melissa and Ashley jumped behind Jenn to survey the new find.

"Wow!"

"Hubba hubba!"

Kelly grimaced, folded her arms, and placed her head down on the table. "Oh, please, not again!"

"Don't worry, Kel. It's not at all like the underwear model. You're safe this time." Melissa patted her arm. "It's a sweet picture of you with one of those EMTs and a bandaged puppy. Can't tell which is cuter, the dog or the guy!"

Jenn took a deep breath and wistfully said, "I'd sure like an opportunity to cheer him up. Do you have his number?"

Kelly scowled. "No, I don't. And you don't need it anyway. He's married."

Jenn sighed regretfully. "Why are the good ones always taken?"

"They're not," Kelly admonished. "Think this through, Jenn. You saw this guy's photo on the internet and you don't know a single thing about him. I love ya, but ya gotta use that girl logic of yours in a more rational way. Then it will keep you on track."

"I know, I know," Jenn muttered. "My internal guidance system is somewhat out of whack. Doesn't that ever happen to you? I mean, what are you obsessing over today?"

Kelly laughed. "I haven't had much time to obsess over it. Adam's sister volunteered to go shopping with me today to find the perfect gifts for his parents."

"Well, that's a good sign," acknowledged Ashley. "Obviously you didn't scare her off Friday night."

"True."

"And you're not obsessing over this?" Melissa prodded ever so gently.

"No, not yet anyway."

"Where are you shopping?" Jenn questioned. "Just yesterday I saw a list of the top ten places to go holiday shopping in Atlanta."

"Thankfully we're not going into Atlanta. We're meeting down on Canton Street in Roswell."

"I love that area!" Jenn gushed.

"Hm-mmm. Sarah said her parents adore that historic district. She texted me that her mom prefers gifts from charming boutiques."

"Sounds promising," Ashley approved. "How long will you be gone?"

"Oh, I'll be gone the rest of today."

"Wow, that's a long time to commit to shopping with his sister. You don't think that's risky?"

"Jenn, I'll only be shopping till about four, and then Adam and I are meeting up."

"Well, when you are with his sister, why not just ask her for ideas?"

"Really, Melissa? Wow! You are *so* clever! Said no one ever." Ashley's saucy remark was left to hang in the silent air. "Sorry. Sometimes my mouth just operates faster than my brain."

"I know. I've seen it on your T-shirt."

"That's a great comeback, Melissa." Kelly extended her arm toward the smug sister, offering a congratulatory high-five. Turning toward Ashley, she continued, "Better up your game or cut back on the Irish cream, Ashley. She's on a roll. And it's probably best if I just figure this gift thing out for myself. Anybody want a refill?"

"No thanks," declined Ashley. "We're now out of Irish cream, and I'm going to need to make a run for it once the liquor store opens at 12:30."

Melissa shook her head. "None for me either. I'm coffeed out. Besides, I think it's time for me to get dressed so I can be the designated driver for my little sister."

"Well, aren't you the thoughtful one!" Ashley winked at her sister.

Jenn closed the lid to her laptop. "No more for me either. Since you're off to go shopping, Kelly, I think I'll take a nap on your behalf. Hope you have a great time."

"Looks like you've got the kitchen all to yourself. Enjoy!" laughed Melissa.

Kelly scrutinized the three sisters as they headed to their rooms. *I sure scored big when I got those three for roomies.* Reaching down to pet her cat that had been circling, she added, "And I scored big when you came into my life, too, Mr. Shrimp."

Her exotic shorthair let out a pleading, drawn-out meow, obviously wanting more of his owner's attention. She bent down and pulled her four-legged companion onto her lap. He contentedly purred. "So you missed me, didn't you!" Kelly stroked her fur baby's back. "I know you were left alone for a long time this weekend." Mr. Shrimp raised his head to look at her. His pupils narrowed and his stare was hard and focused. "What's wrong?" His ears pulled back and his whiskers stiffened. "Don't worry, my friend," Kelly advised. "I might have helped some other felines, but none of them will be coming here to live." She could feel his body relax to her touch as he slowly blinked his eyes at her.

Kelly was so focused on her pet that she never realized Ashley and Melissa had reentered the kitchen. "I see you're working on your cat-whispering abilities again," scrutinized Ashley. "Is darling Mr. Shrimp talkative today?"

"Of course. He's especially thankful I'm not bringing home a four-legged roommate."

"You're not, but I might want to adopt one." Melissa reached out to the center of attention and scratched his chin. "Come on, Kelly. Wouldn't he like a little girlfriend?"

Ashley wrinkled her nose. "Middlest, ya gotta remember what happens when a boy cat and a girl cat get together. Mr. Shrimp might turn out to be a real *Cat*-sanova, if ya know what I mean." She laughed at her own cleverness. "After all, it could be more like a brawl than a courtship."

"Not always. Right, Kelly?" Melissa argued.

Playfully, Kelly confided, "We wouldn't have to worry in this case since," she paused and pretended to cover Mr. Shrimp's ears, "he's been neutered."

Ashley smirked. "Totally forgot about Mr. No-Nuts!"

"Ashley! Have you no shame?" Melissa scolded. "He can hear you!"

"And I bet if you hear an onion ring, you answer it!"

Not to be outdone by her younger sibling, Melissa advised, "Just remember, Ashley: 'Minds are like parachutes.

They only function when open.' My mind just happens to be open to the possibility that animals do indeed understand words. Just sayin'." Ashley shrugged as she turned toward Kelly and rolled her eyes. "You think I didn't see that, Ash?" Melissa questioned. "Well, I did, and if you do that again, I'm gonna grab your rolling eyes and make them my marble shooters!"

Ashley chuckled. "Promises, promises! Let's get outta here and go get those doughnuts we promised Jenn. That half-price special she saw on the net is too good to pass up."

Melissa nodded. "See ya later, Kelly. If you're gone when we get back, hope you have a great day!"

"Thanks, girls. Hope you have fun too." Kelly took a sip of her now lukewarm coffee and turned her attention back to the dozing furball on her lap. "Wake up, sweetie. Time for both of us to get moving." Much to Mr. Shrimp's dismay, she gently placed her four-legged friend on the floor and took her cup to the sink. "You can finish that nap in our room. I really need to get going or I'm gonna be late."

The pulsating cascade from the perforated shower nozzle worked its magic, and Kelly found herself revitalized and on her way in record time. Although she didn't go to Canton Street often, the hamlet was high on her list of preferences. She loved that the old homes bordering the tree-lined street had been converted to various boutiques and restaurants. It oozed historic charm, despite a miniscule touch of twenty-first-century sophistication.

Even though the day was chilly, throngs of people filled the brick sidewalks, creating a lovely holiday scene with a sense of excitement floating in the air. Every patio table was occupied with caffeine-consuming adults and their smiling kids sporting hot chocolate mustaches. Kelly checked her watch. *I'm early. Perfect . . . Even time for another cup of coffee.* As she waited in the sluggish line, an equally slow Southern drawl grabbed her attention.

"Goodness gracious. Just look who's here. Haven't seen you since you were counting zipper teeth!" Kelly turned toward the voice with elongated vowels and was spontaneously embraced. "I was just thinking of you the other day. How have you been?"

"Good, Charlotte, and how about you?" Kelly asked as she stepped out of the lagging lineup.

"Finer than frog hair split four ways, sweetheart! Looks like I'm gettin' that Broadway role I auditioned for last month, and I am so excited!"

"Wow, congratulations."

"Thank you, dear. I'll be movin' at the end of next month, so maybe we can get together before I leave."

Kelly graciously agreed. "I hope so."

"Wish I had time to chat now, but I gotta get over to Yumyum's Doggie Deli."

Peering over Charlotte's shoulder, she saw the designer double-wheeled pet carrier the actress was pulling. "Mmm. Taking Itty and Bitty for their weekly ice cream fix, I see."

"Gotta spoil my babies and then take some home for Bosley. He's with Maggie at his favorite dog park right now. So it'll be a nice treat when he returns all tuckered out. Be sure you wish that sweet man of yours a Happy Hanukkah or Chrismukkah or whatever he called it at the party."

"Sure will. And please give . . ." But before Kelly could finish her sentence, Charlotte had once again continued on her way.

Seeing the caffeinator queue had barely advanced, Kelly rejoined the pedestrian crowd. As she weaved her way between window shoppers and individuals laden with shopping bags, there was a skip in her step. She was thankful and eager to have Sarah's help in accomplishing this important task.

"Hey, Kelly! Wait up!" She turned to see Adam's sister navigating the crowded sidewalk. "Sorry if I'm a bit late. Had a last-minute meltdown to handle."

"You're not late. Everybody okay?" Kelly asked as she tried to fall into step with Sarah's power-walking pace.

"Yes. It was just Noah. He wanted spaghetti for lunch so I reheated last night's, and then he didn't want *that* spaghetti. I swear he acted as though I'd ruined his life!"

"That's too funny."

"It is now, but it wasn't at the time." Sarah paused, as if trying to catch her breath. "So, do you have anything, and I do mean anything, in mind that you're looking to get?"

"I've racked my brain and haven't come up with a thing. That's why I'm so happy you volunteered to help. If it weren't for you, I'd still be searching the internet with my three roommates scrutinizing every click of my mouse. Much more fun being out and about."

Sarah smiled. "Kockeputzi always has a mishmash of stuff. Hope my friend Becca is here. She's never failed me in the past when I've searched for that perfect parental gift." Sarah grasped the ornate, oversized, angel wing handle and pulled open the shop's heavy wooden door, holding it so Kelly could enter first. "This is something else, don't you think?"

Kelly stood motionless as she surveyed the plethora. "This is incredible, Sarah. It's like an over-the-top upscale homeowner's garage sale on steroids." The oddly pictur-esque entry was jam-packed with treasures in a clever floor-to-ceiling display behind the crowded front counter. From the distressed cabinets filled with collectibles, to the antique workbench covered with pitted metal oil lanterns, to the bicycle precariously suspended overhead, Kelly was sure she would find the perfect treasure to win over Adam's parents.

"Well, let's head on back to my friend's booth and do some poking. I've shopped there long enough for her to know my mom's and dad's preferences."

Kelly grasped a handheld shopping basket and fol-lowed. They passed displays of vintage Christmas decora-tions and farmhouse-style furniture, but Kelly immediately fell behind when she stopped at Han's Wooden Puzzles booth. An intricately carved Nativity had caught her eye, and right alongside it was a Jewish menorah candle puzzle. Impulsively placing them both into her basket, she hurried to catch up to Sarah.

A lighted marquee, rhythmically flashing HAVE I GOT A DEAL FOR YOU, welcomed them to Becca's back corner, a true mélange of miscellany! The booth appeared to be a happy blend of tempting tabletop items and underneath, a staggering, somewhat hidden inventory of unmatched cartons bursting at the seams.

"I just love old stuff," Kelly gushed as she set the basket down and ran her fingers across a pink snakeskin evening bag.

Returning a Depression glass plate back to its holder, Sarah chuckled. "You're definitely gonna love my folks then. They act even older than these items."

Kelly focused on Sarah as she eyed another delicate, crystal-clear piece. "You like Depression glass?"

"Mmhmm, but my mother doesn't. Did your mother ever have any favorites?"

Kelly reminisced. "She loved anything Cadogan Classics. See that porcelain pig with the vegetables?" Sarah approached to assess its appeal. Kelly continued, "My mom would have loved that. Not exactly my style, but I love it now because it reminds me of her."

Sarah investigated the unique item. A voice called out, "So you're thinking of gifting that pig to your parents? I do believe you've either lost your mind or your heritage, Sarah!"

She whirled around to face the apron-clad woman. "You know me, Becca. I'm a real troublemaker!" Her snorting laugh only made the situation more comical.

"Yes, you are trouble, especially if you bring that little unkosher porker home!"

Once the duo's giggles subsided and introductions had been made, Becca asked, "So, Kelly, what do you think of Kockeputzi?"

"This store is charming! I've already found a couple of things for me."

"Really?" questioned Sarah. "What'd you find?"

Kelly pulled out the two items for her fellow shoppers to evaluate.

Sarah immediately grasped the menorah puzzle. "I've never seen this before. Very cool."

"Everything that Hans creates is top-notch," agreed Becca. "And he's such a nice man too. Sure wish he was here today so you could meet him. This is the weekend he donates time teaching woodworking to kids. 'Service above self,' he always says, and he lives it too."

"Good to know. Might be something Esther would enjoy," added Sarah.

"How about for Morty and Freida, Kelly. Anything special in mind?" Becca asked.

"I'm just not sure what to choose. I don't want to get some generic gift, but I don't want to give something they will think is *too* personal. Honestly, Becca, Sarah speaks so highly of your track record that I'm looking to you for some suggestions."

"We'll figure this out. Why don't you take a look at those back shelves while I pick Sarah's brain? I'm sure Morty and Freida have some new interests."

"Not really," interjected Sarah. "My dad is still a self-proclaimed entrepreneurial genius and my mom continues to keep herself occupied with other peoples' business."

Kelly cracked a smile. "Looks like you've got your work cut out for ya, Becca. Hey, what about a book?" She stepped toward a walnut cabinet. "Does your mom or dad like to read? There's a bunch here . . . especially cookbooks . . . and they're Jewish! Perfect!"

"Trust me, Kelly. You don't want those," admonished Sarah. "My mom donated those to Becca last year when she was bargaining for a music box. I don't think a single one's sold, has it?"

Becca playfully nudged her buddy. "Those books may not sell, but they make the cabinet look great."

"Your mom likes music boxes?" interrupted Kelly. "What about one of those?"

"Unfortunately, her fascination with those is over," acknowledged Sarah.

Kelly noticed her cohorts were now on the floor, poring over other items. "Hate to say this, ladies, but it looks to me like I'm back to flowers, candy, or some other boring gift." She contemplated the finality of her words before forcing a smile. "I do appreciate your help, though."

Sarah stood, sidestepped the cardboard box, and placed her arm around Kelly. "Hey! You're not putting the kibosh on this yet. There's still a multitude of possibilities hidden in these boxes. Give us a hand."

Somewhat reluctantly, Kelly set her hand basket down and planted herself on the hard cement floor. As she sorted through box after box of paraphernalia, a small glimmer caught her eye. She retrieved the partially wrapped item and peeled back the yellowed tissue paper to showcase an impressive set of lures. "Hey, Sarah, does your dad like to fish?"

"He attempted it once when he was trying to find a hobby but never tried it again."

"Too much peace and tranquility in nature?" Becca wisecracked.

"Not a chance. My mom went along and promised to sit quietly on the dock and read. You know the rest of the story."

"Sure do . . . How about this?" questioned Becca, pulling a set of embroidered napkins from a smaller container. "Tag here says they're made of the finest Ethiopian cotton . . . Oops, never mind."

"Why?" questioned Kelly as she checked the time on her watch. "They look nice."

"They do until you read the embroidered comment, 'What's said at the seder, stays at the seder.'"

"Sounds appropriate to me," snickered Sarah.

"Hold on, girls. I think I've found it." Kelly joyfully lifted a hand-painted ceramic serving piece from a mountain of foam peanuts. "Adam once told me your mom is the dish queen. Isn't this pretty?"

Becca gave her approval. "Sure is."

"Best of all, blue is my mom's absolutely favorite color,

so it will go with everything," Sarah added. "You've hit a home run, Kelly!"

"Thanks to you girls for not letting me quit. However, I do have to leave now."

"You can't go yet. You haven't found anything for Morty," protested Becca.

"I know, but Adam's picking me up, and I don't want to be late."

Sarah stood and gave Kelly a hug. "Becca and I will keep on sorting through these boxes and I'll text you a photo if we see something my dad might like."

"Thanks. I still have a couple days to find something, but if not, I can bring a boring gift."

"Hey, Kelly, my dad has never been disappointed in a bottle of Marischeblitz."

"Thanks, Sarah. Nice meeting you, Becca. Hope to see you again soon."

Kelly grabbed her shopping basket and walked to the front of the store. As she waited to place her three items on the countertop, the customer ahead of her touted the treasure trove of pet costumes filling the entire space.

"I never thought I'd find a striped shirt for my sweet little Pucci that matched the one I bought for myself last weekend! Isn't it unbelievable that I would have such luck? Now my Pucci is Gucci!" She barely paused to catch her breath before continuing. "And this reversible rain-coat! Pucci can be a sunny canary yellow or an adorable polka-dotter. Hope I can find a poncho for me that matches at least one of those!"

The clerk never looked up from scanning the multitude of items but nodded in agreement and announced the total.

"Such a bargain for my baby!" commented the happy

consumer as she inserted her card. "Your Posh Pets booth is just the best. See you next Sunday."

"Yes, ma'am," the clerk replied. "Have a great week."

Kelly smiled at the young cashier. "Is that the most unusual sale you'll have today?"

"Oh no. We get lots of 'doggie-twinning' clientele. It just amazes me how many people spend so much of their money on dog or cat apparel. Seems highly indulgent to me." She carefully wrapped the ceramic serving tray. "I mean, I've heard of 'therapy jackets' that might help a pet deal with a thunderstorm or lessen arthritis pain. Those make sense, but dressing your pet for special occasions? Would you do that?"

Kelly tapped her card. "Not me. Doggy outfits aren't my thing. I could never be one of those crazy people who forces their pup to get dressed every day. How about you?"

"Same here." The employee handed Kelly her bagged items and laughingly whispered, "I actually support dog nudity!"

"You're a riot! Hope you have a great afternoon." Kelly grabbed the bag and strode outside. As she weaved her way through the crowded sidewalks, her mind kept returning to the Pucci Gucci owner at the shop. *I know a wardrobe is necessary for warmth sometimes, and as long as it doesn't stress the pet, I guess it's okay. But when someone is so obsessed with daily wear for their pet . . . that woman must be either really lonely or just needs lots of control. Oh well. Glad I don't know anyone like that!*

Chapter 11

ADAM

Kelly wasn't the only one who had slept late that Sunday morning.

The sun was high in the sky when Adam first opened his eyes. In fact, if it hadn't been for Bo's furry muzzle and warm breath breezing his face, Adam might have slept even longer.

"Wow! Twelve thirty? How'd we sleep so late? Sorry, buddy," Adam sympathized, "you're long overdue for a potty break." Bo concurred and pranced to the bedroom door. "Hang in there, fella. I'm moving as fast as I can." Adam rushed to dress. He grabbed Bo's leash and together they headed outdoors.

The air was cool but fresh, and the goldendoodle wasted no time in taking care of his business before setting out for his favorite off-leash park. Bo's upbeat prance transformed the walk into a sprint. Adam knew his dog craved to be unfettered and play in the large fenced area.

"Well, hello there, Adam. Sure didn't expect to see you here. Have you and Kelly recovered from the media frenzy?"

Adam looked up to see Charlotte's personal assistant Maggie approaching, being pulled relentlessly by Bosley. "Yes, thank goodness. We did have a great time at the party, though. Are you leaving?"

"Oh, yes. We've been here for an hour and Charlotte will be coming back home soon with Bosley's favorite ice cream treat. We certainly can't be late and risk it being melted."

"I can understand that. Maybe we'll bump into each other another time."

"Doubt that will happen. Charlotte's taken that new role in New York City, so I've decided to leave her employment and move back to New Hampshire to be closer to my grandchildren. I've already taken a new position with a best-selling author."

"Wow, congratulations. I certainly wish you the very best."

"Thanks, Adam. You take extra good care of Kelly. She's a great girl, and I'll really miss working with her at the Humane Society."

"Thanks, Maggie. I'll tell her."

An hour later, Adam and an exhausted Bo were back home. The loveable teddy-bear canine quickly followed his owner into the bedroom and bounced onto the bed. "Time for a snooze, buddy?" He laughed as the goldendoodle rolled onto his back with his belly up and his legs in the air. "While you cool off, I'm taking a shower, and then I'll let you in on a little secret." Bo rolled onto his side and cocked his head, as if to ask what the secret could be. "You'll just have to wait, buddy."

Adam emerged thirty minutes later with a towel wrapped around his waist and quietly finished dressing so as not to awaken the snoring canine. Unfortunately, the annoying sound of an off-track drawer caused Bo to open one eye. "Stay put, fella. Just need to get the important items for tonight," he whispered as he removed the two objects and zipped one of the pieces into his jacket pocket. "You be a good boy, okay? Go back to sleep. Probably going to be late getting home, so don't wait up."

Adam never saw the road as he drove to meet Kelly. He was on autopilot, and with joy in his heart, his eyes were fixated on tonight's endeavor. His preoccupation caused him to drive straight past her building, forcing him to circle the block before seeing her standing in the portico. He quickly pulled up to the curb and then dashed to her side so exuberantly that he almost flattened her.

"Whoa, fella!" Kelly laughed. "I'm glad to see you, but I really don't need to be squashed!"

"Sorry," Adam apologized. "Didn't mean to over-power you. It's just I've missed you so much since Friday that I couldn't wait to see you." He enveloped her in his arms, gave her a sweet kiss on her neck, and then whispered, "I have a surprise for you."

"Really?" Kelly disengaged. "What is it?"

To Adam, her face radiated the zeal of a ten-year-old, and he found her childish enthusiasm charming. "I can't tell you, but I will show you. Let's go." Taking her hand in his, they walked briskly to the car.

"Hey, what's that in your other hand? Something for me?" she pried.

"Yes." He extended the mysterious handheld object.

"What's this? A neck gaiter?"

"Yes. Now put it over your eyes and enjoy the ride."

Kelly's eyes narrowed as Adam started the car. "What's going on here?"

"You, my sweet captive, are going to have to wait to find out. Now just blindfold yourself, like I asked."

Kelly nodded and ever so slowly adjusted the gaiter to completely cover her eyes. "Is this one of Jenn's spontaneous 'trust' challenges from the internet?"

"It's kind of a trust challenge . . ."

Kelly furrowed her brow and let out a weird little giggle. "Well, you might think you've got this whole thing under control, but I am going to figure it out."

"Have at it." Adam glanced at his blindfolded passenger. His camo gaiter might have masked her alluring features, but there was nothing that could conceal the beauty he'd found in her soul. Kindness, humor, gentleness, generosity, humility, tempered with a sprinkling of spiritedness and sass . . . That was Kelly to him. Adam knew he would be forever lost without her, and it was that thought that made him question tonight's game plan. Was it foolproof? He hoped so! What more could he have done? He'd spent hours over the past four weeks orchestrating this evening. He was determined that this occasion would be nothing less than perfect. After all, how often do you ask someone to marry you?

As he pulled into the parking lot, Adam remembered how he'd invested a hefty amount of time contemplating potential locations for popping the big question. His first thought was to propose at Will's Pet Haven, where their forever love story had begun. It would bring their relationship full circle . . . but there had to be a more romantic spot than her workplace! His next thought was to propose where he'd first said "I love you." Adam remembered how that lazy Sunday afternoon had been cut short when Kelly's pager vibrated. He'd found himself tagging along with her on the requested vet call to a North Georgia winery where an expectant nanny goat was in distress. Subsequently, as they'd toasted the triplets' arrival with a crisp chardonnay and drank in the beauty of the panoramic view, he'd said those three little words. Even now in December, the view that only Yahweh could have created would be the perfect background for a proposal—unless those goats made an entrance! No, it was not worth taking the chance. Idea after idea came and went. To Adam, nothing would be the adventurously romantic occasion worthy of being retold. That is, until he saw the brochure. Adam slowly pulled into a parking space and turned off the ignition.

"Are we finally here?" Kelly questioned.

"Remove the gaiter, girl!"

Kelly whipped off her eye covering and squealed with delight. "Really? Oh, wow! I can't believe we're going to Fly Time!" She threw her arms around him. "Thank you, thank you, thank you!" she whispered. Then, loosening her tight grip, she continued, "But didn't you say you're afraid of heights?"

"I did say that, but I know how much you've been wanting to try this. Just thought I'd give you one of your Chrismukkah presents early!"

"Wow, you did great! Really great!" Once again she threw her arms around him, but this time she forcefully met his lips with an intoxicating seductive twist, initiating reactions all through his body. Adam yearned for this moment to last forever. He was enveloped by her and had no desire to leave her warm embrace, despite a recurring *tap-tap-tap* on the window. When it became clear that the knocking would continue, he gently disentangled himself from her embrace and rolled down the slightly steamed window.

"You all right, ma'am?" the stern-faced security guard asked.

"Never better, sir."

"This guy's not bothering you?"

"No, sir." Kelly suppressed a giggle. "Not at all!"

Obviously disappointed that he would not be rescuing a damsel in distress, the officer mumbled, "Then I suggest you two move along and take your business elsewhere."

The mall was bustling with holiday shoppers. As they strode toward the venue, Adam put his arm around Kelly. This was it! Love was definitely in the air, and he planned to appreciate every single moment. Once inside, he led Kelly to the desk area to officially register and sign the required waivers.

Reading the attendant's name badge, Adam greeted her with a huge smile. "Hello, Carla." *So this is the wonderful person who's been helping me.* "My name is Adam Cohen and this is Kelly. We are here for our six o'clock reservation."

"Wonderful, Mr. Cohen. I believe I spoke with you on the phone about the waivers but forgot to mention that a film crew was scheduled to be here tonight shooting some footage for an upcoming commercial. I hope that you both are okay with being filmed."

Adam shook his head. "I don't know, Carla. I'm afraid of heights, and I'm not sure how I'm going to do with this flying stuff. I'm probably not the best candidate for advertising your company."

"Oh, come on," Kelly coaxed. "Be a sport. You'll do great!"

Adam grimaced. "Oh, all right, but only because you think I'll do great."

"I know you will!" she encouraged.

"Everything is set, then, except for your signatures. Please review the documents and sign where the yellow check mark is," instructed Carla. Kelly began scanning the form as Adam's cohort in crime winked discreetly at him. *So far, so good.* His plan was working.

With the signatures completed, Carla fastened their wristbands and directed the couple to take the staircase to the mezzanine, where they would meet their instructor in the training room. As the couple began climbing the open-riser staircase, Adam clutched the cold iron railing. He held his breath as he took a quick look downward to see if Kelly was wearing shoes that laced. He'd forgotten that was a prerequisite for flying. Unfortunately, his eyes shot beyond the laces and the floating stairs to the ground floor. A mixture of shoe relief compensated for the low-grade panic that commenced.

"Are you really looking down between the treads?" questioned Kelly. "That's pretty brave. No more acrophobia?"

"Not totally. And this wind-tunnel adventure might help me with it."

Kelly squeezed his hand and smiled. "It's so sweet of you to put your fear aside to do this with me. Maybe we should make a bucket list of adventures to share. Got any ideas?"

Adam cracked a smile. "Oh, I've got ideas, all right. We'll make a list if I survive this."

"Oh, you'll survive. I'm sure of it. Just remember, you are *not* falling—you're flying."

Oh, you are so right. I am flying . . . toward an exciting future with you, Kelly!

Adam held the door for Kelly to enter the training room. "There's no one else here," Kelly whispered to Adam, who shrugged.

Almost immediately a side door opened and a young man wearing a white flight suit entered. "Hi. My name's Eddie and I'm your Fly Time instructor this evening. You must be Kelly and Adam." The pair nodded. "Well, you're in luck tonight. The other people who were scheduled to fly in your group had to cancel due to a family emergency. That gives you two some extra flight time." Adam smirked. He knew there was no other family booked. *She has no idea . . .*

Eddie continued, "First, we're going to watch a short video together. Be sure to pay close attention to the section on hand signals. It's really important that you know those so we can communicate in that noisy wind tunnel. Any questions?"

"Not for me."

"Me neither."

"Great. Then grab a chair and let's get started."

Adam's mind wandered as he stared at the screen. He had watched this instructional internet video a multitude of times, knowing that when this moment arrived all he would be able to think about would be the proposal. Once again he recited his eloquent speech and then glanced in Kelly's direction. Seeing that her eyes were totally fixated on the video, he unzipped his jacket pocket and verified that the ring was still safely hidden. All was going according to plan. He breathed a silent sigh of relief.

"Time to gear up," Eddie announced as he flipped on the lights. "Let's go to the locker room next door and get your flight suits. Just slip them over your clothes and you'll be ready for takeoff." Adam found the uniform to be surprisingly comfortable, but transferring the ring from his jacket to the suit's inside chest pocket proved to be a real challenge. On his third attempt he thought for sure the jig was up.

"Why are you fidgeting?" Kelly asked, twisting her hair into a loose bun. "Something wrong with your suit?"

"Something is poking me."

"Let me help," offered Kelly. Adam quickly recoiled. "Hey, let me help!" she insisted.

Adam shook his head. "No, I've got this." He patted his chest and felt the ring's outline. "You just get your pretty hair tied. Don't want those red tresses getting snagged on anything." He zipped the pocket closed while Kelly turned her attention to the mirror. Once outfitted with the appropriate gear, Eddie led the couple to the antechamber. "Take a seat. The couple currently flying is doing a demo for the commercial. You folks will be next."

"Wow, they're really good," observed Kelly. "We are not going to look like them. They're whizzing around doing fancy tricks like pros. You sure you want to film *us?*"

"Absolutely. It's important to show that anybody can do this."

"Well, Eddie, let me be clear," Kelly jokingly said. "Adam and I are *not* just anybody!"

Their instructor chortled. "Yes, ma'am. I totally agree with you." He knowingly nudged Adam. "You may not have the choreographed routine of this couple, but I guarantee you will love seeing yourselves on film! So, who's going first?"

Adam did not hesitate. "Kelly. Absolutely!"

"What? You aren't chickening out on me, are you, Adam?"

"I just think you should go first, Kelly."

"Well, I just think you should go first, Adam. Be brave, my courageous Machabee in shining armor!"

"Sounds cool. What's a Machabee?" asked Eddie.

"A Jewish warrior, just like my guy here. Right, Adam?"

Before Adam could reply, Eddie interjected, "Look, one of you needs to go first. The other couple has finished their showcase flight for the film crew. Who's it going to be?" Neither participant spoke. "How about it, Kelly? Why don't you lead the way?"

Adam smiled. *Eddie knows the plan: we each take one turn,*

and on Kelly's second flight, when she descends, I'm on one knee, ready to propose.

Kelly stood. "All right. I'm game. I have wanted to do this for a very, very long time!"

Adam gave her a thumbs-up as she proceeded to the tunnel's entrance. *Oh, how I love that girl! Fly safe, my love!* Once airborne, she made it look easy. With just a little help from Eddie, she floated smoothly like a cloud rising above the horizon. Adam had a hunch that he was about to embarrass himself. *No way am I going to look that good!* The sixty-second experience was quickly over and he cringed. It was now his turn. He'd never liked even getting on a ladder, and now he was choosing to lift both feet off the ground at the same time.

"Hey, you okay, Adam? You don't look so good." Eddie nudged his next student.

"Yeah. I'm fine. Just a little nervous."

"It'll be fun. Go give it a try, sweetie," encouraged Kelly. "I bet once you're flying, you'll love it!" Adam stood, somewhat reluctantly, and hugged his advocate before following Eddie toward the tunnel's entrance. It was then that he noticed Carla had joined the group of people who had stopped to watch the experience. Seeing her discreetly holding the sign with the all-important, preprinted question on it gave him a momentary burst of courage. *I can do this. Just need to get through sixty seconds . . .* Adam tapped Eddie on his shoulder.

"I hope I don't pass out before popping the big question."

"It'll be fine. I won't let go of you. It's safe. Trust me." They both inserted their earplugs, and Eddie stepped into the tunnel.

Adam edged closer to the tunnel's entrance and glanced

upward. The tall shaft swirled before his eyes, and he took a step back. Eddie reached outward, beckoning him to step forward, and when Adam finally did, his instructor eased him into the tunnel. At first, Adam struggled, but Eddie was quick to readjust the rookie's hips and feet into the correct position, and he began to actually enjoy the experience. Even as he floated higher into the tunnel, Adam had no fear of the elevation. *This is incredible! I love it!* He surveyed the shoppers walking beneath him and . . . *No, no, no! It can't be! Not now! Not tonight!* Adam scrunched his eyes tightly closed and reopened them quickly, hoping what he thought he'd seen was a figment of his imagination. His mind whirled at the realization that indeed there was only one woman in the entire world who owned the most ostentatious fur coat ever created, and that was his mother! And here she was, arm in arm with his dad, at the far end of the mall headed in his direction.

Dear God in heaven. They weren't planning to arrive till tomorrow! Why are they here? At the mall, even . . . Adam's mind raced with overwhelming thoughts, but in the end, there was only one option. There would be no proposal. Just like that, his desire to make Kelly his own ahead of meeting his parents, thereby causing less squabbling, was ended. At least for the moment.

Seeing twenty seconds remaining on the clock, Adam flashed the "stop" and the "come down" signals. Eddie cocked his head to the side, obviously questioning Adam's request, but complied. Once out of the tunnel, it was a race against time. "Not feeling good, Eddie. Gotta go!" He hurried to Kelly, who was now on her feet.

"What's wrong? You're white as a sheet."

"Not feeling good, Kelly. Need to get out of here, before something else goes wrong."

"All right. You gonna be okay?"

Adam grabbed her hand. "If we get out of here quickly enough! Hurry!" He was grateful that Kelly understood without further questioning. They rushed to the locker room and stripped out of their flight gear, then sprinted down the open-riser staircase. Upon exiting Fly Time, they passed a perplexed Carla, who hollered, "Hey! What's up? Where ya goin'? What about the sign?"

"Nowhere. We're going nowhere, Carla, because some signs are bigger than others. And right now we're forced to make a detour." The couple continued running back to the Yafah LX and into the night while Carla read her sign and asked herself, "What other signs?" She did not know Morty and Freida Cohen.

Chapter 12

KELLY

Kelly had been nervous all day. Though she knew she could hold her own in most situations, this first official face-to-face encounter with Adam's parents, more specifically Mrs. Freida Cohen, would be quite a challenge. Once she entered Adam's Yafah LX, her stress was evident after just a few comments.

"Got a bad case of the jitters? You don't seem like your usual self, judging by your vibe," Adam ventured.

"Judging by my vibe? I have a vibe? A vibe that's off? Please, Adam, please just tell me what I'm doing right, because all I can do right now is list everything that's off. Not to mention how you were off yesterday evening. It's like every time things seem to be going great for us, suddenly something happens and I'm off or you're off or, hell, everybody's off. That's the whole theme of my life, I swear! I have a roller-coaster love life. One minute we're up and then suddenly we go down! I just want tonight to go well. Your parents already seem dead set against us being together."

"They're too late. We're already together," Adam quipped.

"I mean us together and happy. I love you and they're your parents, so I want them to love me too. I just want them to be happy *with* us."

"I did mention to you along the way that my parents are Jewish, right? They'll never be fully happy with us. Even if they love you, and they *will* love you, they'll still worry and want to fix something about us. That's what they do. It's in their DNA. They throw around worry and guilt like beads at Mardi Gras."

"Ooh. Mardi Gras. My parents and I always spent that day eating up all the junk in the house so we wouldn't be tempted during Lent. I remember it being hard at times, during those forty days, but it made Easter an even bigger celebration."

"Forty days is hard? Try forty years in the desert!" Adam threw down his gauntlet in the battle of which faith was tougher.

"Never mind all that! Tell me how to survive four hours with your parents and win their hearts!" Kelly returned to the original topic.

"Well, my dad will be easy. He's a natural negotiator, so he'll come our way before my mom does. She's the difficult one. My mom is always worried about how everything will look to our Jewish community back home in New York."

"I know that already. Tell me how to survive tonight! And hurry! We're almost there. I feel like I'm forgetting everything." Kelly was becoming downright panicked.

Adam slowed the car to buy more time. "Breathe first. Then simply be yourself. You're beautiful inside and out, and if my parents can't see that, then we'll take out the heavy artillery."

"Which is what? What artillery?"

"Me. They adore me and I adore you. So, if they won't have you, then they won't have me. And I can't imagine them not wanting me in their lives. But I'm telling you, they're going to fall in love with you sooner or later. If you want it to be sooner, and I know you do, then just impress them with the wonderful Jewish prayers and Yiddish you've learned. They'll appreciate it and all your effort will finally pay off. Oh. And my dad thinks you have a fantastic figure after seeing the pictures I sent, so that's already a step in the right direction." Adam was greeted with a playful swat on his arm. "And we've arrived," he added. Kelly leaned over and gave him a quick peck on the cheek.

"Thanks. That's the pep talk I needed."

The couple exited the car and Kelly smoothed out her clothes while grabbing a quick peek in the sideview mirror. She carefully handled the beautiful bouquet of blue and white hydrangeas they had preordered for the occasion.

She walked up to the front porch while Adam maneuvered a tote with two classic bottles of Marischeblitz wine they had purchased with respect for his parents' tastebuds.

Kelly was already at the door of the Weinberg home and noticed Adam was only just closing his door and locking the sports car. *Oh my dear God! I'm so nervous that I just came straight up here without him by my side. God, please help me. I know it's two different faiths, but make 'em play nice with us in the sandbox, and Lord, please keep it sand. No mud-throwing! Oh my God, I'm a wreck! Which one do I say again? Shalom aleichem or Aleichem shalom?* Kelly practiced a smile and a lovely handshake. *Kelly. Kelly Leary. So happy we can finally meet. Shalom aleichem.*

"Adam! How are you, my son? Good to see you! Very nice shoes. What did you pay for 'em? Don't tell me it was retail. I'll drop dead right here, I swear!"

Kelly spun around to see Adam laughing and hugging a shorter cigar-holding balding man in the middle of the front walkway. *Must be Adam's dad! Where did he come from? Was I that deep in my thoughts? Well, it's not how I pictured it starting, but here goes nothing!* She walked back down the steps to meet Mr. Morty Cohen. Adam introduced the two and Kelly greeted the older man with "Shalom."

"Shalom. It's nice to meet the lady who keeps my son so busy these days. You didn't happen to be with him when he bought his shoes, did you? Tell me he didn't pay retail. That's what we would both agree is a sin, correct? Nice-looking girl like you, I'm sure, is a good shopper."

Relief washed over Kelly as she giggled. Adam was right. His father would be an easy sell. Mr. Cohen did not wait for a reply. "So, tell me, Miss Kelly, did the meeting go well?"

She looked at Adam and he returned the same confused face. She faltered in her reply. "Meeting? What meeting?"

Adam's dad inhaled his cigar and let out a puff. "Why, the pretend person whose hand you shook while smiling up on the porch. Did it go well?"

Kelly blushed with embarrassment as she rode back up her self-induced roller coaster of stress. "Uh, well, to be quite honest, I was practicing meeting you and Mrs. Cohen. I care deeply about Adam and want our first meeting to go well, and I hope I get points for this bit of awkward truth-telling."

"Mmm. You do, you do. I'll give you even more points if you tell me whether Adam paid full retail or not for those spiffy shoes he's wearing. Good quality doesn't mean you have to pay full price is all I'm saying. Sometimes my son is too eager to give his money away."

"Never mind that, Dad. What are you doing smoking a cigar?" Adam saved Kelly and himself from any further embarrassment.

"You see, your mother is always insisting that she better not see me smoking cigars. She can't see me out here. And there you go."

"But maybe she'll see you through one of the windows," Kelly suggested.

"Are you kidding me? She's in her glory managing everybody else inside. By the way, that reminds me. Did Adam tell you I'm easy? I'm not as easy as he always thinks I am, but I can work with you. In this case, it's your first time so you had me out the gate at shalom. See? You try, I try too. Teamwork makes the scheme work. Right?"

"Tate, it's teamwork makes the dream work," Adam corrected.

"Yeah, that works too." Morty dismissed his son before continuing with Kelly. "Now my wife, she's a different story. She'll most definitely be a tough customer. Selling the idea of the two of you together will be like selling a toaster with a bathtub. Both great things, just not together."

"I hardly think we're the same as a toaster and a tub. C'mon. Put out the cigar and let's go inside." Adam tried to put an end to the conversation but Kelly's insecurity intervened.

"Do you really think she'll be that hard?

"Yes, and she's relentless." Morty offered very little hope.

"Relentless? Really?" Kelly felt another climb begin on her emotional roller coaster.

"That's right. Except for a few words here and there, I haven't really talked to her in almost two years," the long-married man informed her.

"Why not?"

"I don't want to interrupt her! That causes trouble. So see what I mean? But hey, you can always try. As a matter of fact, you're Catholic, so you must believe in miracles. Pray for one of those. Not out loud in front of her, though, unless you've learned some Jewish prayers too."

Kelly's eyes grew wide as she flashed a stiffening look of panic at Adam. An escalating battle of what appeared to be short Yiddish comments between son and father erupted and it ended as abruptly and awkwardly as it had commenced. Mr. Cohen adjusted his stance, cleared his throat, and politely showed his palm, inviting Kelly to ascend the porch stairs ahead of the men.

"Shall we go inside then, so you can meet Adam's mother?"

Kelly shot the younger Cohen another quick look, this one conveying a question mark, but Adam gave a quick shake of his head and mouthed the word "later." The threesome ascended the steps of the classic-bricked dwelling.

"We brought Mame's and your favorite wine for tonight." Adam offered a verbal olive branch.

His father accepted. "Oh, good. Hey, uh, back to the shoes. I want you to tell me what you paid for them! I can probably get you a better price off my list of wholesalers. I'll get you a copy so you'll know them."

"Dad, I don't need to know your wholesalers. I'm doing well here. Really," Adam declined.

"Mr. Fancy Shoes," his father countered, "I'm just telling you, knowledge does not take up much space and I've never heard anyone complain that he saved too much."

"Fine. If I take the list, will you stop with the shoes?" Adam relented.

"I can stop with the shoes, with or without you having the list," his father assured him. "What I am going to do, though, is buy you a new wallet."

"Why do I need a new wallet?" Adam inquired.

"Because the one you have now must have a hole in it," Mr. Cohen replied.

"Ooh. That's a good one," Kelly smirked. "Didn't even see it coming."

Morty Cohen nodded toward her. "Thank you."

"You just met my father and already you're on his side?" Adam playfully objected.

"Smart girl you have there, son."

Adam gave Kelly a quick side hug, being careful not to damage the hydrangeas while replying to his father, "Finally! Something we can both agree on for now!" Kelly smiled, realizing now that this exchange must have been the usual banter for the two, without anyone really being angry.

The trio touched the mezuzah on the door jamb and lightly kissed their fingers before entering through the front doorway. Adam gave Kelly a look of contentment and took her by the hand so he could guide her to his side. Morty called out to no one in particular, "You have more visitors!"

Kelly smiled when Adam mouthed, "One down, one to go." Joel showed up first with the children, followed by Sarah with Mrs. Cohen in tow. Adam's sister welcomed everyone and took their coats. Kelly's line of vision collided with that of Mrs. Cohen, who stood behind Sarah and Joel, waiting to be introduced. From there the two ladies' eyes played hit and run, with Kelly's darting away upon each visual connection. While donning a polite smile, she hastily prayed deep within any prayer that popped into her head.

There was a Catholic one, a Jewish one, and one that started out Jewish and somehow finished Catholic. She prayed for what seemed like everything short of world peace and finished it all with praying for an actual miracle. Adam's voice brought her full focus back to the current conversation.

"Kelly, I want to introduce you to my mom. Mame, this is my girlfriend, Kelly."

Mrs. Cohen was shorter than Kelly but gigantic in presence. She offered a curt hello as she extended her hand. The two ladies shook but the older woman hastily withdrew her hand while her gaze remained locked. Kelly felt like Adam's mother was already jockeying for dominance with her body language and a gut-wrenching panic enveloped her. Adam's mother seemed so calm and almost calculating. Suddenly Kelly remembered her preparation for this very moment.

"Shalom, Mrs. Cohen. It is so nice to finally meet you. I'm Kelly." She immediately detected a touch of nervousness in her practiced reply and hoped it didn't show.

"Yes, Adam just mentioned your name, but I'm glad you confirmed it." Kelly blushed but would not succumb to intimidation. She offered the stunning fresh-cut bundle of panicle hydrangeas to the older woman.

"These are for you." Kelly hoped her smile was contagious.

Mrs. Cohen accepted the bulbous bouquet of multiple blue-and-white hues. "Mmm. Very nice. Hydrangeas are one of my favorite flowers. I'll have Sarah take out one of her Hanukkah vases to hold them. Of course, they'll have to stay here because we can't travel on the airplane with a container of flowers filled with water. So I guess these are really for me *and* for Sarah. Thank you."

Kelly was at a loss for words. Had that been a condescending remark or an expression of gratitude? She was
relieved when Adam jumped back into the conversation.
"Mame, Kelly is a veterinarian. She's very good at what
she does." His commendation soothed some of the sting
from Kelly's initial interaction with his mother.

"That's nice, honey. Not everyone can be a doctor, so
I'm sure a veterinarian is okay too."

The sting sunk in deeper as Kelly's gaze moved downward. Sarah extended her arm and invited everyone to
take a seat in the sitting room. "Shall we? Joel, perhaps you
and the kids can bring drinks and appetizers for everyone,
while I take care of a few last things for dinner?" Her husband agreed and set about his task while everyone else sat
down.

"Why don't you just bring us some of that Marischeblitz
that Adam and Kerry brought tonight? I'm sure Mr.
Moneyshoes bought the best." Mr. Cohen smirked and Joel
looked at Adam for his endorsement before taking the two
bottles of wine, along with the children, into the kitchen.

"It's Kelly, not Kerry, Tate," Adam corrected.

His father replied, "Sure. Of course it is."

Mrs. Cohen called to Sarah, who had already left the
room herself, "I don't mind helping so we can move dinner along, Sarah, honey."

"Unless you want me to join you so I can learn more,"
Kelly offered to help as well. She was willing to do anything to avoid any more swings and misses with the
mother of her boyfriend.

"Tonight's probably not best for teaching, Sarah, but
help is never out of fashion," the older woman insisted.

"I'm good, ladies," Sarah called out. "Nothing here that
needs help or teaching. Enjoy your chat."

Adam obviously wanted to address his mother's last comment to him and appealed to her, "Mame, about what you said earlier. A veterinarian *is* a doctor, and she has to learn about all kinds of animals, not just one."

"Yes, dear, but they don't get paid as much, do they? Hmm. I wonder why that is. I'm sure she'll figure it out. Where's that Marischeblitz?"

Joel entered as if on cue and delivered the Jewish wine to the foursome as the children walked around the group, offering cheese fritters and stuffed mushrooms. Adam protested to his mother, "Mame. I feel vets are actually underpaid and undervalued for all that they do. After all, pets are family members too."

"Well, Adam, don't take this the wrong way, but the reality is, pay and professional respect are not based on feelings, and some living beings are more complex than others. It's that simple. But, like I said, vets can be okay too."

Mr. Cohen leaned over and whispered audibly to his son, "Think before you get your mother started, Adam. Besides, your girl's still hot as hell. I can see why you're attracted to her."

"Tate, I'm sure you were just as attracted to Mame when you were both our age."

The older man returned to what he thought was whispering. "Adam, I'll tell you, our Lord only gives us what we can handle sexually, and clearly He never expected a whole lot from me." Mrs. Cohen scowled at her husband before he called out to his son-in-law, "Joel, could you bring me another wine, please?"

"But I just brought you one," Joel stated.

"This one will be done when you bring the other, rest assured," the father-in-law replied. "The longer the night feels, the shorter the wait should be between refills."

"Okay, but we just got started," the young rabbi asserted.

"What can I say? I drink coffee to change the things I can and wine to accept the things I can't," Mr. Cohen insisted.

"Hey, Tate, be careful with yourself," Adam joked. "Many bad decisions can turn a man toward bad living and hell."

Forgetting himself, the older Cohen responded in a regular voice, "I'm not afraid of the devil. I've known his sister for years." Freida Cohen's eyes shot her spouse visual daggers as a warning. He turned to Adam and Kelly. "My wife is an angel, whom I have loved for so many years, oh, so many, very many years." He finished his wine in a single gulp. "Marischeblitz refill here yet?"

Adam changed the subject. "So, the two of you must have questions about us, no? Sarah and Joel did. Don't you want to know how we met or anything like that?"

Freida jumped at the invitation to ask questions, but they weren't the ones Kelly had prayed. "Tell us, Adam, why do you think it's a good idea for a fish to fly with a bird? Hmm? I mean, your father and I need your help here. Are there any good reasons for you to sin and jeopardize all your chances for Yahweh's greatest blessings and heaven's eternity with Miss Kelly here? We're just curious, you see."

Adam looked how Kelly felt, shocked at his mother's words. "Don't do this, Mame. It's not a sin for a Jew to date a Catholic, and she's a woman, not a fish."

"Yes, definitely a woman. A fish could never walk like that," Morty offered. His wife pinched his arm. "Ow! Not the damn arm again!" Joel instructed his children to leave the appetizers and go.

Adam ignored his father's comment. "Look. Kelly respects Judaism and I respect her faith. No one is trying to convert anyone at all. We both love Yahweh and we're going to let Him decide what happens each day. In the meantime, we look for what we have in common and enjoy our time together."

Kelly added, "I agree. Yahweh will decide. Or God. Whatever you want to call Him."

"Whatever name? Oh, Morty! Help me, please. Suddenly I feel faint."

"Yes, my angel. It must be those Southern vapors we hear about." He winked at Adam and rolled his eyes.

Adam clearly didn't want to play along like his father. "Mom! You're not fainting! C'mon. Let's keep tonight simple. I just wanted you to meet Kelly and enjoy dinner together. We can talk seriously another time."

"Joel, instead of this wine, please, bring me something stronger to drink, something from the liquor cabinet."

"Stronger than the wine? Are you sure? I just brought you the refill."

Freida interjected, "Morty, that's so sweet of you to think of me! Do you think it will do well to help me?"

"You'll be fine. It's for me," Morty stated. "I'm absolutely certain it's going to be a long night now. Joel, make it a double, please." His son-in-law reluctantly left the room to fulfill the older man's request.

Adam let out a heavy sigh. "Look. Just so you both know, Kelly and I love each other and have already agreed that we would make the hard decision to remove anyone from our lives who will not support our relationship. The world is filled with enough negativity; we don't need more of it." Kelly was surprised they hadn't even touched dinner yet and Adam was already taking out his biggest weapon.

"Wow. That's a serious statement right there," Morty asserted as he took the drink Joel delivered. "Surely there's some wiggle room for something less severe."

"Tate, I love the two of you, but it's nonnegotiable."

"Nonnegotiable?" his father objected. "Everything's negotiable."

"Not this time." Adam looked in Kelly's eyes and took her hand. "Nonnegotiable." Morty quaffed his new drink in one shot.

"Does anyone care at all if I'm feeling fainter by the minute?" Freida put a pin in the bubble of the awkward moment. She put her arm up to her forehead.

Kelly was sure she could put a better light on the topic at hand. "Perhaps it would help if we took a more positive approach."

"I'm positive this is going to be a long night," Morty interjected while holding up his empty glass. Joel said nothing, slowly collected the glass in resignation, and left the room to refill it.

"Seriously," Kelly countered. "Why don't we all insist on concentrating on our commonalities instead of our differences? Okay? I'll start. Mrs. Cohen, I may be Catholic, but I follow Jesus and Jesus was a Jew. See?"

Freida, feigning weakness, replied, "Ha! Jesus. Yet another Jewish boy who left his mother for a different religion." Kelly's hope was sucked out of her heart and face with one quick swoosh.

"Mame!" Adam snapped. His mother looked at him with disbelief that her son would use such a tone with her. His father was busy continuing his own deliberation.

"Nonnegotiable. That's ridiculous. Everything's negotiable. Well, except maybe my marriage. That seems to be nonnegotiable and as permanent as death and taxes. Oy," the older man mumbled through his self-inflicted debate.

When all seemed lost to Kelly, a small white Maltese sauntered into the room. The miniature canine wore a blue-and-white knit sweater with a Star of David emblazoned on the front of it while a small yarmulke adorned the dog's head. Above the star icon Kelly could see the name Davey. "Well, who do we have here? Nice to meet you, Davey!" She was happy that the topic could change to a more pleasant one. *No one can argue over a small cute dog. Right? Okay there, fella. Thanks for arriving in the nick of time!*

"It's Dah-vey," Mrs. Cohen corrected.

"Sorry. Hi there, *Dah-vey*," Kelly enunciated. "Come here. Come here, Davey. You're just a regular happy fella, aren't ya!"

Freida rolled her eyes and took a deep breath. "Davey is not a *regular fella*. He happens to be a highly trained dog of good Jewish taste who is held in high regard within our community back home in New York. I'm sure, as a *vet*, you can appreciate that."

"Of course," Kelly politely replied to avoid more conflict. *Lady, there's no easy topic with you for me, is there?*

Joel reentered the room and delivered a Moscow Mule for Mr. Cohen. Kelly put her hand out as the Maltese made its way closer to her, stopping to inspect Adam first. Davey enjoyed Adam scratching behind his ears as he continued his scrutiny of his infrequent play pal. The pooch finally made its way to Kelly and sniffed her hand thoroughly. *Finally someone friendly! Someone to make this evening much easier. And you don't care if I'm Catholic, do you, sweetie?* Davey lifted his leg and peed on Kelly's shoes.

"Oh!" she gasped.

"Davey! No!" Adam exclaimed.

"Davey! Bubbeleh! You poor thing. I'm glad I have extra outfits for you. Come with Mame and I'll let you pick out a new outfit to wear." The dog happily headed over to Mrs. Cohen.

Morty took a swig from his drink. "See? Even the dog knows how to negotiate. Everything's negotiable. Everything."

Adam called out to his mother as she rose to leave the room with her furry loved one. "Mame. You need to scold Davey so he doesn't do that again. Kelly's shoes may be ruined!"

"Mm. Yes. You're right," she agreed. She picked up the Maltese and spoke to it up close. "You thought you were protecting us, didn't you, Bubbeleh. It's okay. You are a good judge of character, my little one. Maybe she did something to provoke you that she didn't realize was aggressive, huh? We'll get you changed. Say sorry to Adam about his girlfriend's shoes now. And I'm sure she's sorry too." The older woman calmly stroked the dog and started walking. Joel returned with wipes and paper towels. It surprised Kelly that Morty spoke up next in the middle of this mishap.

"Davey! Say sorry for what you did. You should never ruin a good pair of shoes, especially expensive ones that were probably purchased by Mr. Moneyshoes here! C'mon! Say sorry to Kerry!" The dog barked while exiting with Mrs. Cohen.

"Tate! It's Kelly!" Adam exclaimed while helping Kelly to clean the puddle and the shoes.

"Okay. I say Kerry and you say Kelly. Close enough. I told you. Everything's negotiable." The older man's comment went unheard as Sarah entered the room with a plastic bag for the wet socks and shoes. She offered Kelly a pair of her own socks and some slippers to use for the evening.

"Thanks. You're a lifesaver! I don't know what got into Davey to do such a thing. I've really never had a dog do that to me before now," Kelly explained.

Sarah replied, "Don't you worry. Besides, dinner is ready, so let's eat!" Morty announced that he would check on his wife and get her to the table quickly. Once he left the room, Sarah continued, "I know it's not going as you hoped right now, but you have plenty of lifesavers here to help you navigate the stormy waters. Just signal Adam, Joel, or me, and one of us will rescue you!"

The two couples headed into the dining room, joined by the children, and the adults strategically chose seats that put some distance between Kelly and Mrs. Cohen. The elderly Cohens arrived a few minutes later with Davey in tow, who wore a black shirt that showed a colorful dreidel. Under it was emblazoned "I love you a Latke." The Maltese also sported mini black leggings to match his shirt. Kelly thought he looked adorable but wondered what the dog thought about having to wear clothes. She also wished he had worn the leggings earlier, as perhaps it would have stopped him from piddling on her shoes!

"All better. Hopefully Davey wasn't too traumatized by the whole mishap in the sitting room. I'm going to have him sit next to me while I eat, just in case he feels out of sorts." Freida sat down. "You know, I heard on a popcast that a dog's demeanor can change if you don't attend to their mental health. So I'm not going to chance it, because Davey has a wonderful disposition."

"Podcast, Mame," Adam corrected. "It's a podcast, not a popcast."

"As long as you knew what I meant. That's what matters, dear."

"Okay. I don't know about everyone else, but I want to

start eating," Joel announced. He stood up to help Sarah serve what looked like a mouth-watering Judaic collection of food. The rabbi and his wife sat down and Sarah asked Joel to say the dinner prayer. Joel deferred the task to Adam, mentioning his chance to impress his parents with the fact that nothing of his heritage was forgotten just because he was dating outside of his faith. Adam, with a great deal of pride, deferred the honor of saying the prayer to Kelly. She cleared her voice, scanned the faces before her, and bowed her head. She had practiced this everyday blessing over food repeatedly and focused on it sharply.

"Baruch atah Adonai Eloheinu melekh ha'olam hamotzi lechem min ha'aretz." Adam reached his hand under the table and gently squeezed Kelly's hand. She looked at him and saw a growing smile on his face and she released her breath. *Thank you, Catholic God, for helping me with Jewish God! Ha! Probably the same guy, and Mrs. Cohen probably would've had Davey bite me!*

"That was great, honey! Couldn't have said it better myself." Adam beamed. Kelly soaked in the congratulations and praise that followed from every family member gathered at the table, except for Freida, who offered some critique.

"You did okay with the blessing, Kelly. I mean, the words were pronounced correctly, but the tone seemed off to me."

"The tone? Please, Mame, be fair in your judgment," Adam protested. "This is Kelly's very first time with the whole family *and* she's reciting one of our prayers. So maybe you can take that into account when you comment."

"I was fair," Freida defended herself. "However, I will also correct where correction is needed, no matter who it is that needs it. It is important to do things correctly so that

Yahweh is pleased with our diligence. As a matter of fact, I was just about to advise Sarah to stick with making a traditional brisket, instead of this one she made. She should cook it in the oven instead of her low cooker, and use our Israeli tomato sauce instead of ketchup and a packet of onion mix. Sarah, dear, you do not wish to offend your husband."

"As long as we're correcting, it's a *slow* cooker, Mom," Sarah advised. "Slow not low."

"I'm not offended. It's good," Joel added.

Freida countered, "Of course you're offended. You should be. You're a rabbi."

"But it's still kosher, so a contemporary version is okay. The kids love it, too, so that's a plus," Joel explained.

Adam entered the debate. "Mame, I'm sure if Joel, who is indeed a rabbi, is okay with the brisket, then it's fine enough for the rest of us."

Mrs. Cohen unfolded her napkin and placed it on her lap. "Ah, yes. My son, with a shiksa, should know everything about what is acceptable in our faith and our rabbis. You know, we may be here in America, but we must still make Israel, our homeland, proud."

Adam countered, "I agree with you, but America can also be a place to combine the best of both worlds."

"You were not raised to *combine things!*"

Morty injected a rare comment into the rising tension. "Well now, combining things sometimes creates new opportunities and new opportunities bring more sales and more sales bring us a comfortable life. That we must also remember. And the brisket is still kosher soooo . . . meh. Eat it already."

Freida's glare locked on Morty. "I am not finding you very helpful right now!"

"Eh. Tell me something I haven't heard a thousand times before now. Someone please pass me the salad."

Sarah passed the bowl of finely diced vegetables to her father. Cholent, challah, and brisket continued to be passed and enjoyed as well while the mealtime discussion centered itself upon lighter topics. Everyone enjoyed sharing reminiscent family stories as the children intermittently added further questioning and humorous reactions to the exchange. Kelly was finally beginning to feel comfortable.

She noticed that Davey had started to stroll around the table, looking for tiny morsels of anything dropped to enjoy, so she grabbed her opportunity to forge a new friendship. Kelly purposely dropped a tidbit of the succulent brisket. Davey strutted over to collect the moist treasure and sat looking up at the newcomer. Kelly grinned. *Ah! I've got you now, don't I? We're going to become friends, you and me, and then you'll help me win over your owner.*

Kelly cleverly coughed some of the cholent into her hand and then let it drop to the floor. Davey was on it at the same time it landed. He sat closer to Kelly, staring at her while waiting for the next piece to fall, but before she could disguise another gifted action, the canine disappeared. She deliberately dropped her napkin and bent down to retrieve it in order to disguise her search for her newfound friend. Her jaw dropped slightly when she spotted Mrs. Cohen sneaking a bit of brisket to Davey. Kelly sat up and wondered if the older woman had spotted her bribery first or if she did this on a regular basis. She snuck a larger gravy-slathered chunk of brisket into her hand, dropped it, and held her breath, praying the dog would come. She needed this alliance! She looked down and saw the Maltese scoop up the meat and then lick any leftover liquid from the floor. "Yes!" Kelly exclaimed in an oversized whisper.

"Yes about what, duvshanit?" Adam asked. He brought Kelly's attention back to what was happening above the table.

"Uh. Yes! This food is delicious. We'll have to get all these recipes from Sarah so I can make them at home."

"I'm glad you like it enough to want to make it," Adam replied, "because you'd have to fight everybody else here to get any leftovers the next day, probably even Davey!"

Everyone laughed while the two ladies made eye contact and maintained their stare like a showdown between two cowboys. One chose her next drop to be a chunk of brisket while the other chose a handful of cholent mixed in with a piece of challah. The staredown continued while they waited for the dog's decision, each shooting a quick look downward to check for victory. A large smile grew on Kelly's face as Freida began to silently fume. Kelly momentarily forgot the immediate circumstances and basked in her victory. Then the unthinkable happened. The two women looked at each other with slight confusion. Davey had just walked away from the table and was now unceremoniously upchucking his overfed feast of meaty treats. Both women rushed to the dog, Kelly in a natural career reflex and Freida in the role of master.

"I can take care of him if you'd like," Kelly volunteered.

"I'm his mother," Mrs. Cohen disputed the offer and snatched up the Maltese.

"Okay, but you might want to wait until—" Davey heaved up another piece of undigested matter. The older woman immediately regretted picking up her dog as remnants of food rolled down her clothes. She placed the canine back down on the floor.

"I'm actually going to let Davey finish, um, doing what he's doing and then I'm going to change him yet again!" Freida proclaimed. "Next time please don't feed the dog unless you know what you're doing."

"But I was just . . . and you know that you gave him . . ."

Kelly sputtered, trying to choose her words delicately. The whole family was now watching.

"We both know it always comes down to the mother knowing what's best. I think, down deep inside, we all truly know that." Mrs. Cohen smiled contemptuously.

Kelly had many responses in her mind, none of them polite. The evening had somehow become a dueling shootout and she was lying on the ground wounded. She chose her words carefully. "It doesn't mean that a mother—" Adam arrived in the corner, jumping in to prevent any further escalation.

"Mame! Kelly! Stop. You both know me and care for me in different ways. It's not one or the other. I love you both."

"What?" the women asked in unison.

"Aren't the two of you arguing about me?"

"No," they stated with unanimity. The two women gave each other a long look, both knowing full well that he had just laid out the bare truth hidden underneath the doggy duel.

"I must go change Davey now that he's done." Adam's mother lifted the Maltese into her arms. "Kelly, let's just call this a misunderstanding. No need for further discussion really."

"Agreed. No problem," the younger one offered her an olive branch.

"Yes. It was all just schmegegge."

"I know that word! It was indeed nonsense. On the bright side, I can't wait to see Davey's next outfit." Kelly feigned adoration for canine fashion.

"Oh, they're all adorable, aren't they? Of course, Davey is also more handsome than the average dog." Mrs. Cohen smiled at the furry ball in her arms. She left the dining area with one more comment, directed toward the dog, but it was obvious it was meant mostly for Adam. "Davey, I'm so sorry you were overfed. A mother does usually know best in family matters, and I'm thankful to Yahweh that I still have you at least. Otherwise, I'd be a forgotten mother." The Cohen siblings looked at each other and rolled their eyes.

Adam and Kelly returned to the table and the meal was finished without further trying moments. Everyone helped to clear the table, except for Mr. Cohen, who excused himself to check on his wife. When Kelly happened to glance outside through one of the dining room windows, she noticed the older man puffing on a cigar. She grinned at his incorrigibility, as well as his excuse. Anyone married to Mrs. Freida Cohen would probably need some form of bad habit to release the tension.

The group sat back down and Sarah delivered the much-welcomed dessert. She had baked an impressive batch of chocolate rugelach and the children's eyes, partnered with their smiles, grew twice in size. They jockeyed themselves to grab their first choice of pastry and awaited their mother's go-ahead. Joel and Adam teased them at first and Kelly enjoyed the banter. Family time could be the most fun and then, at times, the most trying. Morty joined the table and had the honor of taking the first rugelach. He immediately added a second one to his plate as well, with the excuse that the pastries looked a tad smaller than usual.

"Ah. Just like last time!" Joel exclaimed.

"And the other times before that!" added Sarah.

Morty suggested that they not focus on the past and everyone laughed.

Joel observed, "That's all you've got to say? I've noticed your defensive strategies have been weakening."

"So has my willpower. Everybody, take some already, so I'm not the only one eating dessert here."

Everyone was enjoying the generously filled pastries when Freida arrived with her dog in tow. "I've decided to put Davey in his pajamas, seeing he looks tired to me, probably from his incident." The Maltese was wearing a black cotton tee that proclaimed he was "Mommy's Little Matzo Ball." Kelly was indeed starting to like the idea of these outfits. They didn't hurt anyone, she guessed, and she started looking forward to seeing what would adorn Davey next. *Okay. Score one point for crazy dog dressers!*

"If people don't mind, I'm going to excuse myself from dessert. I think I need to sit with Davey while he falls asleep. I want to make sure he's okay. Kelly, it was, um, interesting to meet you."

Kelly got up and walked over to give the matriarch a hug goodbye. There was an awkward moment during the attempt as Freida kept adjusting the canine so they could hug, and yet not hug. Kelly couldn't tell and finally just shook hands with the older woman. She then gave Davey a few strokes under the chin and a quick peck on the head. "Good night, Davey. You and your clothes are adorable!"

"Thank you," Mrs. Cohen replied and left the room. That was it. Kelly's big first impression challenge was gone as quickly as their exchange had intensified. But she knew there would be more challenges ahead during these holidays. *I just know I can win her over, and by the time Chrismukkah is done, I hope she likes me like Davey—a latke.*

The start of a new discussion brought Kelly back to the table's conversation. Morty came to life with his endless passion for starting a business with his son. "I'm telling you, we'll hit the jackpot, Adam. You don't like my last idea, that's fine, but what happened tonight could inspire an empire! We could sell kosher doggy mixes for Jewish dogs!"

"No, Tate. Great idea, but not interested in it myself. But I think you should do something with it. Joel is a rabbi, so you could have him be a commercial spokesperson or something like that."

"Those clothes Davey wears seem popular too. We could start our own fashion line for dogs. We could call it Kosherrific or The Canine Line. Everyone is going pooch-crazy these days. Let's do it, you and me."

Adam shrugged. "I don't think so. Why would I do clothing when I enjoy creating jewelry at Dan's store?" He grinned. "After all, I love telling people that I make women happy for a living." He wiggled his eyebrows at Kelly while maneuvering his pretend cigar.

"That you do," agreed Kelly.

"By golly, that's it!" Morty blurted before slapping his hand on the table. "A jewelry line for dogs! It's genius! It's so useless and decadent, people will snap it up to show their pets how much they love them. And we can do a special devotional line for Jewish dogs. I'll handle the business and you can handle the designs, my son. We'll pierce every canine ear and hang a chain on every neck. Hey! We could do matching owner and pet sets too!" He waited for Adam to respond.

"It's actually a great idea," Kelly chimed in on the suggestions.

"Well?" Joel and the children could no longer hold themselves back. Everyone was waiting for an answer to yet another one of the older Cohen's brainstorms.

Adam hesitated a bit longer. He looked back and forth between his father and his girlfriend and then scanned the faces of his other relatives. "There must be something wrong with me. I actually like this idea, and maybe I can make women *and* their fur babies happy for a living. The creative aspect really intrigues me."

Kelly and Adam's family cheered his response and Adam squeezed her hand. "We'll talk about this later, Tate, just you and me. Then we'll see where this leads." Morty was thrilled. He rambled on about people to contact, paperwork to start, and plans to be made.

Standing up he announced, "I'm going to bed to dream about this new opportunity. I'm a happy man, and we're going to make big plans that will bless us with great riches together. Not to mention, we have the Hanukkah Festival tomorrow night. Joel, you too should go to bed, along with the children. It's a big event for you at your temple. And, Adam, you won't regret your decision! We're gonna get, how do you say it, people jacked!"

"Tate! You said that right!" Adam replied with great surprise. Laughter followed. After goodnights were wished Adam added, "Tate, enjoy starting our business, but leave urban speak for us."

"Who's Urban?" Morty Cohen waved off the group's continued laughter and left the room.

"Festival night is a big night, and even bigger when all the Cohens are there . . . plus one." Joel winked at Kelly. "So I think the rest of us are going to head to bed soon."

After clearing the table, Sarah left with the children while Joel saw Adam and Kelly to the door. The three agreed on a time to meet at the temple the next evening, as they were going ahead of the others. This way Joel could show Adam and Kelly where they would oversee the Menorah Walk, a display of the rabbi's impressively growing menorah collection. While walking to the Yafah LX, Kelly contemplated what had transpired and felt that her place with the elder Cohens was probably slightly better than it was before the evening's dinner.

Eh. Overall, not a bad night. I'm pretty sure I'm close to winning over Mr. Cohen. Then I'll score FrankenFreida before she can break up Adam and me! She was amused by the implausible thought of breaking up while leaving the Weinberg household arm-in-arm with the man she loved so deeply.

Chapter 13

ADAM

Adam and Kelly arrived on time the next day to meet Joel at the Jewish Community Center of Atlanta. They were looking forward to helping with the Menorah Walk before exploring other areas of the Hanukkah Festival. During their drive, Adam had explained to Kelly that, besides the walk, there would be a photo booth, carnival games, live music and dancing, crafts, scrumptious foods, and a very popular silent auction. He could tell Kelly was excited to experience her very first Jewish festival and it delighted him. They dropped off a large batch of sufganiyot for the food pantry before heading to the rabbi's office. Adam explained that the delicious pillowy doughnuts would be distributed along with other boxed foods to marginalized families in time for the first night of Hanukkah.

"Speaking of the first night of Hanukkah, I really wish we could be there with your family, but you know I had already promised my Aunt Julie that I would take GG to midnight mass. Sorry again about that."

"No worries. Besides, I'm actually looking forward to midnight mass at, uh, six o'clock." Adam smiled with amusement as they arrived at the door to Joel's office.

"I know that sounds funny, but GG likes to go to Christmas mass at her nursing home's chapel. Her childhood friend lives there too. Imagine that, best friends for longer than you and I combined have been alive! Anyway, the elderly there grew up going to midnight mass. It's sentimental for them, but they can't stay up that late, so they offer it at six o'clock." Kelly shrugged. "It is what it is. But you're all set for tomorrow, right? GG will expect us to be dressed nicely. I told you that, I think."

"Yes, ma'am. My suit and shoes are ready to showcase your trophy boyfriend. We'll pick up GG and her bestie at the nursing home and head to the chapel, all while I charm them with my impeccable manners and brilliant repartee. We'll also impress the rest of the crowd, causing you to fall deeper in love with me, while worshiping and celebrating the birth of Jesus, who created a new religion, thus disappointing my own mother, who's going to be even more disappointed because we've apparently sacrificed Hanukkah for the sake of Christmas. However, we know she'll get over it for my sake. See? I've got it all down pat."

"You're such a smartass." Kelly grinned.

"And those were the exact words Mary said to encourage the donkey while she and Joseph traveled to Bethlehem for the great census. See? I'm ready for any quiz you've got!"

"Smartass and my kind of guy. I love you so much, babe."

"Mmm. And how much is so much?" he teased. The two embraced and found their way into a deep, long kiss. Adam pressed Kelly against the wall. He wanted to sweep her away and make love to her over and over again, and he knew she desired that as much as him.

As if on cue, the office door opened and Joel remarked, "I had a feeling two people were out here smooching like a couple of hormone-induced teenagers, so I thought I'd help and open the door for you."

"Your timing is terrible, dearest brother-in-law," Adam countered while Kelly and he quickly disengaged from their entwined stance.

"That may very well be, but my ability to recruit volunteers is astonishing. Shall we head out? The festival is starting in a half hour."

The three walked over to the area holding the rabbi's menorah collection. The event was well organized and decorated in a festive manner. Joel showed Adam and Kelly where to store the submitted tickets and what would be acceptable behavior from viewers while enjoying the collection. It all seemed simple enough. Adam and Kelly had no further questions and they agreed to meet up with Joel at the silent auction once their shift was completed. The entire family was planning to meet there. The rabbi checked an incoming text on his phone and hastily excused himself. He was needed at the main doors to give a blessing for the opening of the festival. The two lovebirds were left to begin their shift and promptly walked hand in hand to check out the menorahs.

The rabbi's extensive collection was indeed popular and the next two hours proved to be busy ones. Adam and Kelly eyed each other as they overheard comments about the craftsmanship of several pieces, including a vintage brass menorah with an ornate pedestal depicting the lions of Judah, a simple early-nineteenth-century candelabrum with bronze branches, including a ninth lamp serving as the shamash, and a modern silver menorah with a Maccabean theme. Adam made a mental note to share some of the onlookers' remarks with Joel, as he was sure his brother-in-law would be pleased with the overall reaction to his collection. That opportunity came quickly as the young couple was replaced by another set of volunteers at the end of their two-hour shift.

Exiting the menorah walk and heading down the hallway toward the silent auction, Kelly shared how happy she was to learn more about Judaism in such a fun way. Adam was thrilled that everything was going better than anticipated, and Kelly's words were music to his ears. They entered a large hall filled with people swarming throughout the silent auction and gathering area. He smiled radiantly at his girlfriend and pictured his parents seeing her through his eyes. He could finally hear his mother's voice of approval too!

"Adam! Over here! Oh. He brought Keely." The bubble of the Jewish son's dream popped at the timing of his mother's actual voice. He led Kelly toward his relatives and the young couple said their hellos before Adam took his mother to task.

"Mame, you should know by now that it's Kelly, not Keely."

"Yes. Well, I wasn't sure if there was a Catholic pronunciation of the name."

"There's no such thing as a Catholic pronunciation of any name," Adam insisted.

The older woman threw judgment to her son-in-law. "Joel. You're a religious man. Your thoughts?"

"He's right. No such thing, and maybe you already knew that. So perhaps we'll call it a small slip of memory."

Freida Cohen apologized in a way only she could. "That's probably it. Sorry my slightly failing memory was such an offense. I guess it comes with age, and I can't control that. So, what was it again? Yes, Kelly." She hesitated. "Hello once again, Kelly."

The ladies' eyes locked as they nodded to each other. Adam couldn't tell what either of them was thinking and didn't want to ask at the moment. He knew his girlfriend, though trying hard to be understanding and polite in a challenging situation, could also hold her own in a verbal sparring match.

"Nice to see you again," Kelly offered anticlimactically.

"You're being sweet, duvshanit," Adam stated before turning to his brother-in-law. "Ah, such a diplomatic and wise man you are." He patted Joel's shoulder. "Has anyone perused the auction items yet?"

"We just got here ourselves," offered Sarah while she took out her wallet. "I'm going to buy something for the children to eat first. Then Joel can sit with them while I go see what I want to bid on this year. My friend Rachel told me her mom spoke with a friend of hers who is on the auction committee, and she said there's some really great items this year!"

"Ah! Telephone, telegraph, and tell a woman! Best ways to pass on gossip!" Morty Cohen was blunt with his beliefs. "I can't wait to see what people are shelling out for some of this stuff. Temple auctions are like retail on steroids."

"Mr. Cohen, I have to ask that you please try to contain your thoughts while my congregation is in a generous holiday mood. After all, it is their generosity that begins and builds great things within our community. It's good and it's fun to boot." Joel was pleasant but stern.

"Sure, sure. I get it. But I still want to check the clipboards, so let's go already!"

Sarah arrived with food for the children and Joel. She then fell in line with Adam, Kelly, Freida, and Morty as they trotted off to the silent auction. The tables were filled with numbered baskets, gift boxes, and certificates, as well as written descriptions of local services, cruises, and vacation rentals. There were treasures big and small to be had by all the declared winners, including a replica of the knotted ring Adam had donated to Charlotte's fundraiser. He was happy to be a donor here as well.

Row after row the group stopped individually to pen in an offer on some hopeful prize. Mr. Cohen was true to his word about containing himself vocally, but his gestures spoke volumes. The younger adults in the family chuckled and shook their heads from time to time when it looked like he would spontaneously implode after picking up a clipboard to read it.

"Whoa. Check this one out," Adam declared in an unusually excited voice at the high-value table. "I'm definitely bidding on this one. But look. There's only a couple of bids, but they're already kind of high. Oh man. I don't know."

The five inspected the item encased in a locked box. It was an antique keychain with a finely detailed etching of the Israeli Yafah LX logo. Adam stated that he believed the color of the olive was made up of what looked to be encrusted peridots and the black background was probably onyx. The fine gold lines were impeccable, right down to where it outlined the letters of the brand name. The group murmured in agreement as they listened to him speak as a jeweler. Adam took out his loupe to take a closer look at the keychain.

"You just happen to have a loupe on you?" Sarah asked.

"Of course! In my line of business, sometimes I bump into customers and they'll ask me to take a quick look at a piece of jewelry on someone who's with them. Sometimes that person is impressed with my observations and starts bringing their business to me. Besides, it's small enough to easily carry." Adam held his loupe and came as close as he could to the glass panel of the locked box. "Hmm. The best I can tell is that those peridots are real. The clarity seems even and pretty good throughout all of them. The white lettering is made with white sapphires, I think, rather than diamonds. This is an incredible piece, and it's perfect for my Yafah LX. I just can't believe it's here! Wow."

"The description says it's been donated by some estate of a late temple member and it comes with certification," Kelly offered.

"So get it already, my son," Freida insisted. "It was certainly meant for you to have along with the beautiful Yafah LX your parents gifted to you."

"If Mr. Moneyshoes can spend so much on footwear, he'll definitely be in for the jeweled keychain. That we can all be sure of!" Morty pointed his finger skyward but promptly pulled it back down after a quick look from his wife.

"Tate. I'm not Mr. Moneyshoes, but I do indeed love this keychain. It's going to be a lot of money, though, and I'm trying to save right now. Plus, it's the holidays with lots of gifts and so forth. I just don't know." Adam sighed and toggled his head back and forth.

"You can skip any gifts for me, my love. I mean, how often is a unique item like this going to cross your path?" Kelly leaned into him and gave him a gentle squeeze.

Adam sighed again. "I don't deserve you, duvshanit."

"You're right. You deserve better, so bid!"

Sarah interjected, "My kids are most likely done eating by now and Joel's probably holding them at bay. So let's bid or move on already! Oy vey!"

Adam moved on without picking up the pen to bid. "I've got better things to get than some keychain." His parents and girlfriend objected, but his decision was final. He did not return to the keychain's clipboard.

The adults arrived at the table where Joel and the children were finishing their desserts. Sarah mentioned how glad she was that the auction group's timing was better than she had calculated. She then went to purchase food for herself and her parents. Adam and Kelly tagged along to get their own delicious meal and sweets. When the three returned from the kitchen's serving counter, Joel left with the little ones for the carnival games. Sarah had suggested they all meet up at the photo booth after the games and then follow that with the Menorah Walk.

Everyone at the table offered so many comments about the food they were enjoying, its flavor, its quality, various versions of recipes, even the history behind certain items for Kelly's sake. For a short time, everyone was actually happily conversing and having a great time. In between remarks, however, Adam had noticed that Kelly excused herself twice to use the restroom. Then she excused herself to check on a couple of items she had bid upon in the silent auction. Then she had to visit the restroom again. She even excused herself to visit the dessert counter after just saying how full she was ten minutes earlier!

What was even stranger to Adam was how every time Kelly returned to the table, his mother would then leave, often mimicking his girlfriend's reasons. He also noticed how the tone of their facial gestures was gradually changing, but he couldn't leave to check on them personally. He was part of a continued conversation with his father about the possible family pet-jewelry venture. Morty had convinced Sarah that she, too, could have an important role in their business and still work from home. Adam became increasingly torn between what his eyes were witnessing and what his ears were hearing at the table. Why would two women give each other glaring looks just because they both used the restroom?

The weirdest moment came when his mother left the table and stated directly to him, "I don't have to tell you everything. I'm the mother!" Why would she say that? And why would Kelly take out a pen for a visit to the dessert counter? Why would his mother return from the restroom clutching a pen with a string attached to it while smugly grinning ear to ear at his girlfriend? There was something going on between them and he was going to get to the bottom of it. Right now, however, he had to pay attention to other details . . .

"Adam! Are you listening to my concerns? I just want to make sure we're all on the same page with this. You know, we could probably accomplish a lot more planning at the house. Oh, good! Dad's back."

Adam was surprised to see that his father had apparently briefly left the table and had just returned to the conversation. The three agreed that Sarah could handle administration and bookkeeping, he would handle designs and jewelry creations, and his father—

"Wait! What?" Adam blurted as he was sidetracked from the talk once again. He saw his mother and girlfriend both holding on to each other in a death grip as they watched the clock hanging above them. "Oy gevalt! What in the world are they doing?"

"We can definitely see *what* they're doing. Actually, *everyone* can see what they're doing, judging by all the eyes in the crowd." Sarah had joined in Adam's line of vision and dismay. "The better question would be *why*."

"Well, I know why and I handled it already, so you're welcome, everybody." Morty made the declaration with great satisfaction. He showed off a handful of pens, some with strings and some without. Adam and Sarah looked at their father and then at each other, searching for the answer to the moment's puzzle.

"You're a female. Any idea?" Adam asked his sister.

"Not at all, except that we need to get up and go end it." Fate answered and the lights in the area flashed. There was a collective noise from the entire crowd and, just like that, the two most important women in Adam's life let go of each other, adjusted themselves, exchanged a few words, and headed back to the table where the rest of the Cohens were sitting. The two sat down and smiled at the group as if nothing had happened. Adam was stuck trying to decide whether to inquire about what had just transpired and risk a recurrence of any disharmony between the ladies. He decided to treat the situation like he would a beehive.

Joel stepped up to a microphone and introduced the silent auction subcommittee. Each person acknowledged their applause and the final volunteer, the chairperson, gave a short speech filled with gratitude before announcing the auction winners. There were intermittent surges of acclamations and jubilation, based on the popularity of each donation. The Cohen group cheered and clapped for each winner along with the rest of the crowd. Everything seemed fine to Adam, until it didn't.

"Um, this next item, I'm going to let our rabbi, Joel Weinberg, announce." The chairperson stepped aside so the surprised rabbi could step up to the microphone and look at the next item on the list, along with its winner.

"Oh. Yes, I see. This next item gives me personal pleasure to announce." Joel scanned the room and then looked directly at his family. "This item is a beautiful one donated from the estate of a treasured and well-remembered person from our temple. It is a boxed peridot-and-white-sapphire-encrusted keychain with the Yafah LX car line logo. It was created in Israel, as was the Yafah LX car line, I might add. Is that correct, Adam? My brother-in-law, Adam, is here with my family today, along with his girlfriend, Kelly, as well as my in-laws, Morty and Freida Cohen. Adam, is my information correct?"

After another round of applause, Adam replied, "It is. And I'm going to guess you must be the one announcing it because it's being given to the temple by the winner. Now you can tell me if I'm correct!" Adam smiled. Joel smiled. Their eyes connected.

"No, you are not correct! I have been asked to announce this item for a special reason that I fully understand now."

"So tell us already." Adam was growing more curious.

"Not so fast," Joel insisted. "First of all, I want to address the two ladies who got a little out of hand bidding on this item, trying to outdo each other."

Adam started putting pieces together and suddenly the puzzle's full picture became quite clear. He looked over at Sarah, who gave her brother a look of successful puzzle-solving in her own mind as well. He smirked and leaned heavily into Kelly. She quickly defended herself, "Well, I could tell how much you instantly fell in love with that piece, so how could I not want it for you!"

Before Adam could respond there was a protest from his mother. "I noticed how much you loved it first, naturally. If you look at the list, you'll see that I signed it first. So the keychain was mine first to give to you for Hanukkah, my bubbelah."

"That's because you grabbed the pen when I was reaching for it!" Kelly insisted.

"I'm Adam's mother. I should be first."

Kelly opened her mouth to respond but Adam stopped her. "I must be the luckiest man on earth. I have two women who love me so much that they're arguing over who can give me a valuable gift. And that love, in itself, is the *real* gift!" Both ladies reacted with faint smiles and adoring eyes. Random sounds from touched hearts murmured throughout the crowd.

"Well, that's pretty much what I was going to say," Joel offered, "but I think you said it better. I can't wait to have you as a speaker at the temple sometime!"

"That's okay," Adam countered. "The temple is your area of expertise. Right now, I just want to know which one of my beautiful ladies won the keychain." The plaudit from those gathered endorsed his intention.

Freida and Kelly looked at each other and shrugged before Kelly explained, "We're not sure anymore who signed last. It did get a little crazy, I'll admit. So, yeah, we lost track."

"That's fine. Our favorite rabbi is about to announce it anyway," Adam replied. "Right, Joel?"

"And we're finally back to where we need to be!" the rabbi interjected. "And that's where I announce who won the item! So, without further ado, I am personally pleased to announce that the winner of the Yafah LX keychain is . . ." Adam felt Kelly squeeze his hand. He glanced at her face and saw she had closed her eyes as well.

"Me! It's me! Just say it already, before I plotz!" Freida exclaimed, unable to contain herself.

"Mrs. Cohen, my dear shvigger," Joel informed her, "you will not explode, but I must say it is not you."

"That cannot be! Oh Morty, hold me. I don't feel so good!"

"Why should both of us not feel good?" Morty objected and the elderly couple entered into a brief battle of facial expressions.

"Mame. Tate. Please stop," Adam muttered.

"It's all good," Kelly crowed. "Your son will still get the keychain. And it's thanks to his girlfriend!"

Adam smiled weakly, no longer sure how to handle the tug-of-war between the two women.

"Morty, is the room spinning?" Freida lifted her arm to her forehead.

"No need to worry, everyone. I'm sure my shvigger is just entertaining us," Joel announced before continuing. "Kelly, you did not win either."

"What?" Both women shot up in unison, surprised by the revelation.

Joel cleared his throat and declared, "The winner of the jewel-encrusted Yafah LX keychain is . . . my father-in-law, Mr. Morty Cohen."

The adults in the Cohen family turned and stared at him in disbelief as the hall filled with applause. The grandchildren ran around the table to hug him and whooped, "Zaydee! Zaydee! Zaydee won!" Joel checked his watch and moved on with the crowd to the next items on the winners list. The conversation between the Cohens continued privately.

"Why, Morty? Why would you take away my chance to surprise our son?"

"Yes, Tate. Why did you join in the bidding? You always say it's better to sell at auction than to buy. It's just not you." Adam was curious as well.

"The old man is sharper than you think! I saw what was going on and waited until the last minute to put in my bid. And it wasn't easy with pens coming and going, I tell you.

Women always complicate everything." The elderly man basked in the glory of his achievement.

"That's nice, Tate, but we want to know *why*," Sarah clarified.

"Well, if Kelly won, Freida would have been very angry, and I don't want to live with her kvetching every minute about losing to a shiksa," explained Morty. "And if Freida won, Kelly would probably be upset, and I don't want my son to live with that! So I want my wife back for me and my son to enjoy his girlfriend. These two ladies are going to rip us all apart fighting over Adam! Besides, it's a Yafah LX keychain. If things don't work out, we can always sell it at a higher street value through Dan's Jewelry Store and make a good return on my investment."

Adam shook his head. "Well, that was noble of you to save us from being ripped apart in today's tug-of-war. And, I have to say, the last part of your explanation is more your style."

Morty addressed the two ladies directly. "You both lost to me. Now you have something in common with each other besides my son! Work with that."

"Well, it flatters me that you still want me just for yourself," Freida conceded, "and at least my dear son will have his keychain from our beloved Israel. So Kelly and I will accept this for now."

"Mame! You said Kelly! You got her name right. See? It's getting better already."

The elderly woman shifted to hide her surprise. "You think I'm that simpleminded that I can't even get the name of a shiksa right?"

There was a pregnant pause while the young couple processed what would be their replies. Adam countered first. "I didn't mean it that way. And we've been correcting you constantly, so I think we—"

"Adam, it's okay. I *am* a shiksa. Your mother is right." Kelly accepted her label.

"Yes, but she doesn't have to make it sound like you're a second-class citizen."

"I never said that," his mother refuted.

"But you did, like you always do, in your own way." Adam stood his ground.

Sarah interjected to thwart the building exchange. "Hey, the kids are getting restless so I'm going to bring them home now. Hanukkah starts tomorrow, so there's a lot to do and we're all going to need some serious bedtime tonight."

"Well, it's the first night of Hanukkah for those of us who choose to be there," Freida provoked.

"Mame, you know we already had a commitment to bring Kelly's grandmother to midnight mass Christmas Eve. I can't control holidays from falling on the same date. Please be realistic and understanding," Adam insisted.

"Yes. I believe that's the religion with midnight mass at six o'clock," Freida gibed, apparently still upset from the twists she endured throughout the evening.

"Just at this nursing home, for the sake of their residents. It's all understandable, actually," Kelly explained.

"And on that note, I'm saying thank you for coming, everybody, and good night!" Sarah jumped in while she could. Hugs were exchanged with Sarah and the children before they left the table.

"Let's go, dear," Morty prodded Freida before any more words could be exchanged between his wife and son. "We need to go pick up my auction item and head to Sarah's so we can get some needed sleep ourselves. It's been an exciting evening, to say the least!" Polite words and gestures were reciprocated between the two couples and the parties went their separate ways.

Kelly and Adam found Joel and thanked him for the evening. Once the young couple was alone in the parking lot, Kelly observed, "It doesn't take long for your mom to bare her fangs when things don't go her way."

"Yeah," Adam sighed. "That's my mom, sworn enemy of shiksas worldwide."

"She's a force to be reckoned with, but I think I'll be okay. Lost a little of my confidence tonight, but I'm still madly in love with her son."

"And I love my sexy determined shiksa! She's no quitter, and she also doesn't have a fear of little people." Kelly grinned at Adam's attempt to make her laugh.

They leaned into each other and embraced, kissing for a moment before Kelly added, "No fear of little people, but maybe a fear of Jewish moms." They hugged each other in shared solace.

"We'll be fine," Adam assured his girlfriend, hiding his own lack of conviction in this comment. The two got in the Yafah LX and headed out into the night.

Chapter 14

KELLY

Kelly opened her eyes to a lingering tail in her face. A hungry Mr. Shrimp was brushing up against her with his usual bed stroll. She had slept past the alarm but still had time to get ready for the clinic. There were only a few short appointments today, so she'd be back early enough to get ready before Adam drove them over to the nursing home.

Remnants of dreams deposited themselves at the edge of her memory and left her feeling bothered. She lay still for a moment, staring at the ceiling, thinking about what had taken place the previous night. Never had Kelly experienced someone who didn't like her simply because of her religion. How could her and Adam's relationship work if the ones closest to them opposed them as a couple? If they were married, how would they raise their children? What example would be set if Adam's mom fought with her about everything, just to fight?

She squeezed her eyes closed. Just that thought made her feel emotionally drained. *I'm tired of investing time into relationships that never work out. Am I doing that again? "Birds don't swim with fish." That's what she said to Adam.*

Dammit! She's getting into my head! I know there are birds that actually swim, and I'm sure there's some kind of fish that can fly in this whole world. Might be rare, but that doesn't mean they don't exist.

The cat rubbed up against Kelly's head as if to agree. "Okay, there, Mr. Shrimp. I get the hint. Which would you like? Bird or fish?" The exotic shorthair dropped and stretched his body. "Chicken it is! Let's get you fed and me ready for work."

Kelly filled her fur baby's dish and momentarily watched him devour his meal before getting herself ready for the day. She placed Mr. Shrimp in his carrier and, within a half hour, the two arrived at Will's Pet Haven. Kelly was happy to see there were still just the two spays on the roster and the first one was already underway. She followed this welcomed news with Mr. Shrimp's planned checkup and placed his blood vials in the container marked for that day's pickup. Outside of waiting for the ampoules' results, her beloved feline pet was in perfect health. He purred as she stroked his fur, starting with his back and then working her way toward his belly, making him collapse in thorough enjoyment. The door to the clinic opened and Kelly was surprised to see Adam walk in with Bo. "Well, hello there, my two handsome guys! Merry Chrismukkah! Is this a fun visit or a medical one?"

"Merry Chrismukkah, my love. Both. Always fun for me to see you, but it's a medical visit for poor Bo." Adam kissed Kelly and she handed Mr. Shrimp to him. "Here. You can hold him or put him back in his crate. I'm surprised he's not hissing at Bo. He usually doesn't like dogs."

"Bo is a Cohen, and we Cohens are incredibly easy to like. What can I say?" Adam went in for another kiss. Their mouths lingered longer the second time.

"Mmm. I see what you mean. Downright irresistible." She turned toward Bo. "What's happening, buddy?" The canine rushed to lick her in between the repetitive tilting of his head and rubbing of his left ear. "Not yourself today, huh?" She frowned. "Let's take a look at you." Kelly examined the dog's slightly red and swollen ear flap.

"I'll just keep good ol' Mr. Shrimp out of his carrier and in my arms. I happen to be achondroplasiaphobia-free, so you're in luck."

"Funny guy patting you, Mr. Shrimp. Thanks, Adam, for reminding me of my ex. Not!"

"Sorry, I had to say it. It was just too easy."

"I know, I know. I probably would've gone for it too. You know the saying, 'go for the joke and apologize later.'"

"Yeah, let's apologize to each other later. Great idea!"

"Adam, stop. We can talk and get cozy tonight after we take care of GG and her friend Lou with midnight mass and all. They'll be all a-fluster if we arrive late for mass. Then GG will tell my aunt and uncle, and I'll be in the doghouse."

"Well, if you're there, I'll join you and we can still get cozy!"

"Adam, you are incorrigible. We'll never get cozy if we're not on time. I need to concentrate and get this done. Hmm. There's some crusting on Bo's pinna. He's got a basic ear infection and he tried to scratch it a bit." Kelly used a medical ear cleanser to thoroughly clean both of Bo's ears and then rewarded him with a treat. She handed Adam some sample-sized tubes of medication to apply on the infection at home. "Follow the directions on the tubes. Make sure his ears are dry before applying this and then massage the ears to work in the medicine. It's okay if he shakes his head right after, and then give him a treat so he's okay with having the treatment."

"Got it. I love it when you talk sexy vet to me," Adam flirted.

"Everything is sexy to you," Kelly bantered.

"Only with you, metuka." Adam embraced his girl-friend while cradling Mr. Shrimp in one arm. Bo nudged his way into the cuddle. "Look at our little four pack. I'm a lucky man, overly blessed by Yahweh!"

"Wait! I know metuka. That's sweetie! And for you, I would say matok, right?"

"Correct! You get a prize, so you win my heart. No, wait. Hold on. You already won that the first time we met."

"Aw. Did you think of that, or did you hear that some-where?"

"A Cohen never reveals the origin of his artillery of lovefare."

"Artillery of lovefare?" Kelly repeated.

"Yeah. It's like warfare, only it's lovefare. I'm good at making love, not war." Adam flashed his boyish grin. "Want to find out?" He looked into her eyes and she re-turned his gaze for a long moment.

Ask me to marry you, Adam Cohen, and I'll say yes in a heartbeat! Then we can enjoy all the artillery of your lovefare. The animals escaped the cuddle, leaving the young couple to retrieve their pets and abandon Adam's question.

"I'm so sorry to interrupt you two," the flushed vet tech apologized.

"No worries. Everything going all right in the back?"

"Well, the first spay is done. Sully's all gloved up and sterile, so she sent me out to see you because there's a com-plication with the second surgery. She's going to need your assistance."

"Sure thing. I was just finishing up with Bo, who had a minor emergency himself. What's the complication with the second spay?"

"Dioctophyme renale. Worms in the right kidney."

"Wow, don't see that every day! Be right there to help."

"Thanks."

"So where were we?" Adam coaxed.

"I'm sorry, matok," Kelly tried to practice her Hebrew, "I really have to go. Sorry I keep disappointing you. I'm making us miss the first night of Hanukkah, your parents don't like me, and now I'm rushing you out of here!"

"Hey, you're not making me miss anything. That was my choice, and I'll choose being with you every time. As for my parents, be patient. Change takes time in this world, especially for those who cling to old practices. And look at you. How can they not eventually fall in love with you? I know for a fact my father already loves your fine figure, so that's a start!"

Kelly burst out laughing. "I love you, Adam. You have all the right words at the right time."

"Remember that tonight when we get cozy!"

"I will. But now I really have to go!" After one last quick kiss, Adam left the clinic with Bo as Kelly returned Mr. Shrimp to his carrier. She moved on to assist Sully in Room Two. The rest of the day went smoothly and Kelly was able to return home with ample time to shower and change before Adam's arrival.

The twosome made the short drive and arrived at the nursing home to collect GG and Lou before heading to mass. Adam and Kelly smiled as they watched the two elderly women hold hands like young schoolgirls while they navigated the hallways, talking without realizing just how loud or deaf they were. The group of four accessed the elevator and got off on the first floor.

Lou couldn't help herself and stopped to survey Adam slowly from head to foot before commenting on his amazingly handsome looks. GG followed this with her own compliment. "You know, not everyone looks good as a couple. Sometimes you wonder why one is with the other at all. I mean, beauty is only skin deep, but ugly goes clean to the bone. But you two, you look great together. I just hope, Kelly, that he doesn't knock you up before getting married!"

There was an awkward pause as the young couple blushed almost immediately. "That is not going to happen!" Kelly exclaimed. "Now that my parents are gone, I try very hard to make them proud by being a good Catholic and honoring my faith."

"Well, that's good, honey. You know how men are. They tend to think with one end instead of the other."

"Mrs. Delmore, I want to assure you that I think with my head. Your granddaughter is an amazing and beautiful woman, who is worth waiting for, in my opinion."

"Well, that's refreshing to hear these days," Lou responded. "Especially seeing as I thought you made a move on me earlier when you held the door open for us."

"Don't be foolish," GG admonished her friend.

"You never know, honey, you never know! Love is blind sometimes and I appreciate it when that blindness works in my favor," Lou countered.

The four arrived at the gathering space, where Adam read aloud the words on a large print entrance sign. It proclaimed the celebration of the midnight mass would commence at six o'clock. Kelly saw Adam chuckle to himself and knew that the discrepancy in time still brought him great humor.

"It's not *that* funny," Kelly chided in a whisper. "It's usually celebrated at midnight. But, c'mon. These people can't stay up that late. Heck, I have a hard time staying up until midnight myself!"

"I can think of something for us to do to help us stay awake until midnight," Adam teased.

"Me too. Doesn't mean it's happening in the near future," his girlfriend bantered.

The elderly women shuffled their way to center seating. Kelly recognized their usual tactic of positioning themselves so as not to miss a single action or piece of gossip. She gave them their space and chose the two end seats in the row behind them.

"Tonight I shall pray for the strength to wait and you can pray for the will to surrender, duvshanit," Adam continued to jest in a low voice.

"Tonight all I'm praying for is my relationship with your parents and this whole interfaith issue. I just want happiness."

"That's fine, as long as *we* are the ones to define that. We can't put our key to happiness in someone else's pocket."

"Well, then I'll pray we get new pockets, because mine has a super long crazy thread unraveling from it. And we both know who's pulling on it." Kelly bowed her head in quiet prayer and had a heart-to-heart with God. She exhaled before opening her eyes. *Ah. Better.*

People in wheelchairs were being rolled in and placed by the side wall before having the wheels locked. The chairbound residents would have a view of both the mass and the congregation. One elderly woman in particular kept slowly bobbing her head and looking at Adam each time her head was lifted. Kelly noticed the lady had only one eye that would open and, with it, she would stare at Adam intensely as she flashed him a big smile.

"What's with the one-eyed lookum who's ogling me like I'm a mouth-watering Angus steak?"

"Two things," Kelly counseled in a low tone. "One, I'm sure she's harmless. And two, you're my steak and no one else's!"

"Ooh. Let's get grilling!"

"Honestly, Adam, you're incorrigible!" A choir of elderly members began warming up with the director.

"Oh, sugar shoot! Now I need to turn down my hearing aid," Lou complained in what she did not realize was a loud whisper.

"Be nice now or you'll hurt their feelings," Kelly's grandmother advised.

"Then we'll be even because they're hurting my ears."

GG patted her friend's hand once she was finally done adjusting her hearing device. "We'll be fine. You'll see." The opening song began and the congregation stood as a lector, an adult altar server, and a frail aging priest proceeded to the altar at the front of the gathering.

"Oops! Show's starting," Lou announced quite loudly to no one in particular. Kelly extended herself and tapped the closest of the ladies to remind them of their manners along with their volume. With her accessory turned down, Lou was less aware of both and responded even louder, "Oh. We're not leaving yet, honey. Midnight mass is just starting. Might end early, though, if Father drops out before communion, if you know what I mean." Lou winked at Kelly.

As if on cue, the priest began, "Welcome to midnight mass, everyone, as we celebrate the Lord's birth together."

Adam whispered to Kelly, "Carry the twelve, subtract six. I guess it's midnight somewhere in the world." Kelly bit her lip so as not to giggle and encourage her boyfriend.

The mass continued for several minutes without any distractions from the elderly twosome.

Then the priest declared, "Let us pray."

Lou lit up. "That's a great idea! Let's all pray!"

GG tried to quiet her friend, but once again Lou was louder as she pointed. "Shh. We're all praying right now. Except for them in the wheelchairs. They're sleeping."

Kelly heard the response and looked over at the mobile seating area. Every head was drooping and One-Eyed Lookum was drooling heavily. Kelly looked back at the priest, who was trying his best to stay standing at the altar with his arms raised. She sighed and hoped for the best. This was far from her beloved St. Anthony's church, with its contemporary Christian music, inspirational words, and close-knit family. Her parish was truly changing with the times. The choir suddenly came roaring to life, bringing Kelly back from her thoughts. The sopranos hit their peak notes and the entire row of people in wheelchairs threw their heads up and opened their eyes wide. One-Eyed Lookum ogled Adam and offered him a huge smile.

Lou adjusted her hearing aid, but she and GG didn't miss any action as Lou exclaimed, "Why's Adele got that big fat smile on her face, and what is she staring at with her good eye?"

GG responded, whispering loudly, "Not sure, but whatever it is, she desperately wants it for Christmas like a little kid!"

Kelly and Adam squeezed each other's hand rather than dissolve rudely into laughter.

Once again the priest stated, "Let us pray."

Lou shot back, "Already did that, Father. Now you're just repeating yourself." GG shushed her friend.

Lou countered, "Well, he *is* repeating, whether you like

it or not." Kelly's grandmother quieted her friend and the mass continued. At one point, the elderly clergyman lost his balance but corrected his stance in time. Lou couldn't resist commenting, "Oh! He almost went down for the count! Could've had a knockout! That would've definitely made up for the missing earplugs. You know, we should have midnight mass more often."

Adam whispered in Kelly's ear, "Only if it's at six o'clock!"

GG started to complain to her friend, "You're too loud!"

"I'm not loud. I'm whispering," Lou objected. Some people turned and scowled at the elderly women.

GG argued, "You're whispering all right, whispering like thunder!"

"I'm no worse than you, Katie," Lou insisted. "Hey! Let's be lightning instead and flash people after mass."

GG cackled and shook her head at the naughty thought. The two women took each other's hand and were instant childhood friends again. Kelly shook her head. She thought of taking a seat right next to the two but realized it was pointless. She closed her eyes for a moment as mass continued. Adam squeezed her hand again. They smiled at each other as if to say they would still do this any time and as many times as needed, as long as they were together. They watched as some of the people in wheelchairs nodded off again, including One-Eyed Lookum. Kelly looked back at Adam and mouthed "I love you."

He returned the gesture, and as the choir began singing again, he whispered, "I've got to look the other way now. My other girlfriend is about to pop up again and flash me her pearly whites!"

"I guess I have competition." Kelly winked. "Now I just

have to decide whether I want to feed you to her." At the next high note, One-Eyed Lookum was back to staring at Adam with a huge smile. This time she pursed her lips at him.

Adam squeezed Kelly's hand and whispered, "Nooo! Tell me she's not sending me a kiss!"

"Look at you, hottie!" Kelly replied. "You've got ladies of all ages looking at you tonight."

Adam shot back, "That's just wrong!"

"Don't worry, babe. I'll defend your honor and fight them all off 'til the end." The mass continued for several more minutes, with the young couple now on their knees, before Adam leaned into Kelly. "Well, there you go. One-Eyed is going down fast again. Should be in full sleep mode in a minute or two."

"I don't think so. We're coming up on communion. So the choir will start singing again and the priest will walk over to your other girlfriend, ol' Adele, and she'll be receiving the Eucharist. Then he'll return to the front and we'll be walking up in line with everyone else. Maybe she'll grab you and we'll have to play tug-of-war for you. Hope I don't lose!"

"You'll win because you'll be in great shape from all these Catholic calisthenics we're getting with sitting, standing, kneeling . . . and repeat!" Adam flashed an exaggerated grin.

"Touché! Maybe I'll just give you to Adele without a single tug." The two winked at each other. "By the way, don't forget," Kelly added. "It's the same here. You can't receive, but you can be blessed. Just cross your arms in front of yourself like usual, and, uh, good luck with Lookum on your way back."

Adam nodded. "I'll pass on the last part. I already have my hands full with the girl I've got!"

The choir began singing as if prompted by Kelly's prediction. The priest brought the Eucharist to the wheelchair-bound and then returned to the beginning of the waiting communion line. Kelly lost track of Adam after she herself received the body and blood of Christ. She was too busy circling back around to help her grandmother wrangle in Lou, who was trying for seconds on the wine. After a brief and awkward encounter, the group was soon back in their places along with the rest of the congregation. The choir's singing faded as the priest returned to his seat.

"Katie, if he says 'let's pray' again, I'm going to yell at him to get a new line," Lou blurted. "It's bad enough he's cheap with the wine and you only get one shot at it!'"

GG tapped her friend's hand. "You're too loud!"

"I know they're too loud. Wish I had my earplugs with me." The elderly women continued, clearly oblivious to the fact that the priest was talking and people were now glaring at them again.

"We're lucky to have music and a choir," GG defended the ensemble. "I think they sounded good."

"That's because you're deaf and don't hear as well as I do, my friend."

Kelly shook her head. She loved these dear old ladies, but they were clueless!

"The mass is ended. Go in peace to love and serve the Lord." The priest joined the recessional walk with the lector and altar server.

"What did the priest say they're serving?" Lou asked. The congregation sang a chorus of "Joy to the World," led by the director and choir. Residents of the nursing home filed out with smiles on their faces as the staff rolled away those in wheelchairs.

Kelly and Adam escorted the seniors as the two randomly waved and nodded at fellow residents and acquaintances. The young couple reached for each other's hands as Kelly spoke softly, "Look at everyone's faces. Now you know why they do midnight mass at six o'clock. So these people can relive wonderful memories. And that's a great Christmas gift to give. By the way, what happened with Lookum?"

"When I crossed in front of her, she tried to grab my leg. However, it turns out she has a short rounded hook to her reach, so I luckily escaped her grasp."

"Maybe my hook will be a better reach. Thanks for coming tonight."

Adam smiled. "It's the least I could do after you fought so valiantly to win my keychain at the Hanukkah Festival for me."

"Ooh. Look at the goodies that they set up for us!" GG marveled as the foursome arrived at the common area on Lou's floor. There were seasonal tablecloths and place settings on every table. The one nearest Lou's room was adorned with an array of Christmas cookies and a festive punch near short stacks of cups, dessert plates, and napkins.

"Told you," Lou exclaimed. "We should have grabbed some extra wine at mass. We'd have it for our party now if we had." She shook her head.

GG stroked her friend's hand. "It's okay, honey. That wine at mass was consecrated, so we'd be drinking Jesus instead of regular wine. Don't think we're supposed to do that."

"Well, let's look around and see if we can find something to spike the damn punch. It's Christmas, people!"

The group burst into laughter at the words of the vivacious woman.

"If there's a bus going to hell, I think you're driving it, Lou," GG admonished.

"If I'm driving it, I'm dragging you with me! You're my best friend. We have all our fun together!" The ladies hugged while Adam poured the punch and Kelly unwrapped the ornate cookies. A staff member arrived with bottles of wine.

"Sorry that I'm a bit behind." The young girl placed wineglasses on the table and worked to uncork the spirits. "I wish we could have set up earlier, but we're not allowed to leave the alcohol out in the open unattended. Ah! Here we go!" She offered the first of two bottles for Adam to pour, then opened the second while Adam filled the four glasses.

"You read our minds, Linda," Lou bubbled as she reached for the first glass. The group thanked the staff member before she rushed off with her cart of adult beverages in tow.

"Lou, you didn't finish your punch," GG informed her friend. Not missing the opportunity, she, too, snagged a glass of wine.

"I'll finish it later. I've got something here that's gonna give me a bigger punch! Katie, honey, I see you're finishing your punch later too." The elderly twosome laughed while the young couple grinned at the sprightly scene unfolding before them. Lou downed her wine in two long shots.

"Dance when you've got the chance," GG proclaimed. "That's what I always say. Cheers, everybody! Merry Christmas!" She tried to keep up with Lou but was unable to guzzle like her.

"Yes! Merry Chrismukkah!" Kelly resounded, raising her glass higher.

"What the hell is a Chrismukkah?" Lou asked, perplexed.

"Well, the 'Chrism' is for Christmas, for us, and the 'ukkah' is for Hanukkah, because Adam is Jewish," Kelly explained.

"Nah. Don't mix the two. Sounds like you're dirtying clean water," Lou objected. "Mukkah. Sounds like plain old muck. Refill on the wine, please."

"Yeah, plain old muck, all right," GG agreed.

"It's not Chris-*muck*-ah," explained Kelly with slight frustration. "It's *Chrisma*-kah."

"All right. It's a little tricky but we'll let you have it, because your boyfriend is so darn cute. Plus I don't want to lose my chance at second dibs if it doesn't work out for the two of you," Lou responded.

"Can I be third or is that a weird in-the-family thing?" GG asked.

"Stop, the two of you! Honestly, I can see the bus to hell pulling up right now," Kelly admonished the ladies while Adam remained speechless. "Let's just behave and enjoy our little party here."

"Um, sorry to crush your ornament of happiness, but one cannot behave *and* enjoy the party. Katie and I need to tap a couple more refills on the wine, please." Lou raised her glass and GG followed suit.

"Okay, but that's the last of the wine, just so you both know," Kelly stated as Adam poured.

"So . . . they zipped your tip, huh? Is it cute? Did the rabbi or whoever do a good job?" Lou boldly asked Adam.

"Well, I, uh, they . . . what?"

Kelly interjected, "Not appropriate at all. Love you, ladies, but *not* appropriate. At all."

"Who's tall?" GG asked.

"Okay, okay," Lou grumbled. "I was just asking because I might not want second dibs if the chop was a botch."

"What do chops have to do with height?" GG was still in the dark.

"Lou!" Kelly scolded, but bit her tongue and looked away so the party could return to a peaceful celebration. The young couple escorted the elderly matrons back to Lou's room after Kelly suggested the party continue there. The two friends took out Lou's slightly worn album of childhood photos and Kelly smiled to see quite a few pictures with GG in them. It was fun to see her in poses that reflected such a youthful happiness. The ladies reminisced with fond memories, lost in their own magical world set in a different time and place.

Kelly and Adam, standing near the door, watched the two and cuddled. Adam leaned into Kelly and pressed his lips against hers. Kelly's eyes glanced quickly to check on the ladies, who were still busy with the photos. She returned Adam's desire and the kiss changed from a light flirtatious one into a long, burning, passionate one. Kelly's soul melted in the moment and time stood still, until she heard a throat being cleared. Adam and Kelly stopped and saw the two elderly ladies staring at them.

"When someone clears their throat," GG sternly informed them, "that means that's enough of that stuff in public."

Lou thought otherwise. "Maybe *you* had enough, but I didn't. I might be old, but I'm not dead. Go ahead, kids. Don't let two old broads interrupt you!"

GG objected. "I'm not a broad. I'm a lady, and one of those people is my granddaughter. Now I don't mind pecking, but that horny stuff belongs behind married doors." The young couple blushed.

"Okay, but remember, if she gives him the heave-ho, I get him next," Lou instructed. "And dang! I want to be kissed like that!"

There was an awkward moment before Kelly and Adam both suggested, their words tumbling over each other, that it was getting late and they wanted to accompany GG back to her room. The elderly women agreed.

"Can't believe we stayed up half the night with midnight mass and our little party," GG crowed.

"Reminds me of all the exciting fun times we had when we were young and full of it. Especially when we stayed out past curfew," Lou exclaimed proudly. The ladies giggled.

Kelly looked at her watch and mouthed to Adam, "Nine forty-five." They grinned. It was nice to see older people so giddy and happy. But Kelly did know, in fact, that it was late for these two elderly friends who would be busy celebrating Christmas the next day.

Adam whispered to Kelly, "I get it now. I understand why there's a midnight mass at six o'clock. Just look at them."

Kelly replied, "Merry Chrismukkah, my love!" This time, knowing they had spectators, they gave each other just a quick peck. Everyone hugged and said their goodbyes and the three headed into the hallway.

Kelly couldn't believe her luck. *God is good all the time, and all the time God is good!* Sure enough, there in the hallway sat One-Eyed Lookum, Adele. She was now in a bathrobe with damp hair and the nurse was rolling her in the opposite direction from the way they were headed. Kelly assumed the worker was rolling her toward the wing that contained additional private rooms. She could barely contain herself as Lookum made eye contact with Adam and pushed the hand brakes forward to stop the rolling wheel-chair. There was a short, silent moment with GG, the nurse, and Kelly watching the exchange. Finally the one-eyed lady spoke, directing her comment to Adam. "Like what you see?"

Adam's eyes grew wide. The jaws of GG, Kelly, and the nurse dropped. Then Kelly started to grin.

Adam stuttered, "I . . . um . . . I—"

Kelly cut in. "I'm sure he does, but this amazing Jewish man already belongs to a very deserving Catholic woman, me! Merry Chrismukkah, everybody!" She took Adam's arm and the three walked down the hallway toward the elevator. Kelly turned only once to look back at the nurse, who was still gawking while One-Eyed Lookum started to reach out with short right hooks.

Chapter 15

ADAM

Adam was enjoying the company of Kelly and her roommates. It was nice to sleep in late and head to their apartment for an afternoon Christmas exchange. He liked being able to celebrate both Christmas and Hanukkah. Hanukkah was all he knew as a child, and it was steeped in generations of tradition. From time to time he would imagine his ancestors celebrating hundreds of years earlier, doing the same as him, spinning a dreidel and eating brisket and latkes, or telling the story of the temple lantern through the lighting of the menorah. Christmas, too, was enjoyable and he loved celebrating every minute of it with Kelly. He had met her at just the right time, having moved to Atlanta to get away from the drama of his breakup with Golda in New York City. The pressure from his parents had been ridiculous. They had wanted him to be a good Jewish son with a good Jewish job, and marry a good Jewish girl and raise a good Jewish family, and to ignore what his heart desired. He wanted love. They wanted Jewish perfection.

"Judaism first. Always," his mother had preached. "Love and happiness will come later."

Adam chuckled to himself upon remembering his father's added comment: "Much later. I'm still waiting for mine."

"Don't interrupt, Morty! Adam, Bubbeleh, I'm telling you don't worry about such things. Yahweh rewards you with love and happiness *after* you choose your future within your faith, and your future is with Golda."

Nothing could have been further from the truth for Adam. He had arrived at this decision once he realized he was just going through the motions when he was with Golda. Looking back, the whole process had been just short of an arranged marriage. It mattered not what Adam truly felt. Freida Cohen had stated that Golda was a reincarnation of herself and liked her. Morty thought this, too, and so he didn't like her. But she was Jewish and that was what mattered most of all.

Somehow, along the way, Adam had proposed—because it was expected—and they became engaged, though not for long. When it came time to choose a wedding date, Adam's soul reached out desperately, grabbed his heart, and shook it awake. He couldn't go through with a life that was not meant for him. It was then he had bolted to Atlanta, where he could still be close to a part of his family, practice his faith, but be true to his own self. Then Yahweh rewarded him with Kelly, who filled every inch of every corner of his heart. Love, happiness, and faith turned out to be a packaged deal, and none of them needed to come before the others. He remembered how his parents had called him constantly at first, trying to convince him that his life was with Golda in New York City. It was nonstop. Adam and Golda. Adam this, Adam that.

"Adam. Adam! You with us?" Kelly asked.

"Always. I'll always be with you," he replied.

"Mm. Love that. Love you." Kelly leaned into her boy-friend's muscular body that felt molded just for her. Their lips met and the kiss they shared was long and thoughtful.

"Okay, you two," Jenn piped up. "Anything beyond that right there needs to be taken out of this room."

"Ooh, now I happen to agree with that suggestion," Adam replied.

"Behave," Kelly chided him playfully.

"Especially in front of us!" Melissa added. "But hey, I will also offer to make refills for anyone who wants an-other drink. Who's with me?" Jenn and Ashley accepted.

"So inquiring minds want to know," Ashley ventured. "When are you two getting hitched?"

"Ashley!" Adam could tell by Kelly's whispered chid-ing that she, too, was caught off guard by the question. He gave her hand a reassuring squeeze.

"I've got this," Adam addressed the query. "You know, in the Bible, Jacob served seven long years to get Rachel, but that seemed like just a few days for him because he loved her so much. Sometimes it takes time for two people because they want things to be just right."

"Wait a minute. Didn't Rachel's dad trick him with a different daughter at the end of those seven years?" Kelly asked.

"Looks like your little lesson is sinking there, Adam."

"Hold on. He was indeed tricked but still married Rachel and then served yet another seven years. That's my kind of devotion and dedication to making things right."

"Soooo, what you're telling us is it'll take years for one of you to propose? At this rate, you'll be ready to have kids just in time for retirement!" Jenn offered her calculations.

Adam attempted to clarify. "What I meant was—"

"Plain and simple," Kelly interjected. "Love you, ladies, but we don't know what the future holds for us. When we do know, we'll let you know. Sorry, Adam."

"Well said, my love. And no need for apologies." Adam gave her a quick kiss of reassurance.

"No pressure intended," Ashley clarified. "Although I hope we're able to make it to the shower with our wheelchairs and walkers." She chuckled. "Nah, just teasing. We were just curious."

"Well, thanks for keeping us on our toes," Adam reassured the sisters as the second round of drinks arrived. He sat in his thoughts as he cuddled with Kelly while the other ladies drank their beverages and commented on the opened gifts scattered around the room. He would never share his plans to propose with Kelly's roommates. His goal was a perfectly flawless proposal to the woman he adored in ways that numbered the stars. This would involve total surprise, no heads-up, no accidental spilling of the beans, no parental negativity, just pure perfect magic.

I know we love each other madly, so why do I keep wasting time? When we're together it's like the universe is ours, so I'm just going to do it—and I know the perfect occasion! New Year's Eve in front of the whole family . . . by the lake, with fireworks . . . and what a perfect way to start the new year! It will indeed be magic! And my parents will come around eventually because we'll get married and have kids, and I know that's the perfect bribe for them. Grandkids!

Adam's eyes met with Kelly's and they smiled. *If she only knew what was going through my mind right now! So now I need this week to prepare for New Year's Eve. And I won't let anyone stop us from getting engaged this time, including me with my fears!* As he looked at her, his smile grew wider.

"What a smile on your face!" Kelly observed. "What's on your mind to make you smile like that?"

"Magic," Adam replied with an amused look. "Magic and you."

They kissed again.

"Abracadabra," Ashley cracked. "Can you make three more Adams appear for the rest of us?"

"Ooh, yes," Jenn added. "We'll give you a list of specifications as to what works for each of us, but with the same quality of adoration, please and thank you."

"Pin a big yes on that for me," Melissa added.

A spirited discussion sprinkled with repartee followed until it was time for the couple to leave for Hanukkah's second night with Adam's family. He watched as Kelly inspected herself in the hallway's body-length mirror. He could tell her nervousness was growing as she reapplied her makeup, and he yearned to remove that anxiety, making their Hanukkah just as enjoyable as their Christmas. Adam drew Kelly into his commanding arms and pampered her with a long, reassuring hug. He was relieved when she released some of her apprehension through a slow and controlled sigh. They looked into each other's eyes with no need for words.

What left Adam with a few drops of uneasiness, though, was this growing level of panic in Kelly with each passing interaction with his parents. This confirmed the urgent need to propose to her. Surely that would solidify their solidarity, while letting his parents know they were moving on, with or without them. He relinquished his embrace and the young couple shared their thanks and goodbyes with the Harty sisters, who were settling in with a Christmas movie.

Adam and Kelly entered the Yafah LX sitting outside the condo in its vintage elegance. Kelly asked, "I thought you were going to put this car into storage for the winter?"

"I usually do, but this baby stays out as long as my parents are visiting. We need to show them that nothing Jewish goes away because we're together."

Kelly lauded Adam. "You are a wise man." After a short drive, they arrived at the Weinberg house and rubbed the worn mezuzah upon entering. Adam inhaled the wonderfully aromatic and familiar sweet bouquet of Hanukkah scents while Kelly took out two doggy treats. Joel came to the foyer to welcome them.

"Hey, if it isn't my favorite religious man, Rabbi Weinbag!"

"Always so cute, this one. By the way, I answer to them all, Weinbag, Weinberg. As long as *somebody* is listening to me, especially at temple!"

"Ah. You're *finally* here," Freida commented as she approached and hugged Adam. "You didn't leave much time before the lighting of the menorah! There's only about an hour left before nightfall." She kissed her son on the cheek. "But I'm sure it wasn't your fault. Sometimes you're forced to wait when you choose to bring someone with you. Oh well. At least you're here and that's what matters."

Davey appeared, wearing a matching blue yarmulke and bowtie set, and strutted his way directly to Kelly. The yarmulke featured a gold embroidered star of David with payot hanging on the sides. He came looking for treats and was not disappointed with his discreet reward while she bent down to pat him.

"Oh my goodness! Davey is just adorable with his outfit and hanging curls!" Kelly gushed as she stood back up and opened her arms to offer Freida a hug.

"They are called *payot* by those of the Jewish faith," Mrs. Cohen instructed as she hugged Kelly more with her wrists than her arms.

"Going orthodox these days, Mame? Are you going to insist on saying kippah, too, when Kelly says yarmulke?" Adam asked.

"And so it begins," Sarah announced. "Nothing like the quality family time we've been enjoying lately. Shall we head over to the dining room?" She and the children handed out their hugs while escorting the group out of the entryway.

Five-year-old Noah offered a quick update for the holiday. "Uncle Adam and Kelly, you missed the first night of Hanukkah here and Bubbe said it was Kelly's fault. We lit the first candle on the menorah and learned about the Maccabees' victory and how Hanukkah means dedication."

Esther then asked, "Kelly, did you know that already? And did you know that people shouldn't have birds and fish together? I'm not sure why. Bubbe said that's a true fact, though. Then Zayde said anything is okay if the fish is pretty. Do you know why they can't live together?"

Adam cringed and took his girlfriend by the hand in a show of support. Kelly stammered, trying to find her way to a higher road, "Well, I-I do know about the Maccabees and the rededication of the temple. Uh, the fish and the birds, they uh . . . you know, we had already made plans for Christmas Eve with my grandmother before we knew about your Bubbe and Zayde coming for a visit. But next year we can, or maybe next year, if well, if we are even, uh—"

"Kelly knows a lot more about our faith than she gets credit for, kids. At least she's trying," Adam rescued her from the difficult moment. "*Plus*, just because they're different doesn't mean birds and fish can't live together in the same home, especially if everybody loves and takes care of each other, right? And together they're better behaved than older birds who are not very kind in their words!" Freida shot a hurt look at her son. Adam continued, with resolve, "You know what? Joel. Rabbi. I am asking you this from the heart. Would you please allow Kelly the honor of taking the shamash and lighting the menorah this second night of Hanukkah? She has been studying Judaism and knows what to do. She won't disappoint, and I would like to honor her the way she honors me when I enter her house of worship."

After a short eruption of heated debate between all the Cohen adults, Joel abruptly declared, "Stop! This is my home and I say that Kelly may light the menorah. With so many against us, we should be thrilled when there is one who wishes to join us." Everyone stopped with surprise at Joel's raised voice. His words resonated and Adam smiled. It seemed to him that Kelly's eyes reflected a very welcomed relief. He nodded his gratitude to his brother-in-law for the kindness bestowed upon his girlfriend. She attempted to smooth over the awkwardness hanging in the air by offering to hear the children share the story of the Maccabees and why Hanukkah is celebrated. The children eagerly accepted her invitation.

"Then you can quiz me and check on everything I learned about Hanukkah." This offered the children even more excitement.

"What's there to learn?" Morty interjected. "Someone tried to kill us but we won. So we celebrate. That's every Jewish holiday."

"Zayde! You're so funny!" The grandchildren bubbled and giggled as they tried to climb on his legs.

"What are these bugs I have crawling on me!" Morty feigned great concern as the group entered the dining room. "I know just the pesticide to use. Let's see. We have rugelach, cheese fritters, and noodle kugel. Mmm. Those appetizers should draw the bugs to the table!" Sarah allowed the children to choose what they wanted her to serve them after they gamboled from their grandfather's legs. "Ah! Works every time," the older Cohen boasted. "Now let's see what quick little something I wish to serve myself. Who's joining me in a glass of Marischeblitz?"

"Mrs. Cohen, seeing as Sarah is busy with the kids, I was wondering if you wouldn't mind giving me a tour of the beautiful foods here. I would love to learn more about them." Adam recognized Kelly's admirable attempt to once again find a connection with his mother.

"Now there's a career I never tried, a teacher. Ah. But why teach something for nothing?" Freida scoffed. "I'm sorry, dear. But go ahead and enjoy it, as Sarah has learned quite well from her mother." Adam watched hope drain away from Kelly's disappointed eyes.

"I don't mind showing you!" Morty jumped at his chance while pouring himself a glass of wine. "And I'll hold on to you to help keep your plate steady with all these appetizers."

"Tate, I'm afraid of your hold. You just steady yourself with that glass of yours instead," Adam insisted. "C'mon, I'll teach you. We still have time."

"Because the menorah is not lit until just after dark. I remember reading that!" Kelly added. It filled Adam's heart to see Kelly smiling again.

The young couple explored the offerings on the table, stopping to sample each one as Adam explained how the fried foods symbolized the miracle of the menorah oil lasting for eight days instead of one. Kelly could not pick a favorite as she enjoyed them all while Adam chose the rich, nutty rugelach.

"It's an easy choice—it's sweet, it's salty, it's nutty. It's got it all."

"Kind of like us, wouldn't you say?" Kelly jested. They laughed and then tempted each other with another sample of the enticing pastry, flirtatiously feeding the crescent-shaped confections to each other. Adam caught his mother staring at them with what he deemed was displeasure.

Morty mused, "No one ever fed me like that."

"Years and years together and only now you're kvetching about how you're fed?" Freida chided. "I can do that."

"What I could have had then, I don't want now. If the source changes, however, I may reconsider." Freida scowled at her husband's reply and followed it with a *hmph* before enjoying more of her grandchildren's company.

As Adam and Kelly finished their tour of the Jewish appetizers, they complimented Sarah on her excellent cooking skills. She accepted their praise for the items she created and confessed to the ones she purchased. The talk between the adults turned to a short discussion of more details for the proposed future family business. Canine jewelry seemed to be a good fit for all their talents. This time Morty even included Kelly in a suggested role as an overall consultant in what jewelry designs would work safely for a dog's anatomy. Adam was thrilled with his father's idea and the adult Weinbergs quickly agreed that this information could be added to the packaging.

"I thought this was going to be a family business?" Freida disapproved. "I'm sorry to disagree, but facts are facts. Kerry is neither Jewish nor a family member. No offense, of course."

"But it is offensive, Mame. And you surely know by now that her name is Kelly. Please give my girlfriend the same respect that is offered to you."

"Of course. I'm trying. And please do not get upset with me just because I live within reality instead of some pretend world."

"It's time," Joel stated.

"Time?" mother and son asked in unison, both lost in their personal struggle with each other.

"Yes. It's nightfall," the rabbi declared. "Surrender your trials for now and let us light the menorah with peace. Let's all take a breath, release it, and begin our precious ceremony, our blessed and revered tradition."

The family gathered at the ornate table displaying the menorah and quieted. Joel gently smiled and held his hand up in the direction of the shamash as a signal for Kelly to begin. She slowly took the candle and lit it with a flame burning from a small container of blessed oil. Adam felt pride swelling within him as he watched his Catholic girlfriend respect the ceremony of his beloved Judaism in front of his family.

He looked at the exquisite menorah before them made with fourteen-carat gold and dark-blue enamel. It was meticulously decorated with the symbols of the twelve tribes of Israel. At the base the word *shalom* was embossed and the letter *o* was replaced with a star of David. Adam felt it was a work of art to be appreciated and it presented the unique word, *shalom*, standing alone in all its simplicity, to all those who gathered around it. *Shalom*. It was a word of greeting or farewell and the very essence of Kelly's and his future with his family. It could become many joyful greetings for them with his parents' acceptance of Kelly as their daughter-in-law, or one painful farewell as the two of them went their way to live their own life together. Hello or goodbye. Either way Kelly and he would find their peace.

Adam's thoughts returned to the ceremony before him

as the group recited two blessing prayers in Hebrew, led by Kelly. He beamed at her almost perfect recitation of the Hebrew prayers. She only stumbled twice in her pronunciations and the group's memorization helped carry her over them. Joel then interrupted with a few words about Noah, which was followed with Kelly confidently taking the shamash and lighting two candles on the menorah.

"It's very important to light them in the right order," Freida admonished.

"She's doing great," Joel encouraged, smiling with Sarah and Adam.

Freida was quick to reply, "Of course, this would be easier if everyone here had grown up in our faith." Her words were ignored as everyone else congratulated Kelly on her success.

Joel followed with the recitation of the story of the Maccabees and the origin of Hanukkah's celebration. Every person listened intently, drawn in by the rabbi's exceptional storytelling skills, and then the group sang songs with a sprinkle of words and laughter between each one.

Kelly decided to sneak one of her smuggled treats from a pouch she had brought for Davey and quickly fed it to him. Adam smiled; it was a genius idea. She had figured these would win him over easily, thus showing Adam's mother that she was indeed the "good character" that Freida had mentioned her dog could detect when he urinated on Kelly's feet the first time they met. Adam's smile grew as Davey lingered near Kelly. He loved that his girlfriend was clever and determined enough to find ways to dismantle the wall Freida insisted on building. He knew, however, how strong-willed his mother was and hoped Kelly would not give up on the challenge.

During the last song, the two younger couples left to

deliver the food for the night's meal to the exquisitely set table. Freida and Morty eventually arrived with their grandchildren in tow. Everyone sat and Joel recited a prayer filled with gratitude and blessings. Serving platters, bowls, and plates were passed around the table as chatter filled the dining room. Adam was so happy that the most stressful part of the evening was behind them. He was even unashamedly glad that at the moment his mother was taking exception with his sister instead of Kelly or him.

"The wife of a rabbi should set an example for the others in a community and kosher-clean her own kitchen. That's all I'm saying," Freida criticized.

"I'm too busy to do it *because* I'm the rabbi's wife!" Sarah defended herself. "It doesn't matter if I hired someone to do it as long as it's done."

"But how can you be assured that it's done correctly? Oy! How times have changed."

"We trust those whom we have chosen from our community, just as I am sure your rabbi trusts you, Mrs. Cohen," Joel defended his wife's decision. "And hiring someone frees my wife to help me in our service to our community, as well as care for our children, who are the future of our faith."

"This is true, Joel. Thank you for your words of wisdom," Freida respectfully conceded.

"We should use him when my mom gives us a hard time," Adam whispered in jest to Kelly. She grinned politely. "Everything okay?" he asked, sensing his girlfriend's disquiet.

"Um. Sure. Could you please pass the latkes?" Adam handed her the plate filled with the fried potato pancakes.

"By the way, everybody, guess who's in town! You

won't believe it, but it's true!" Freida exclaimed. "She called me and told me herself. I guess she tried to email a text to me, but I told her I'm too old to bother with such things."

"You don't email a text," Adam corrected.

"The one who breaks the rules lately is the one revising my words?" Freida countered.

"So who is it already?" Sarah asked. "Tell us!"

"It can't be good for us if the person called her and she's excited about it," Morty commented. "After years of playing with fire, you can predict what's going to burn."

"Well, you're not going to believe this, especially all the way down here in Atlanta, but . . ."

"Ooh, big burn coming. I feel it," Morty interrupted.

"It's Golda!" Freida burst.

"Golda?" Joel asked.

"New York City Golda?" Sarah inquired.

"Yes! Our New York City Golda is coming to Atlanta for a while."

"Golda? Golda Meir, Golda my ass!" Morty insisted. "Somebody get me some aloe!"

Freida offered her rebuttal. "But Morty, she's just like me."

"True. Better double the aloe," he shot back while serving himself a second helping of brisket. His sarcasm was ignored.

"Golda was in a hurry when she called, but she wanted to at least let us know she was going to be here. Isn't she thoughtful? I told her we'd figure out a good time and place for all of us to get together while she's here for some quick job."

"Atlanta must be short on complainers," Morty continued his digs.

"Mame," Adam finally spoke, "I don't think that's a good idea for some of us. I think—"

"Nonsense! It's just a visit. Now I was thinking that maybe, Joel, you could ask your brother and sister-in-law to invite Golda to their party at Lake Lanier on New Year's Eve. Our family is already going, so it'll be perfect. Right?"

No! This cannot be happening on the one special night I plan to propose and make Kelly my fiancée. Not with Golda there. She might make a scene and ruin it! How do I stop this?

"Right?" Freida repeated herself.

"Wrong! Wait!" Adam interrupted. "Joel, before you answer, please consider my feelings in a difficult situation such as that."

"If that was me, I'd feel weird about it too," Sarah agreed.

"There is no difficulty here or weird feelings," Freida argued. "Joel, I ask you to do this for me, the mother of your wife, while I am a guest in your home."

"And, Joel, I ask that you consider the circumstances. I don't know if Kelly and I could go to a party with Golda attending."

"She is my friend!" the Cohen matriarch insisted.

"She is my *ex!*" Adam and his mother locked eyes as their wills collided.

"Ooh! It's burning already and the ex isn't even in Atlanta yet." Morty threw his comment into the ring. "And I need that aloe. I could be making a million with it right now!"

Joel's usual calmness quieted the group. "To do a favor for someone I love is sweet like honey. But I must let go of the honey, if I believe anyone at all will be stung in its pursuit. Mrs. Cohen, you are Sarah's mother, so you are also my mother. I would do this for you, but there are too many hearts that may be stung by it. Let's not fret, however, for we are here all together, celebrating the festival of lights." The rabbi raised his glass. "Hanukkah Sameach, and I toast my wife, who once again prepared a wonderful meal and evening for us. She does it all, makes it all look easy, and still manages to captivate my heart." The group joined in the toast.

"Well, all except for kosher-cleaning the kitchen," Freida added. Sighs came from around the table. "I'm sorry, but I will not be sorry for being honest."

Everyone helped in clearing the table rather than reply. Once everything was cleaned and put away, the children returned with their dreidel game and Joel supplied a generous amount of chocolate gelt. This time the game was not as lively as in the past due to the tension that had grown during the meal. The children did provide some distraction and everyone cheered when Sarah won the pot. She looked at the clock and suggested that everyone get their Hanukkah gifts for the family exchange. The children opened their gifts first and loved the books, puzzles, and games they received. Sarah and Joel handed theirs out next. Morty and Freida gave everyone Israeli shekels. Jacob asked his grandparents if they could buy something at the store with their shekels.

"No. It's better for you to save them because one day you'll shop with them in Israel when your parents hopefully take you there. Yahweh willing, we'll still be alive to go with you, if the stress of our children's changing lives doesn't leave us too weak and sick to travel." Freida gave a struggling smile and the tone of her voice begged for mercy.

"Mame, is that what you and Tate did with us when we were little?" Sarah asked.

"Did what? I spoke the truth then and now. We did

everything we could possibly do to stay within our faith to raise you and your brother correctly. So it's hard to see and accept how times are changing." Freida picked up Davey from the floor and gave him the affection she herself seemed to desire at this moment. After a few strokes, the dog jumped down and headed straight for Kelly, who discreetly rewarded him from her cache of canine treats. It was evident that Freida was unhappy about her pet's change of attention.

"Excuse me. I need to take Davey outside for a minute. I'll be right back."

While the others' attention was drawn to the children, Adam gathered Kelly into his arms for a long embrace until he saw his mother returning. "And she's back. Kelly, why don't you hand out your gifts and impress the hell out of my family."

Kelly nodded with renewed confidence, stood up, and started by handing out her presents to the two people who made her the most nervous. Mr. Cohen opened the first present to find two pairs of crew socks, embellished with "People like me a latke" and "These socks belong to a mensch." The novelty attire was a big hit. Morty's second gift was an exquisitely framed picture of him holding Adam as a baby. The frame's olive wood was emblazoned at the top with the words "Touch the Future." At the bottom was a saying from the Talmud: "When you teach your son, you teach your son's son." Everyone loved it, and even Freida was no exception. Adam beamed with pride and enjoyed the moment.

Next came Kelly's gift for Freida, which was the beautiful ceramic platter from Kockeputzi. Adam was even more thrilled with his mother's reaction as she gushed about it being a work of art. Kelly gave a big relieved smile and he could tell she knew she had hit a homerun. All was right with the world momentarily, and he was happy she could have that. He noticed Kelly sneaking yet another treat to Davey while Sarah finished handing out her presents to everyone by poking the bear with Kelly. Upon his girlfriend's opening of the gift, Adam saw that his sister had given her an expensive pair of lady's black panties that said "shiksa" on them. He loved his sister's gumption, and the lacy sheer panties were enticing.

"Wear them loud and proud, girl!" Sarah asserted with a wink.

"Sarah!" her mother exclaimed.

"Now there's something you don't see every day," Morty commented. "Wish I could see something worn even remotely close to that on *any* day."

"I would never wear something like that!" Freida objected.

"Who's talking about you?" Morty shot back.

"Okay, okay. My turn now," Adam declared. He loved their Americanized version of Hanukkah. "I know we usually wait until the last night of Hanukkah for these nicer gifts, but I'm glad we're doing it tonight so you can see what I made for each of you all the earlier."

He handed out his gift bags and instructed the group to open them simultaneously. Everyone oohed and ahhed when they saw Adam's sweaters with jeweled highlights creatively added. There was even a doggy sweater for Davey. It was blue and white with an embellished scallop line around the neck containing silver bones spaced apart and a silver star of David in the center. There was a tiny diamond placed at each tip of the star. Freida rushed to replace Davey's other sweater with the new one created by her son.

Adam was happy to see everyone so pleased with their gifts. "Happy Hanukkah, everyone! I'm glad you like the sweaters and, more importantly, I'm even happier to be surrounded by those I truly love for this celebration in our beloved faith." Everyone returned Hanukkah sentiments, except for Freida.

"Well, not *our* faith. Better to say *mostly all* our faith."

Adam closed his eyes and counted. *Thousand one. Thousand two.* He opened them and saw that Kelly had either not heard his mother's comment or she was ignoring it. He decided to do the latter himself. He smiled at her as she left to change her top. She returned to his side within a few minutes and shared how she adored his jeweled design at the top center of her sweater. He had started with a Star of David and then placed a cross in the center of it. A heart-shaped diamond was then placed in the center of the cross and the couple's first initials were engraved to the sides of the diamond. Then there were scattered twinkles formed by mini diamonds surrounding the creation.

"I just love it," Kelly declared. "You're so thoughtful, my love. This will always be precious to me." They embraced and kissed.

"Mine is precious to me, too, and so is Davey's," Freida blurted. "Did you hear me, Adam, dear? Your family loves you and thanks you for these gifts that are treasured because they were made by your hands, the hands that were created and held by your parents for so many years. Thank you deeply, Adam, my bubbelah, from the bottom of your mother's aging heart."

Adam and Kelly looked away from each other to see his mother leaning so far forward in her seat toward him as if the strength of her words could reach and pull him away from the young couple's embrace.

"I'm thrilled that everybody loves the gifts I made. I'll be even happier when everyone I love accepts and loves each other as well."

"Well, we obviously do what we can with what's been brought to us. Or who," Freida stated.

Adam noticed other eyes rolling in unison with his own and shook his head in temporary surrender. His attention was then drawn to Davey, who walked over to Kelly again, this time to the disappointed look of his owner.

"Hey there, buddy," Kelly chirped. She patted the dog and furtively fed him yet another treat. Adam joined in the fun.

"Wow. Davey is really starting to like Kelly. Didn't you say, Mame, that he was a good judge of character?" Davey sat up on his hind legs and leaned against Kelly.

"Do you want up, little fella?" Kelly asked. "Why, of course you do! Yes!" She picked up the Maltese, placed his small body across her chest, and stroked his fur while slipping another treat into the side of his mouth.

"I am really surprised at my Davey. Usually he's consistent in his judgment." Freida shrugged. "Meh. He's just feeling overly excited and festive. Whatever's gotten into him, he'll sleep tonight. That's for sure." Kelly and Adam grinned at each other.

He wanted to grab the opportunity to encourage her and whispered, "Well, at least things are taking a turn for the better with this little one. And he's not piddling on you anymore!"

"Thanks to a little vet know-how." Kelly smiled. "However, I am in need of the restroom right now, so I need to put this guy down or hand him off to you."

"Down's good. I'm going to help myself to another drink while you're gone. Can I get one for you too?" Kelly attempted to place Davey on the floor but something of his was caught on her new sweater.

"No. I'm good. Um . . . ooh. Hold on," Kelly faltered. "Rats. Looks like Davey's Star of David is hooked onto my design. I can't seem to unhook it." Kelly stood holding the dog to her chest.

"Here. I know the designs. Let me take a look," suggested Adam as he rose to his feet.

"Don't ruin my baby's precious brand-new sweater!" Freida exclaimed.

"We're not going to, Mame. Don't worry," Adam assured his mother.

"Careful, honey. I don't want to ruin mine either," Kelly asserted.

"I'm just looking at it for a moment. Besides his star being caught, it seems that the tip of your star is hooked on the ribbing of Davey's knitted pullover as well. Hmm . . ." Adam continued to inspect the double snag. "I should probably go get my jeweler's toolbox from the Yafah LX to disconnect the two."

"If you have to cut anywhere, cut into the stitch on hers," Freida suggested right away. "Davey's outfit is so miniature any cut would easily show."

"But it also would be easier to fix, seeing as it's smaller than mine," Kelly countered.

"Cutting into Davey's sweater will scare him. Plain and simple."

"*Any* cut will scare him, seeing as he is attached to me right now!"

"Ladies, stop! I'm not going to cut anything. I'm going to use my tools to unhook the stars. I'll be right back."

As Adam left the room, Kelly called to him, "Davey and I are heading to the bathroom while you're gone. I really can't wait any longer."

Adam knew he had to hurry before a colossal eruption of wills occurred, ruining what was already a delicate balance between his family and girlfriend. He dashed to the car and retrieved a portable version of his toolbox before returning to the house.

"You missed it," Morty declared to his son.

"Missed what?" Adam asked with a rising panic. Morty explained how his wife refused to allow Kelly to take Davey anywhere without her accompanying them. "So Freida followed them to the bathroom. I tried to follow too because, let's face it, some things are priceless to see and this is one of them."

"So then what happened? They're not back yet?" Adam inquired.

"Well, the two demanded I stay here, which, I assure you, is a regrettable missed opportunity for me. Anyway, we could hear Kelly telling Freida to stay outside the bathroom and Freida insisting she is going wherever Davey goes."

"And then?"

"Do I even need to tell you? They argued. Your mother's stubbornness outlasted Kelly's bladder, of course. They're in there right now, so who knows what will happen. It's like a hurricane meeting a tornado. You don't know which one is stronger but you know, either way, it's going to leave a mess!" Adam looked around the room and connected eyes with his sibling.

She sadly smiled and shrugged before calling out, "Kelly? Do you want me to talk some sense into my mother?"

"It's all good," a voice responded loudly. "I once hung on a stall door in a public bathroom while talking my aunt through a crazy time, so a Cohen and a little dog seem like a small challenge in comparison."

"Don't underestimate either," Sarah called back.

Adam arrived at the bathroom, where he could hear the conversation more clearly. Kelly was asking his mother to at least turn around, to which she replied that she refused to take her eyes off her fur baby. The older woman then suggested that Kelly just take off her sweater, to which the younger responded that she was not going to strip in front of anyone, and besides, she didn't want to take off such a special gift and risk anything happening to it. Adam grinned at his girlfriend's affection for the customized sweater.

He decided to speak up. "I'm really happy that you like it."

"I really do! You know, it's obviously better to take off Davey's sweater instead."

"Hold on! I don't think so," Freida barked. "My son created these gifts with his very hands, and he and Davey are both my children so the precious sweaters mean even more to me, especially during Hanukkah!"

Adam was not surprised by his mother's one-upmanship and shook his head.

"I'm glad you like the sweaters, too, Mame." Adam's father arrived next to him as he opened his mouth to add that his mother, however, should stop this crazy competition of hers. Before he could get the words out, the older Cohen shook his head and signaled his son not to say another word. Adam then watched his dad put his hands in prayer and mouth the word *please* before he slowly thought better of continuing and closed his mouth.

"I always love all your presents, all of them, and all of my children, more than anyone else possibly could. And I just wish Kelly would be more cooperative, instead of rolling her eyes like she did just now."

"I didn't roll my eyes at your words. I rolled them at

this whole ridiculous situation we're in here!" Adam could hear Kelly sigh and then begin to relieve herself on the toilet.

"Well, now I need to twinkle too," Freida decided.

"You mean 'I need to tinkle,'" Kelly corrected.

"You already are, but I need to go too," the older woman made her own clarification. "With everything happening here in the bathroom, how can one not need to go?"

Adam glanced at his father silently laughing to himself and Morty gave him a thumbs-up. Adam opened his mouth to speak and Morty turned his thumb down while putting a finger from his other hand up to his mouth, all while shaking his head. Adam closed his mouth and Morty turned the thumb back up, while he shot his son a beaming smile. The older Cohen tapped the side of his head, communicating to Adam that he had made a smart decision.

The men strained to listen more and could only hear Freida faintly soothing Davey before asking, "By the way, what were you doing hanging on the top of a stall door in a public bathroom?"

Kelly replied, "It's not something I do on a regular basis, but sometimes you do whatever it takes for your family."

"Ah," Freida marveled. "Finally there is something upon which we agree!"

Kelly shouted, *"No!"*

"No, I said I agree with you on that," Freida reasserted.

Adam wasn't sure what was going on behind the door. "Everyone okay?"

Kelly replied to her boyfriend's mother, "No, as in I can't believe this is all happening to me! Davey just wet himself on my chest!"

"He twinkled?" Freida asked.

"He *tinkled!*" Kelly exclaimed with exasperation.

"The dog tinkled?" Adam asked.

"The dog tinkled!" Morty repeated with amusement, forgetting himself.

"Morty Cohen, is that you?" Freida asked.

Adam was about to answer, but Morty shook his head and signaled his son not to tell her.

"Ahhh . . . ooh . . . not good," Adam stated instead. Morty smiled and gave him another thumbs-up.

"Yep. Not good at all," Kelly responded.

"Poor Davey! You're making him so nervous!" Freida stroked the Maltese.

"And poor Kelly!" Adam shot back. "I mean, look at all the craziness she's going through right now."

Morty shook his head and waved his hands, quietly mouthing, "Hurricane, tornado."

Freida exclaimed, "*She* picked up *Davey*, not the other way around! Besides, none of this would even be happening if you had just stayed with Golda." Everyone froze. Morty's and Adam's eyes met.

The father mouthed, "Hurricane, tornado" again. He followed this with a mimed explosion.

Adam's patience detonated as well. "Are you kidding me? Mame, I can't believe you're even thinking that, let alone saying it!"

"I love you and know what's best for you," Freida stated.

"No. I know what's best for me. And *who's* best for me," Adam insisted.

"Sometimes only a mother can see past her children's blind spots."

"Sometimes the mother creates the blind spot!" Adam snapped and immediately regretted his frustration getting the best of him. "Look. Just stop and let's focus on taking care of this problem instead."

"Fish and birds, Bubbeleh, fish and birds," Freida continued.

Adam took a deep breath. "Not. One. More. Word. I mean it." There was a long pause. The toilet was flushed, the door opened, and the ladies came out into the hallway with Kelly and Davey still hooked to each other.

"What are you doing here? I told you to stay in the other room," Freida scolded Morty.

"What? I just got here. I was getting worried about you," he boldly fibbed.

Freida's expression debated his answer.

"Did you get to go too?" Adam asked his mother.

"I'll wait," his mother answered indignantly. Adam chose not to reply and instead pulled out a micro tweezer and a loupe from his jeweler's travel kit. After a close inspection, he went to work and was able to finally disconnect the two sweaters.

"Well, it looks like both tops are wet, so it's a tie. You'll both have to change," Adam announced.

Kelly headed to a bedroom where her earlier clothes were left and Freida returned with Davey to the bathroom so she could relieve herself before handling the task of changing her dog. Adam retrieved Davey's earlier sweater and offered it to his mother as a gesture to smooth his harsh words. She opened the door, took the sweater, and closed the door without any words. He shook his head and left for the kitchen. He found a large plastic bag for Kelly's wet sweater and placed it in the bag when she joined him.

"Would it be okay if we head out now?" she asked. "I'm not feeling my best." Her nose was red and her eyes were puffy. Adam could read full discouragement in her words and body movement. He was so utterly annoyed with his mother at this point, and his father was no help at all.

He replied, "Sure."

They embraced while his frustration wandered off into thoughts. *As a couple, Kelly and I have enough challenges to face in life. We don't need additional hassles from my own damn family! I know Mame and Tate love me, but I'm not a little boy anymore. Thank the Lord that Sarah and Joel have been a big support for us.* Adam's face lit up as he grinned. *Ha! I should have bought Mame and Tate a birdbath for Hanukkah. One where a bird could perch and sing and a goldfish could swim, all in the same birdbath! Hmm. Maybe Mother's Day. But living in New York City, where would they put it?*

Adam's eyes connected with his father's. Morty frowned and shrugged, and then repeated the earlier mimed explosion. Adam let go of Kelly and returned with his own shrug. The young couple collected their belongings and made their rounds to say goodnight to everyone, hugging almost all, but only getting a polite acknowledgment from one, along with a whimper from her pet dog Davey. Joel and Sarah escorted them to the door and wished them one final Hanukkah Sameach before the exiting couple walked toward the Yafah LX.

Hanukkah Sameach indeed! I'm done. Next time we spend an evening with my parents, they'll be watching Kelly and I get engaged. Then I'll get Mame the largest damn birdbath I can find!

Chapter 16

KELLY

Kelly searched the refrigerator shelves and contemplated her snacking options: leftover salmon and a sliver of chocolate cheesecake, both from a lunch with Charlotte. A deliberately loud meow announced Mr. Shrimp's entrance.

"Well, hello there. I bet you didn't think I'd be back so soon from my manicure. Did I wake you up?" Kelly questioned her beloved companion as she stared at the sparse refrigerator. "I assume you are also looking for a snack, am I right?"

"Meow."

Grabbing the salmon, she closed the door and turned her attention toward her buddy. "Personally, I'd rather indulge in the chocolate cheesecake, but that sure wouldn't be good for you." Mr. Shrimp wrapped his tail around her ankle, giving his mistress a hug. "Want to spend some time together? It's been such a busy week with Sully out of town, I've hardly seen you." The silvery-gray furball followed her to the table and unexpectedly jumped up onto the sideboard. "What are you doing? You know you don't belong on furniture out here!" The feline never moved but cunningly began slow-blinking his eyes at her.

"You are a very bad boy," she facetiously scolded, "especially cuz you know I can't resist your toying with me!"

"Mew."

Kelly chose to forfeit the furniture battle and extended a smidgeon of salmon to the victor. "All right, you can sit there. I don't feel like arguing with you. Want to hear about tonight's New Year's Eve plans?" Mr. Shrimp's sandpapery tongue was preoccupied with the mildly flavored, flesh-colored morsel and he paid her no attention. "I see how it is. You got what you wanted and now you're pretending I don't exist?" She laughed. "Sorry, sir. I've had one heck of a week, and you need to be my sounding board." Mr. Shrimp responded with his high-pitched gurgling sound. "So, you *are* listening." Kelly was just beginning to vent her frustrations when she heard a knock at the door. "Don't move. I'll be right back."

Checking the peephole, she was surprised to see her three roommates. Before opening the door, she challenged, "And the password is?"

The queen of sarcasm quickly demanded, "Not a good time, Kelly. Melissa can't find her keys and we both need to pee!" Kelly opened the door, clearing the way for the sisters to make a mad dash toward the bathrooms.

"Can you help me drag all these bags inside?" Jenn pleaded. "Those two left me with a mountain of luggage."

"Sure," Kelly consented as she grabbed an oversized bag, a backpack, and a small leather satchel. "Welcome home, by the way. How was New Hampshire? I didn't expect to see you girls till next week."

"We didn't expect to see you till then either, but a nor'easter was in the forecast so we thought we better get out while we could. And New Year's Eve was the only date available," explained Jenn. "A lot cheaper too."

"I need to remember that."

"What do you need to remember?" asked Melissa as she led the way from the bathrooms.

"All you need to remember is that your cat shouldn't be on the furniture," Ashley snarked and harshly shooed Mr. Shrimp from his resting place. "And he's eating salmon? Has he developed a snooty palate?"

Melissa readily came to the feline's defense. "Better that he eats salmon than the last remaining Christmas cookie. Kelly, this is delish!"

Shrugging off the compliment, Kelly asked, "So, how was the time with your parents?"

Ashley quipped, "Let's just say Santa knows what he's doing. There's a good reason he only visits once a year!" Laughter ensued as the sisters shared other details, but they soon maneuvered the conversation to the question they wanted Kelly to answer. "No proposal?"

"No, not for me," Kelly sighed, "but I do believe Adam almost got one Christmas Eve."

"Really? You were going to ask *him*?"

"I don't think I'd ever do that!" Kelly laughed. "But I forgot to tell you girls about a bizarre, little old lady at midnight mass that took quite an interest in him. If she was fifty years younger, she'd definitely be some stiff competition."

"Not a chance," countered Jenn. "Adam's crazy about you! You're definitely on the same page."

"Agreed," piggybacked Ashley. "You'll be sending out a left-hand photo with an 'I Said Yes' caption before you know it!"

"Which brings us to New Year's Eve," acknowledged Melissa. "Tonight could be the night, Kelly! What are your plans?"

Kelly hesitated. Saying it aloud would make it real. "We're celebrating the last night of Hanukkah with his family."

"What?" the three collectively shrieked.

"You're kidding, right?"

All three scrutinized Kelly's deadpan expression, waiting for her to admit she was bluffing, but that never happened.

"No romantic dinner or cocktails overlooking the city?" asked Jenn.

"No special Atlanta events?" pried Ashley.

"No countdown among thousands of people?" questioned Melissa.

Kelly shook her head. "We're going to Joel's brother's home on Lake Lanier. Adam said it should be a lovely evening, but with so many people there, I doubt he would propose."

Always the optimist when it came to love, Melissa speculated, "It could still be tonight, Kelly. I'm sure Adam is just waiting for the perfect moment."

"And what if there is no such thing as a perfect moment?" Kelly challenged.

Ashley couldn't resist stating the obvious. "Then it will happen at an imperfect moment."

"There have certainly been plenty of those this month." Kelly's mental rolodex of Failures with Freida spun faster than a merry-go-round on steroids.

"Thanks for your encouragement, ladies, but I've been having second thoughts lately. I need to think this through for myself."

"But you do realize—" Melissa began.

"No comments right now, okay? So, have you girls decided what you're doing tonight?"

"Not sure yet. Just happy to make it home." Jenn shrugged.

"Hey! Let's go to that cute place up by Lake Lanier for some drinks and buffalo chicken dip," suggested Melissa.

"Yeah," Ashley agreed. "They're even having fireworks. Let's go out and have some fun."

"All right. You talked me into it," Jenn conceded.

"Good! Sounds like fun." Kelly stood and pushed her chair back under the table. "See you girls in a while."

"You're done hanging out with us? What time is Adam picking you up anyway?" Melissa asked.

"Five o'clock."

"That early?"

"Yes. We need to be there no later than five thirty because the menorah gets lit shortly after sunset."

Kelly lovingly lifted Mr. Shrimp and headed toward her room. Closing the bedroom door, she whispered, "How about you, my salmon-loving boy? Are you happy the threesome is back?"

Flashing a look of indifference, he leapt from her arms to the bed and began to roll on the chenille coverlet. She snuggled up to her purring fur baby and gently stroked him over and over. In response, his eyes closed. And then, so did hers.

Kelly's eyes fluttered in response to a soft *tap-tap-tap*. "Hey, Kelly? Are you awake? . . . Kelly?" She rolled over to face her alarm clock. "Hey Kelly, it's Melissa. It's four thirty and Adam just pulled up. Are you awake?" Slowly the digital dial came into focus and she pounced out of bed like Mr. Shrimp chasing a laser beam.

"Adam's here? No! I'm up . . . I . . ."

Kelly tore into the bathroom full speed and became a whirlwind of action. She knew Adam would be understanding if they were late. Unfortunately, his mother would be a different story. A delayed arrival would most definitely trigger Freida to pull out one of her poisonous verbal arrows. As Kelly dressed, she contemplated potential reactions to Freida's diverse behaviors and murmured, "Take the high road. Just like your mother always told you, 'Take the high road!'" Kelly smiled and seized the moment to embrace her mom's indoctrinated advice before inserting the diamond earrings and dabbing perfume onto her pulse points. As she slipped into her new angel-wing stilettos and closed her bedroom door behind her, she was determined to make every step tonight a happy one.

Adam was standing in the kitchen and greeted her with a dazzling smile. "One word: incredible!"

Jenn looked up from her laptop. "Ooh. Nice! Looks like you're ready for the red carpet."

"I love your dress, and those shoes are to die for, Kelly," raved Melissa.

"True," Jenn conceded. "I would have gotten them in silver cuz I'm not a gold-wearing girl, but you do look fantastic."

Ashley chimed in as she leaned against the door. "I agree. You're lookin' lit. Adam, you sure you still want to go to that party? Looks to me like you two should be goin' out on the town instead. Just sayin'."

"Nice thought, Ashley," agreed Adam, "but avoiding the last night of Hanukkah is just not an option. We'll escape as early as possible, though." He grabbed Kelly's hand and walked to the door. "And by the way, don't you girls wait up. I plan to keep Kelly all to myself as long as possible. Happy New Year, ladies!" He closed the door before anyone could reply and pulled her close. "Oh God, how I've missed you this week!" She pressed into his chest and could feel his heart palpitating. Her heart was racing just like his. He slightly released her from his embrace and lifted her face to his. When the tender kiss ended, she rested her forehead once again on his chest.

"We really need to be on our way so we're not late."

Reluctantly, Adam agreed. As the Yafah LX roared to life, Kelly inquired about the night's celebration.

"It should be a fun time," Adam responded. "Joel's brother Isaac has always been a great host, and his wife Leah is very sweet. They own a chain of bakeries that make the best pastries you've ever tasted. You'll really enjoy whatever they're serving!"

"That sounds great, but what about the religious stuff?"

"Tonight is really going to be more of a New Year's Eve party than a religious observance. Believe me, Isaac might be the brother of a rabbi, but his Judaism ends there."

"And Joel is okay with that?"

"Surprisingly so. The only person who'll be offended is my mother, but then again, when isn't she?"

Now that Adam had mentioned his mother, Kelly was in a quandary. All week long she had battled internally regarding their future as a couple just because of his parents. "Speaking of your mother—"

Adam smirked. "I haven't seen you all week, and you want to talk about my mother?"

"I'm serious, Adam. I've done a lot of thinking about her this week. She's made it so clear that I am perfectly imperfect for you, and I don't want you to always have to defend me like you did on Christmas Day. I want you to be happy!"

Kelly forcefully swayed to the left as Adam pulled the Yafah LX to the curb, slid the stick shift into park, and intensely gazed into her eyes. "Kelly ... dear, dear, Kelly ... Happiness is a choice, and I choose you." She lowered her face, but Adam reached out and lifted her chin.

"Hey, look at me! *You*. You are my happiness!" He cupped her face and pressed his lips against hers. As he pulled her toward him, Kelly maneuvered, hoping for a little more leg room, unintentionally nudging the stick shift so the car began rolling. "Whoa, I better hit the brakes!" Adam blurted.

Kelly straightened her dress. "For a second there, I thought the earth was moving."

"Just give me a chance and I promise I'll move the earth for you. Too bad we can't take this to the back seat."

"But there is no back seat," acknowledged Kelly.

"Exactly! Too bad!"

Once again the roadster vroomed to life and they continued on their way. As they pulled up to Joel's brother's residence, the golden light of late afternoon showcased the charming cottage. The storybook design projected happiness and Kelly hoped this evening would be filled with the same. Adam carefully parked. "Ready to go inside?"

"Mmmhmmm," Kelly answered, still admiring the dwelling. "I don't know why, but somehow I pictured an estate. This is so much more to my liking."

"Me too." Adam got out and circled the car, opening her door.

As they walked the cobblestone pathway, Kelly asked, "What are their names again? I forgot already."

"Isaac and Leah." Adam rang the doorbell and the door flung open. There stood Isaac, beaming with pride.

"Come on in! Good to see you, Adam, and welcome to our home, Kelly. I've heard a lot about you and your monopolizing of Adam's time. So very nice to meet you." Kelly could feel her cheeks reddening. Leaning toward her, Isaac spoke in a hushed tone. "Don't worry. It's all good." She relaxed. "Why don't you folks get a beverage before the candle lighting? It's in the large area off the dining room. And Kelly, after you get that drink, I want to introduce you to Leah. She's looking forward to meeting you."

Adam led the way into the large family room with its massive arched window that perfectly framed a breathtaking view of Lake Lanier. Adjoining the family room was a softly lit oversized area. Small dining tables clothed in fine blue or white tablecloths, enhanced with vases of white lilies and blue faux stems, were strategically placed around the room so it was still possible to freely mingle. In the middle of the room, the massive dining table displayed an array of rich, flaky pastries and savory hors d'oeuvres. Elevated in the center of that table stood Joel's vintage brass menorah with the ornate pedestal depicting the lion of Judah. Kelly paused to admire it, but Adam took her hand, signaling her to move along toward his dad, who was gazing out another enormous picture window.

"Dad, Hanukkah Sameach!"

"Thank you. And to you and Kelly as well. I'm glad you could join us, Kelly." Noticing her shoes, he added, "Did Mr. Moneyshoes buy those heels for you?"

"No, he didn't. When I saw them, though, I just couldn't resist."

"I can see why." Turning to Adam, he asked, "Perhaps we should reconsider going into the shoe business and forget jewelry?"

"Can't do that, Dad. Mom will never forgive us, especially when she thinks Davey will model every creation." Reluctantly, Morty agreed and lifted his empty glass.

"Time for a refill, kids. Let me buy the first round." He elbowed his son and addressed Kelly. "What's your pleasure?"

"A glass of cabernet, please."

"Prefer any particular one?"

"I think I'll rely on your expertise, Mr. Cohen."

"You are a trusting soul, my love," laughed Adam.

"And for you?"

"The same. Thanks, Dad."

"Pour me another one, too, Morty. God knows I need it," complained Freida as she and Davey joined the group. "Hanukkah Sameach, Adam! So nice of you to arrive *almost* on time." Freida took a sip of wine before adding, "Hello to you, too, Kelly."

"Hello. Hanukkah Sameach." Kelly hesitated to say anything more than the simple greeting but could not resist reaching out to pet Davey, once again wearing his matching blue yarmulke and bowtie set.

"Mame, we are actually a little bit early," offered Adam as he, too, greeted Davey.

"Not according to my watch, Adam, but you are here, and that is all that matters to me, except for one other thing." Freida turned to Kelly and cautioned, "You must stay close to us tonight, Kelly. We can't have you doing something wrong in front of this group since you're a Gentile."

Kelly took a long sip of her wine rather than offering a multitude of reckless, sarcastic replies struggling to be released from her mouth. The last thing she wanted was another skirmish with Adam's mother before the celebration had even begun.

"So, Mame, where is Sarah?"

"She went looking for Joel." Turning to speak to Kelly, she continued, "You really should go see the powder room tonight. The vanity sconces are one of a kind!"

"Mmm . . ." *Like I care about vanity sconces.*

"Adam! Adam! Where are you? I know you're here. Come give your Auntie Meshuga a big, wet kiss!"

The familiar voice so startled Freida a stream of wine escaped the rim of her glass. "Oy Gevalt! Who invited her!" Not wanting to attract anyone's attention to the small spill, Freida quickly rubbed her shoe into the carpet to conceal the stain.

"Mame, behave!"

"Adam, who's Auntie Meshuga?" inquired Kelly. "You've never mentioned her."

"Her real name's Ruth. She's Joel and Isaac's aunt on his mother's side."

"We go way back, before Sarah married into this crazy brood," Freida added with contempt.

Ignoring her snide remark, Kelly continued, "If she's from Joel's side of the family, how did your parents know her before Sarah and Joel got married?"

Morty jumped at the opportunity to answer. "Freida and I were living in New York City and Ruth lived across the river in Jersey."

Seeing the confusion on Kelly's face, Adam clarified. "When you're Jewish and you live within ten miles of the New York City Diamond District, everyone knows everyone. Plus, believe it or not, my mom and Auntie Meshuga went to school together in Israel, and Auntie Meshuga stole my mother's boyfriend from her years ago and married him." He turned to address his mother. "So there's no love lost there, is there, Mame." Without waiting for a response, Adam continued. "On what my mother considers the bright side, Kelly, the man died and made Auntie Meshuga a widow." Turning again toward his mom, he said, "I'm sure before this night is over, you'll remind us that Ruth may have gotten your love, but you got the one that lasted."

"What do you mean he was your mother's love? I'm the love of your mother's heart," lamented Morty.

Freida smirked and patted her husband's arm. "Sure you are, dear. Sure you are. And that woman didn't steal him from me. I decided to let her have him."

"Mame, please!" Adam admonished. "Let's not have another battle of the wills."

"Last time I did not battle, Adam. I conquered. I will do the same again and show everyone what a small person she is."

Morty intervened. "Freida, remind me that we need to make an eye appointment for you very soon. There is nothing small about that woman!"

Adam seized hold of Kelly's hand and pivoted to escape hearing any further derogatory comments made by his parents, but it was too late. Auntie Meshuga was slowly hobbling along, supported by Sarah, and heading straight for him.

"Ooh! There he is! What a punim! It's a good thing they're not serving you on a platter, because I would eat you all up by myself!" Auntie wrapped her arms around Adam in a suffocating hug. "How have you been? I have so missed seeing you!" she gushed. "Not to mention those lovely, wavy curls of yours."

"Doin' great, thank you. I've missed you, too, but what happened to you? Why are you wearing a boot?" Auntie Meshuga ignored his question and pulled him close for a second bear hug.

Once released from the garishly affectionate embrace, Auntie Meshuga staggered backward and scrutinized Kelly. "So this is the precious shiksa who has won our Adam's heart after he left Golda and us NYC folk."

"Really? New York City?" Sarah quipped and nudged Kelly. "Our Auntie Meshuga sometimes does stretch the truth a bit."

"Well, I'm actually from Hoboken," continued Auntie Meshuga, "but close enough, right?"

Kelly knew next to nothing about New York geography but nodded in agreement.

"Sarah's been telling me all about you, Kelly. I must say your gain is our loss. Did you know he designed all this lovely jewelry for me when he was just learning the business?" She wiggled her sun-spotted, flawlessly manicured hands that were adorned with multiple gems. "You might as well have won the lottery, girl. He's a real catch!" Seeing that Morty and Freida were quickly approaching, Auntie Meshuga murmured, "Gird your loins, you two. Queen Yenta is approaching." Kelly could see Adam stifle a snicker. "Hello, dear friends! Hanukkah Sameach!"

"Yes, Hanukkah Sameach," Morty began. "It's good to see you, Ruth, but what's with the walking boot? What happened to you?"

"I was—"

"Hanukkah Sameach to you as well," Freida taunted.

"Oh, I'm sorry that the middle of my sentence interrupted the beginning of yours."

"Well, I'm sorry for talking while you're busy trying to interrupt people," Freida fired back.

"Mame, please. Let Auntie Meshuga finish," Sarah cautioned.

"I broke my ankle, had surgery, and was told I would need a couple months to heal. So, I called Isaac to rescue me from the frozen north, and here I am."

Morty looked perplexed. "So, you're staying here with your nephew? Why don't you head to Florida like all the snowbirds?"

"Because Isaac's place is free!" Freida replied with disdain.

"Meh. Can't argue with that."

Freida stared at Ruth in a condescending manner before inquiring, "So basically, you invited yourself? Isn't that asking a lot of Isaac and Leah to care for you while you're recuperating?"

"Let me clarify," responded Ruth. "I brought my own help."

"Sure you did," murmured Freida. "You are so full of schmegegge!"

"I did! And she is standing directly behind you!"

The group watched as Freida spun around, shrieked, and enveloped the unidentified helpmate in her arms. Kelly had never seen Freida so jubilant. Turning toward Adam, she expected him to mirror the same happiness. Instead he stood frozen, staring at the embracing duo. Kelly grabbed his hand and whispered, "Are you okay?"

"No. No I'm not," Adam huffed. "This is Golda." Kelly's heart sank.

Releasing the petite brunette from the overly affectionate greeting, Freida gushed, "This is just the best surprise ever! And to think Isaac and Leah invited you to this party!"

"Oh, no," corrected Golda. "I'm staying here with Auntie Meshuga."

"No matter," enthused Freida. "At least now there's finally something good about you coming here, Ruth. Or should I say someone. Thank you for bringing Golda to Georgia!"

Golda beamed. "The timing couldn't have been better for me since I'm in between jobs and don't have to hurry back. Plus," she added, with color rising in her cheeks, "I thought it would be nice to say hi to Adam."

Golda's heartfelt disclosure unleashed a deafening silence until Freida urged, "Adam. Aren't you going to say anything?"

Adam momentarily flashed a disgruntled expression toward his mother before responding. "Hello, Golda. You're looking well."

"Isn't she though," gushed Freida.

"And I'm Kelly." Kelly extended her arm and was the recipient of a very sweaty palm with a knuckle grinder of a handshake, causing her hand to cramp. When massaging it provided no relief, she handed her drink to Adam and commented, "Freida, I think I'll take your earlier suggestion and check out those vanity sconces you mentioned. Excuse me, please."

Freida was all smiles. "Down the hall, and it's the last door on the right. No need to hurry back."

Kelly locked the bathroom door, turned on the cold water, and submerged her throbbing fingers. *No wonder Freida's ecstatic! Golda's her number-one choice!* A heavy feeling moved from deep within Kelly's stomach to her chest. Her heart began to race and suddenly the room seemed void of oxygen. She quickly dried her hands. Waves of laughter rolled toward her through the hallway as she scurried to rejoin the group, which now included Isaac's wife, Leah.

As Kelly took her drink back from Adam, she broke into the conversation. "You must be Leah. It's very nice to meet you."

"Nice to meet you too. I'm sorry I didn't greet you at the door. I was busy with the children."

"You have such a beautiful home," Kelly admired. "Thanks for having us here tonight."

"We're glad you all could come."

"Leah," Freida broke in, "I just had a great idea! Why don't you take Kelly out on your back deck to see the beautiful view you have here."

"Sure. I'd love to, but I just need to check on something fir—"

Kelly cut in with a comment for Freida. "I thought you wanted me to stay close tonight."

"Nonsense! It won't take long. The rest of us have seen it. You're the only new one here."

"You're so busy being a wonderful hostess. I'll take her," offered Sarah.

Adam grabbed hold of Kelly's hand. "Why don't I take you, Kelly."

"No, you won't," Freida countered.

"What? Why not?"

"Because you must discuss this jewelry business venture with your father."

"Really, Mame? Right now? Tonight?"

"Yes, tonight," lectured Freida as she forcefully nudged her husband into agreement. "It cannot wait, as we may find suitable investors here."

Kelly squeezed Adam's hand. "Hey, business is business. We won't be gone long." Leah moved on to her hosting duties while Kelly followed Sarah onto the back deck.

"Nice view, huh?" asked Sarah.

"It's beautiful," Kelly agreed as she leaned against the deck's railing.

Sarah put her hand on Kelly's. "You know, Kelly, I believe my mom means well, in her own way, but Freida just has to be Freida."

Kelly replied, "I agree. Just wish she was more open-minded." Seeing Sarah's face, she probed, "What is it? Did I say something wrong?"

"Not at all. It's just that I overheard a discussion the other day between my parents, but I'm just not sure I should say anything."

"What kind of discussion?"

"A surprising one for me."

"Really? Well, now I need to know."

"All right," Sarah conceded. "I was on my way into the kitchen when I heard my mom say, 'You know, Morty, maybe it's time we have her to our place alone. We can teach her all the ways of our faith and how to do things correctly. Of course, it'll take a lot of hard work and time. A lot. Unless, of course, something else happens.' They stopped talking when they saw me. I never got the chance to reopen the discussion, but since we'd just been talking about you celebrating Hanukkah with us, they must have been talking about you!"

Kelly's eyebrows lifted high. "Sarah, did I hear you right? Are you sure they were talking about me?"

"I can't think of a reason that it could be someone else."

Joy flashed through her like a lightning bolt. "Oh, Sarah! This is so wonderful! Thank you!" Kelly threw her arms around the bearer of great news before adding, "I have to go!"

Kelly could not wait to share this encouraging news with the love of her life. *There is hope for a bird and a fish! Thank you, God—and thank you, Sarah, for sharing the conversation you overheard! Not sure if it was about me, but I can hope.*

Bursting through the French doors, she scrutinized the room. *Where is he?* She methodically scanned the area for her soul mate. A beaming Morty, with a forbidden cigar in hand, was her first find. Not far from him stood Freida, wearing an even grander smile than when she first saw Golda. *They look so happy. I've never seen both Mr. Cohen and Mrs. Cohen look like that at the same time! They must have changed their minds. They must have finally realized that a bird and a fish can live together . . . huh? They're both looking in the same direction with those huge smiles. What are they looking at? This is just so—so—What? WHAT? Wait a minute.*

There, huddled in the corner, were Adam and Golda having what appeared to be a great time—as he leaned forward and kissed his ex on her cheek. *What the hell? He just kissed her! Now she's kissing him even longer and she's pushing herself into him! His ex! HIS EX! What the hell is going on here? Has Adam been playing me? Have I frickin' wasted my time in yet another relationship? Adam, how could you do this to me? I trusted you!* Her face turned a deep red. It took every ounce of her being to keep any tears from falling. *I will not be made a fool! I can't believe this nightmare is happening to me! AGAIN!*

Her eyes widened as the terrible realization overwhelmed her. She continued to stare at them in disbelief. Hopelessness invaded every muscle as her world spun out of control. The doubts she'd had for a beautiful future flashed before her, making her want to run and keep running. She turned to escape but was frozen. *I've got to cut my losses and get out of here. I'm not sticking around for the rest of it!* It was then she felt the warmth of his hand on her shoulder.

"Hey! Glad you're back. I need you." Adam took her hand in his, strolled back to the center of the room, picked up a spoon from the Hanukkah-themed table, and tapped a glass to obtain everyone's attention.

Once the conversations in the room ceased, he began, "Hanukkah Sameach, dear family and friends. I'm so thankful we can all gather together this evening. I would especially like to thank Isaac and Leah for their hospitality." The jubilant crowd applauded and Adam paused as he surveyed the room. "This has been a wonderfully memorable year for so many of us, especially for Kelly and me."

Turning back to Kelly, he continued, "I just want to finish this year off in the best way possible and start the new year in the same way, so, that being said . . ." Adam dropped to one knee. A cyclone of gasps swirled through the room as each guest vied for a better vantage point. "My sweet Kelly, my duvshanit, love of my life . . . Will you—"

Wait . . . What? Kelly's face epitomized shock. *You are kneeling but you were just kissing your ex. Minutes ago you were huddled in the corner with Golda, but now you're down on one knee? Sarah said your parents were going to welcome me to the family, but . . .* Her eyes lined up with Freida's crazed glare. *You! YOU! What is your problem with fins and feathers?* She shook her head and tried to make the dark spots forming in front of her disappear. *I love you, Adam, but how can we build a future together with your mother's unforgiving judgment plaguing us all the time? Plus, you seem to still have feelings for this Golda woman. I can't make sense of this! I just can't!* Kelly forcefully shook her hands from Adam's loving grasp and turned to run, stumbling past the gawkers watching her race to escape.

"Kelly! Wait! *Wait!*"

Wait? I can't! I just can't! None of this makes sense! Kicking her shoes off and grabbing them so as not to trip again, Kelly fled into the darkness. Her feet burst into flames as she pounded the pavement, never looking back to discern if she was being pursued. When it became impossible to catch her breath, she found refuge behind what appeared to be the neighborhood pool house. She bent forward and took several deep breaths. The rhythmic throbbing of her feet brought a sudden realization. *Crap! How am I going to get home? I don't even have a car! Oh my God, I can't believe this is happening to me all over again! I swear, they're just all born cheaters.* She collapsed onto the swath of dormant

Bermuda grass. *Think, girl, think . . . hmm . . . no way to pay. Okay. Call Sully or . . . ooh! I can call my roomies! Thank God they're at some bar up here.*

Grabbing her phone from her tightly clutched evening bag, she called Melissa. It rang multiple times before her roommate answered. "Hey, girl. Tell us you have some exciting news!"

"Exciting, yes. Good, no." Kelly hesitated so as to choose her words carefully. "Tonight was not 'the night.' In fact, probably won't ever have 'the night.' We're breaking up. I just need a ride home."

"*What?*"

Battling the urge to cry, Kelly snapped, "You heard me, Melissa. I just need you and your sisters to come pick me up, please." There was no response. Heartbreak penetrated the silent moment as tears streamed down her cheeks. In a much softer tone, she pleaded, "I need a ride, Melissa. I just . . . p-please." She sniffled. "You girls still up at the bar on the lake?"

"Yeah, we're here. We'll come get you. No worries. Do you know where you are?"

Not seeing any street sign, Kelly groaned. "No."

"Hey, don't worry. I'm sure Jenn's got that tech stuff that can find you. We'll come get you, Kelly, but . . . but, are you okay?"

There it was. The first of what Kelly thought would be probing questions that she had no desire to answer. "No . . . No, I'm not . . ." She punched the End Call button.

Kelly tugged at her form-fitting dress, trying to get comfortable while sitting on the grass. The minutes dragged on and she began to shiver as she massaged her hurting feet. She had almost given up hope of her roommates ever finding her when she finally saw headlights.

As she put on her shoes and slid into the front seat, she quietly confessed, "I just want you to know I'm not up for any discussion other than to say that I really appreciate you coming to give me a ride home and that I'm truly sorry I spoiled your evening."

"You didn't spoil anything," offered Melissa.

"No big deal," added Ashley.

But to Kelly, it was a big deal. Magical New Year's Eve, the night she thought would be a celebratory event like none other. *And just like that, the clock will strike midnight and I will have nothing to celebrate. Once again. Tonight is just a mirror of all the chances I've ever lost in the reflection of my life. Oy.*

Chapter

ADAM

Adam rolled his chair back from the bench and briefly closed his eyes as the Swiss chalet cuckoo clock warbled a single irritating chirp. Ever since the New Year's Eve debacle, insomnia had been his constant companion. *Only four hours to go.* Lifting the loupe to his face, he firmly pressed his thumb against his cheek and positioned the glass squarely over his eye. He leaned his elbow on the table, hoping to steady the loupe's position as he gazed at his jeweled creation. The three-carat ideal-cut diamond had full frontal sparkle. It was a simple, yet elegant, four-prong platinum mounting that went against his regular sensibilities, but he wanted only the very best for Kelly.

"Hey, I thought you'd have that put away in the safe by now," probed Sam as he set the brown paper bag on an adjacent bureau. When Adam didn't acknowledge his return, Sam continued, "Look what I brought. Just what the doctor ordered, and honestly, it always works for me."

"Really?" Adam smiled mirthlessly as he released the loupe and set Kelly's engagement ring on the polishing cloth. "If it's that goat yoga gift certificate your sister gave you for your birthday last week, nice try, but I'm not interested."

"That's your best guess?" Sam retrieved the deli cartons from the sack and set the containers in front of his friend. "Come on. Try again."

Adam grumbled, "I'm guessing you're a good friend who is trying to cheer me up, but there's nothing you can do about this. By my calculation, I've already moved through denial, anger, and bargaining. I'm in the middle of depression and I plan to stay here. And definitely not moving on to the last stage of acceptance. I will *never* accept that Kelly and I are over!"

Attempting to lighten the moment, Sam retorted, "I just wanted to know if you'd guess I went to Meemaw's Deli for her Jewish chicken soup. It's guaranteed to be good for anything that ails you."

"Thanks, Sam. You're a good friend, but I'm just not hungry. You go ahead."

"You sure?"

Adam nodded and once again picked up Kelly's ring to admire it. He had devoted many hours to creating that beautiful symbol of his commitment. Now the ring would need to be packed away. As he slowly placed it atop the classic blue velvet ring box, he continued to admire its brilliance.

Sam set his plastic soup spoon down. "You're missing out, Adam. Nobody makes matzo balls like Meemaw."

"Really? Meemaw's Deli? That name alone proves it can't be kosher."

"Hey, Meemaw is just flaunting her Southern hospitality. My bubbe can't make matzo balls as good as these."

Never taking his eyes from the treasured piece, Adam muttered, "Hmph. Mushy cracker balls."

"What?"

"I said mushy cracker balls. That's what Kelly used to call them."

"No matter what they're called, Adam, Meemaw's are delicious. Anyway, enough about soup. What's still on the to-do list?" Eyeing the other ring on the workbench, Sam asked, "Have you finished repairing Mrs. Goldstein's ring yet?"

"No."

"Have you started?"

"No."

"Want me to take care of that repair?"

"No."

"You sure? I do know how to repair a broken claw."

Adam walloped the workbench and snapped, "I know you can do the repair!" Immediately he regretted the impulsive whack, as both rings were airborne and subsequently rolled out of sight. After a serious ten-minute search-and-rescue mission, the men had not only retrieved the precious jewelry but also regained their temperaments. "Hey, I'm sorry, Sam. Never should have exploded like that or given you the impression you don't do good work."

"Apology accepted. I owe you one, too. Never should have pressed you about Mrs. Goldstein's repair. I know you two have a special connection, and of course you would want to be the one to follow the transaction through to completion."

For the first time that day, Adam genuinely smiled. "Yeah, we go way back. Mrs. Goldstein has brought us a whole lot of business, and she's actually the one responsible for me meeting Kelly."

"I know. I remember her coming into the store with Bo. I also have *not* forgotten the diamond disaster I caused. You know, I don't think you ever chewed me out for that."

"How could I? Your blunder led to a second vet appointment and cleared the way for a date with Kelly."

The door sensor interrupted the flashback and Sam peered through the one-way mirrored glass. "Hey, it's your sister."

"Really?" scowled Adam. "What is she doing here?"

"I'm no Sherlock Holmes, but obviously it's not to see me."

"Well, I don't want to talk with her."

"Well, I don't think you have a choice cuz here she is."

Sarah flung open the door and strode into the workroom. "Good afternoon, baby brother." Her words were tinged with a trace of frustration.

"Hello, Sarah. Don't you think you should knock or something?"

"Why? I doubt you would answer the door and let me enter." Her face reddened when she realized they were not alone. "Excuse me, Sam. I didn't realize you were here. I just need to speak with my brother . . . *alone.*"

Ignoring the penetrating stare from his coworker, Sam grabbed the paper towels and glass cleaner. "There's nothing I love more than battling fingerprints on glass display cases, so I'll be on my way. Nice to see you, Sarah."

She nodded in response, and once she was alone with her brother, her tone softened. "So. You're not answering my phone calls or messages." Adam met her persistent gaze but did not answer. "Are you going to tell me what's been happening since New Year's Eve?"

Adam leaned forward, putting his head into his hands, and massaged his temples. He had replayed the past few days over and over again as his brain tried to make sense of the ordeal. The whole thing made him sick to his stomach. "I don't know what to say, Sarah. I still haven't had the chance to speak with Kelly, so I still have no clue why she ran or what she's thinking or anything at all. It's driving me crazy. If I knew what it was, I could at least try to fix it, but I don't even have that!"

"So all you did was call?"

"No! Of course not!" Adam paced back and forth. "I went back to her place multiple times and knocked on her door, but no one answered. The last time I went, I pounded on her door until her new neighbor, who happens to be a police officer, threatened me with a disorderly conduct charge, so I left."

"Left? You left? Unbelievable . . ."

"Yeah. I went home. No different than when you ditched Joel one summer night."

"Hey, we're not talking about me, Adam." Sarah's retort mirrored his defensiveness. "And you didn't make any phone calls to anyone else?"

"Of course I did. And I bet I've left her hundreds of voicemails and texts as well."

"Who are the other people you called?"

"I've called her roommates, her Aunt Julie and Uncle Mike, Sully at the vet office, her friend Charlotte . . . I even talked with Father Charles at her parish."

"Well, what did they tell you?"

"They all said the same thing verbatim. 'I'll tell her you called.'"

"That's it?" He quickly looked away from his inquisitive sister. He was tired of reliving the debacle and wished she had never stopped to see him.

"I'm so sorry, Adam. I didn't mean to be so pushy." *Yeah, right. You ARE our mother's daughter.* "How are you doing?"

Adam's eyes narrowed until they were almost closed.

"How do you think I'm doing? Pick a word: miserable, heartbroken, depressed, devastated, rejected, hopeless . . . I really am one lost soul without her, and no matter how often I tell myself that this will all work out, I'm cynical."

Sarah shook her head. "You need to stay optimistic, little brother. Why not come over to our house tonight for dinner and a movie? Joel's been waiting to watch some spy thriller, and I know he'd be glad to see you."

"Ah, I don't think so. Dinner and a movie sound great, but the last thing I need is to be coerced by our mom to find a really nice *Jewish* girl. I've already listened to her voicemail rants and can't take any more of it."

"Well, you won't have to bite that bullet. I just finished dropping the snowbirds off at the airport for their three o'clock flight. *Please* come over, Adam. Besides, the kids would love to see you."

After not really eating the past three days, Sarah's cooking did sound enticing. "All right. I'll be there. What time's dinner?"

"Six o'clock sharp, of course." Sarah laughed and gave him a sisterly hug. "And Adam," she winced, "make time for a shower before you come over. You stink."

"Gee, thanks."

"Better me than your nine-year-old niece who always speaks her mind," Sarah taunted. "See you at six."

Adam returned to his ergonomic stool. *So I stink, huh? Not as much as this breakup does.*

"Glad to hear you're going to your sister's, my friend," offered Sam as he returned to get more paper towels. "It'll do you good to see somebody other than Bo."

Adam shrugged off Sam's comment and picked up Kelly's engagement ring. "I guess it's time I put this away in the vault. No need to keep carrying it around until I know I'm going to be seeing her." He carefully inserted the ring with the polished gem alongside the channel-set eternity wedding band, clicked the velvet box closed, and placed it on the vault's top shelf. He guided the heavy door to a closed position and vigorously spun the dial in both directions. After checking the security multiple times, he whispered, "Pure love from first sight until the fading light of last sight."

"What'd you just whisper?" asked Sam. "I didn't catch it."

Adam smiled. "I tell you what, Sam. You fix that broken claw and then read the notes on Mrs. Goldstein's customer card. I wrote that quote down the day she gave me Bo." Grabbing his jacket that was draped over the back of his work stool, he added, "I'm heading out early. If you need anything, just call my cell."

"Sure thing, Adam. Hope you have a good time tonight."

"Thanks."

Adam darted to the Yafah LX, trying to dodge the unwelcome rainy weather. Ordinarily, he'd appreciate these conditions because they'd provide an ideal time to cuddle up with Kelly and watch one of their favorite movies, but today it just made him feel more depressed. Once inside the coupe, he sat for a moment and opened his cell phone. All day long he had checked for a call or a text. *Still no response, from Kelly or anyone. Why?*

He tapped the camera icon and scrolled to his favorite image. It wasn't the most flattering photo ever taken, but it held the magic of love and laughter they'd shared many times. He longed for one more chance to tell her in person how special she was to him and how he yearned to build a life together with her. Tossing his phone onto the seat, he started the engine and forged ahead, weaving in and out of traffic, never considering his reckless maneuvers on the wet pavement. Adam definitely felt out of whack. He had taken care of Kelly and she had taken care of him. There was forgiveness, sacrifice, and a deep perception of security between them, and now that appeared to be gone. As he pulled into his townhome's garage, lightning and thunder blasted forth from the skies. *Thank goodness Bo is fearless and will go on demand.* Adam had to laugh. He opened the door and there was his shimmying pal, with his tail wagging at supersonic speed. *Well, at least YOU still love me.*

Bo bounded forth. "Happy to see you too." Adam half-smiled as his four-legged roommate danced around him. "Now, go potty!" A cloud-to-ground lightning flash stopped Bo in his tracks. "I'm not kidding, buddy. You've gotta go." Reluctantly, Bo hung his head and took off for his favorite tree. He returned in record time. "You're fast. I'd be soaked to the bone if I were you," muttered Adam, grabbing the towel he kept in the garage for just such occasions. After ruffling up the curly coat and wiping Bo's paws, Adam suggested they go inside. "Let's go play hidden treasure. What do you say?" Bo immediately headed toward the door. "That's my boy."

After a marathon of games, and consuming an unending stream of mini-bite treats, Bo ran to the bedroom, jumped onto the bed, and curled up nose to tail. "Guess you've had enough fun for today, huh?" When Bo didn't move, Adam added, "Good. Glad at least one of us is content. I'll be in the shower if you need me."

Half an hour later, Adam reentered the bedroom to find Bo sound asleep. *Hate to wake you, buddy, but you need to go out one more time before I head out.* He tapped the hind end of the fluff ball, and in a low voice, encouraged his companion to leave the comfort of the bed. Bo opened one eye, giving his master a questioning glare, followed by a healthy dose of canine flatulence.

"Good grief, Bo! Never should have given you so many treats. You need to get outside. Let's go!" But Bo never stirred. "Come on, Bo. If Kelly was here, you'd have obeyed and already finished." Almost immediately the beloved pooch jumped to the floor and headed down the hallway. *Unbelievable. Just saying her name makes my life easier . . .*

Once Bo was back inside, Adam got into the Yafah LX and headed out to his sister's. While he wasn't especially eager to be going there, Joel and his dry sense of humor could provide a welcome diversion. Plus the thought of having a decent meal was appealing. *Brisket, latkes, roasted potatoes, fresh-baked challah . . . That does sound good. Probably shouldn't be coming empty-handed, though.* Adam made a quick left turn, pulled into the corner mart for purchases, and then finished the ten-minute drive. Armed with two bottles of cabernet and a bouquet of alstroemeria, he rang the doorbell.

Sarah opened the door. "Well, look who's here. Glad to see you didn't renege."

"Renege? How could I possibly resist a home-cooked meal? What are we having anyway? Brisket? Latkes? Can't be latkes. I don't smell any oil."

"Pizza! We're having pizza!" Esther cheered as she bounded into the foyer. "Isn't that great, Uncle Adam? Mommy said we can have pizza cuz it's a special night since you're here!"

Not wanting to shatter his niece's exuberance, Adam leaned toward Sarah and whispered, "Really? No meat and potatoes? I could have stayed home and popped a frozen one in the toaster oven."

Sarah rolled her neck from side to side to loosen some kinks. "I've spent more than a week catering to our mother's preferential cuisine and kosher kitchen obsessiveness. I deserve a night free from critique and I'm taking it."

For the first time Adam noticed his sister's haggard appearance. "Okay. I get it. Pizza it is," and the threesome headed into the kitchen. "Want me to uncork that wine?" he asked.

"If I can find the corkscrew. Mame rearranged my utensil drawers, so it may take some digging. Never mind. Here it is."

Adam leaned against the wall. "So, what kind of pizza are we making?"

"We're not. Joel ordered from The Pizza Deli. It's that new place off Roswell Road," Sarah explained as she set two wineglasses onto the counter.

"Hmmm. Haven't heard of it." Adam cut the foil below the lower lip of the bottle and inserted the screw into the center of the cork.

"He's been on a soy protein kick, so I guess we'll just wait to be surprised." The doorbell chimed and Esther darted out of the room. "That must be the delivery. Guess we won't have to wait long till we know."

Adam poured the cabernet and handed a glass to his sister. "I would like to propose a toast."

"All right," Sarah agreed as she raised her glass. "To what shall we toast?"

"To peace, and to quiet, and . . . to the two people who have left, creating that peace and quiet!" Adam proclaimed.

They clinked glasses. "Love it!" Sarah professed. "I love them dearly but, boy, are they a challenge sometimes."

After two sips, Adam placed the glass on the counter

and held the base down with his index and middle finger. He started moving the glass around in circles, watching the dark ruby liquid swirl.

"So, Sarah . . . What should I do?" A look of bewilderment crept across his sister's face. "Come on, sis! You must have some kind of suggestion to help me?"

"Who needs help?" questioned the overly concerned Freida as she burst into the room. Seeing Adam, she exclaimed, "Adam, honey! I will help you, my beautiful son! My health has barely held on with all my worrying about you." She threw her arms around her baby, who was frozen in place and feeling as frosty as a pint of ice cream in a freezer. Stepping back from her son, she kvetched, "What? You're not happy to see the woman who gave you life? What's wrong with you?"

Sarah shook her head. "Mother. Enough. Leave the man alone."

Freida shot a hurt look at her son. "I'm sorry, but I will not be sorry for being honest."

"And so it begins," Sarah whispered to Adam as she walked to the cupboard to get two additional wineglasses. "Well, welcome back. But why aren't you on your flight? I dropped you off at the airport with time to spare. What happened?"

Freida quickly placed her hand over Morty's lips. "No need to elaborate. These things happen. Besides, now we can help our favorite son."

Adam shook his head. "Mame, I am your *only* son."

"Yes," she declared, "and our favorite."

The doorbell's chime cut through the room's tension.

"Pizza! Pizza!" squealed Esther as she disappeared.

Sarah filled the glasses and handed them to her parents. "And there were no other flights today?"

Freida shrugged. "Meh."

"Of course there were other flights," Morty interjected, "but I could not convince your mother to leave. She has been kvetching every minute, fearing the worst has happened to our son. She doesn't realize that times have changed."

Freida's eyes widened. "Morty, the worst *has* happened. He did not follow the advice from the shadchan and his wife, and took up with a shiksa instead! There were so many problems with her, and then she tossed him away like he's nothing. Our son. She did that to him. And still somehow he is holding on to her," Freida gibed. "It is painful to watch such a thing, and now I have to accept how times are changing?"

"You don't need to accept anything, Mame," Adam countered.

"You're wrong, my son," Freida scoffed. "You should marry a nice Jewish girl, like Golda, so none of this would happen. But instead, you are still chasing this girl from another faith, with all these problems, and without our blessing. That, my son, is wrong."

Adam wanted to hurl the wineglass across the kitchen. Looking directly into his mother's eyes, he fought to keep his composure. "I love her, Mame. I would certainly love to have your blessing, but I do not *need* your blessing to marry her." He set his glass on the counter and headed toward the door. "Your rules are strangling my heart. Kelly makes me want to live out loud, live freely to be the best version of me, not what some rules dictate. I love our faith, Mame. I really do. But sometimes love is stronger than rules! Haven't you ever wanted to just follow your heart's desire? Even just once?" He left the room.

Freida turned to follow, but Morty firmly grasped her

hand. "You must remember, my dear wife. My parents did not approve of you or offer us their blessing, and yet, here we are. I believe Joel, with his rabbi's wisdom, said it best. 'With so many against us, we should be absolutely thrilled when there is one who wishes to join us.'" Letting go of Freida's hand, Morty tried to catch up to Adam, but he was already outside, with his cell phone to his ear.

"Hi Jenn." Adam spent the next hour in deep conversation.

Chapter 18

KELLY

Kelly was already awake and stroking Mr. Shrimp's chin. Although she was miserable, he seemed quite content to receive her extra attention. Kelly was in her fifth day of limbo trying to navigate her way through the tempest of her feelings.

"Mew," Mr. Shrimp whimpered as he stood up and brushed himself against her. He had to remind her to continue his massage when the rubbing stopped due to her distracted thoughts. She realized she was squinting as if this would help her see the answers more clearly. The cat stretched and lazily plopped himself back down next to his owner once the massage continued.

Today, like the day before, found Kelly in a fog-filled void of feelings, simply wondering what to do next. She had been in so many wasted relationships. There had been supposedly noncommittal Joey who was then suddenly married to his achondroplasiaphobic lover. After him, there had been a revolving door of guys who played chess with her heart and left her losing to checkmate each time. Kelly regretted ignoring telltale warnings and investing her time and energy on these past relationships that had gone nowhere. It was finally okay, though, because she had her faith, which told her to believe that God had a reason for everything and everyone in life. She believed everyone was exactly where and when they needed to be on their journey. These beliefs worked for her, and they kept her devoutly strong. Then God had brought her Adam. He was the one, her ride or die, the God-sent owner of her heart. He had even been about to propose!

Kelly's thoughts scrambled. She couldn't unsee what she had seen. She couldn't undo what she had done in reaction to that sight.

These memories were followed by the constant repetition of Jenn's words the last few days: "But how is it fair to Adam for you to judge him, based on past boyfriends, without even asking for an explanation of his actions? You have to take his call. He deserves that much." The words haunted her over and over again.

Damn it! I really wasn't fair. I just automatically thought the worst. And I ran. And I did it to him in front of everyone. I let my past experiences be the judge and jury. Of course, the stress of his mother didn't help any. Kelly let out a heavy sigh. *So what's the plan for a do-over? I have to let him explain things at the very least.* She tapped her fingers on her pillow. *Ugh! Where's that open window, Lord, when the door closes?*

Jenn burst into the room. "Yeah, I'm not apologizing for not knocking. Oh wow. It's dead in here. You should open a window and get some fresh air."

Kelly began, "I—"

"Save it, whatever it is, because I have some interesting information for you!" Jenn opened the bedroom window. "So the three of us were talking last night and we decided we really like Adam and he deserves a chance to explain himself."

"Yep. I agree. I realize that now," Kelly replied. "I'm just not sure how—"

"Doesn't matter. We decided to represent you and I took one for the team," Jenn explained.

"Took one for the team?"

"Yeah. I called Adam and talked with him for a long time and told him I'd pass his explanation on to you. That was after I told him why you ran and why you're ghosting him. So here's the tea on the whole situation."

"I can't believe you—"

"Well, I did. So here's what he said."

"But . . ."

"Yeah, about those buts—don't be a butthead. Listen, learn, and you can shower the three of us with gratitude later. So it turns out Adam's mother was indeed trying to push that Golda woman and Adam back together again, although Adam and his father had no interest in that happening. You're his one and only, girl! Now when you walked into the room, you saw Adam giving Golda a kiss. But it was a quick goodbye and good luck kiss! He apparently gushed and gushed about you to her and then shared how he was about to propose to you. Golda congratulated him and then gave him a kiss back. I asked him why, then, were you under the impression that it was a long kiss? He told me he found out later that Golda made it longer to make sure there was nothing left between them, a last-ditch attempt. He said it was a kiss that turned very awkward. So he pulled away, saw you, and decided to make his statement to everyone, his mother and Golda included, by proposing to you at that very moment. Girl, he's a keeper and is head over heels for you."

"But his parents were watching and smiling like they knew about something going on between them. Plus I ran out on him."

"They knew nothing at all! They made the same mistake you made. Mrs. Cohen does like Golda a lot and thought something was being rekindled, and Mr. Cohen just thought his son was getting lucky double time. You know, the whole playah thing. Adam cleared up everything with them after the whole incident. He looked and looked for you and finally came back to the party to say his goodbyes and try to figure out what happened. Then they asked him to stay at least until midnight to ring in the new year. He flat out said there could be no new year, or anything, for him without you. I'm telling you, Kelly. Grab that man and keep him! You can figure out the rest later. He doesn't care that you ran. He just wants you back."

"But I embarrassed him in front of the whole crowd, and I refused to talk to him for days on top of that."

"Doesn't care."

"But his mother doesn't even—"

"Doesn't matter."

"Did he—"

"Shut up and call him already! Your besties did the heavy work for you."

"Yeah, call him already! We're getting stiff necks out here listening from the hallway," Ashley interrupted.

"Plus, we do love a good ending! Don't forget that," Melissa commented as the two joined their sister in the bedroom. "Ooh. I love the fresh air. Your room is much better now."

"Thank you, guys! I don't know what I'd do without the three of you."

"Not much apparently," Ashley shot back. "Just kidding. We love you. You know that."

"That's right," Melissa added. "Go for the joke and apologize later."

"C'mon, ladies. Let's get out of here so she can call." Jenn herded her sisters out into the kitchen so Kelly could begin to save her relationship.

Kelly turned her cell phone over and over again while considering what she would say, then placed the call to her beloved. Adam answered almost immediately. Her pulse quickened at the sound of his voice. What had she been thinking to run out on the man she loved with every inch of her being?

The couple stumbled over their words as they rushed to explain themselves to each other. The conversation flowed for well over an hour as they discussed their missteps, apprehensions, and future challenges with a familiar balance of humor and seriousness. They were in sync once more, learning from their recent trouble and vowing to never let negative assumptions go unchecked between them again.

"So let's just pretend that evening never happened and we can pick up where we left off," Adam suggested. He sighed. "You don't know how completely happy you've made me, my dear sweet duvshanit. I am so glad we're together again. Any issues, just tell me. Anything you want, just ask."

That's it! The idea struck Kelly the moment she heard the words. *We can pick up where we left off . . . just tell me . . . just ask.* Her plan picked up speed and grew as soon as it was born. "Hey, babe, I'd love to talk some more, but I have to get going. I have a ton to do today and tomorrow. Tell you what. Tomorrow night, why don't you wear something nice, pick me up at the clinic at six thirty, and we'll go out for a fancy celebratory dinner? Okay? Oh! And it's perfect. It'll be Epiphany! So it'll be our very own Little Christmas, literally. We can give ourselves the gift of being together again!"

"I'm in! Like I said, just ask. I love you so much, Kelly. Can't wait to hold you in my arms tomorrow night."

"Love you too, babe. Gotta run." The call ended. Kelly suddenly had lots of calls to make and what seemed like a million things to do. She jumped up from her bed, which annoyed Mr. Shrimp enough to make him jump off as well. She explained her plan to the sisters, who excitedly agreed to help in their assigned roles.

"Now you're talking!" Jenn explained. "And, you know, if you want, I know some people who are neighbors with some famous singers, and I could see if we can get someone to do a serenade, or I know someone else who—"

"I know people too. Just because I'm the middle sister doesn't mean I don't know anyone. I mean, they're not celebrities, but I could hook you up with some decent flowers for tomorrow night or a professionally made playlist," Melissa offered.

"Of course. She has to offer because I offered," Jenn countered. "I was just trying to help."

"So was I. We all know people. I'm just saying."

"Ignore those two," Ashley suggested. "However, I think you should ask Sam to hold on to Bo and he can stand next to me while I hold on to Mr. Shrimp. That way the pets are all together."

"Yeah, and that way, you and Sam are together. Don't think we can't see through your idea there, littlest," Jenn bantered while Melissa shook her head and smiled in agreement.

"Hey, you two know all kinds of people, and he just happens to be people I'd like to know," Ashley countered with a clever grin.

Kelly chimed in after the short eruption of laughter. "I didn't know you were interested in him. I love the idea, though, Ashley. I'll ask him. Okay, ladies, I have a few calls to make and then I'll be on my way. Thanks for saving me from myself! C'mon. Group hug." The four gathered and embraced among scattered "love you's."

Kelly placed her first call after the group hug to Adam's coworker and friend, Sam. After a short discussion he agreed to meet her for lunch away from the jewelry store. Next she called Sarah and made arrangements to stop by her place after lunch so she could explain her plans and what she needed from Adam's family. She also asked, if the older Cohens were still in town, that they be included in the afternoon's discussion. Her next call went out to Sully so she could swing by the clinic near closing time to share her agenda in detail with the owner and cherished confidante. Hours later, having met with everyone, Kelly found herself content with the goals she had achieved. That night she slept well knowing that all the pieces to her plan were in place.

Can't wait to be in Adam's arms again. Can't wait to see him. Can't wait to kiss him. Mmm. Feels so good. Kelly and Adam. Adam and Kelly. Kelly . . . Kelly . . .

"Kelly! Wake up! Ah, finally! Melissa is out taking care of her stuff and Ashley and I are heading out to pick up the candles you'll need. The three of us are planning to arrive at the clinic late afternoonish. Need anything else at all?" Jenn asked. "And just so you know, it's midmorning already. So I figured you'd want to get up instead of doing whatever it was you were doing with your lips in your dream."

"What? Lips? Oh. Oh yeah. I'm all set. Thanks for asking. I guess I overslept a little bit. Where's Mr. Shrimp?"

"He left you, my dear. He's stretched out and sunbathing on the windowsill in the living room. I fed him already." Kelly thanked Jenn for taking care of the cat and for waking her up before the sisters left for their errands. She went quickly about her tasks as she washed, dressed, and had a quick coffee and muffin, all while humming her favorite love songs. It was a great day to reconnect with the love of her life, and there was still plenty to do to ensure her surprise was a success. Once she had everything in hand, including her garment and makeup bags, she left the apartment for the clinic, this time with Mr. Shrimp in tow.

"Well, hello there!" Sully greeted Kelly and Mr. Shrimp before unhooking the latch to the carrier so the furry divo could strut out onto the exam table. "Hey there, buddy." She showered the cat with strokes and scratches.

"Happy Epiphany!" Kelly offered. "What a perfect day for a perfect surprise!"

"Everything in place? How are you feeling? Hell of a lot better than the previous few days, huh?"

"Everything's looking great, and I feel amazing now that all's right with the world," Kelly responded with a glow. "Now let's hope Adam likes my surprise tonight."

"How can he not? It involves you," Sully asserted. "Now get me a few treats for our buddy here and let's get on with the plan. This turn of events makes me happier than a tick on a fat dog!"

The older vet returned Mr. Shrimp to the feline's favorite blanket in his carrier and deposited some savory morsels for him to enjoy. The two women went about the next few hours completing all the veterinary tasks Sully had listed for that day. The sisters arrived late in the afternoon as planned and the group happily completed the clinic's charming transition. Kelly and Sully took turns showering and changing in the staff's overnight room while the sisters began placing bowls and trays of appetizers onto counters and converted exam tables.

Kelly could feel her nervousness growing as she returned to the front room. She began to question everything as her mind sprinted through her list of worries. What if Adam didn't like her surprise? What if it all backfired? What if the Cohens changed their minds and embarrassed her in the moment?

"Breathe, girl! I know that face!" Jenn smiled. "Let it go and just enjoy. Live in the moment."

"Mmm. You're right," Kelly agreed.

"Of course I am," the oldest sister quipped. "And here we go. People are arriving!" The two put on their best smiles. The Cohen clan entered the clinic and were greeted by those already there. The children almost immediately began their requests to visit with any animals and were delighted to meet Kelly's pet. Sully offered to give Davey a mild sedative to calm his nerves, but Freida insisted, with her eyes scanning and judging the room, that her Maltese would be just fine.

"Dr. Sully, it's nice to meet you," Morty began. "You know, our family is going to be starting a certain pet business venture, to be disclosed at a later time. As a friend of our growing family, I can cut you in on a share at a great price, and your credentials would be quite helpful in getting it off the ground. We should talk."

"Um. Sure." Sully shook hands with Mr. Cohen.

"Are you of the Jewish faith?" Freida asked bluntly.

"No. No, I'm not," the vet replied.

"Maybe you shouldn't talk later then," Adam's mother directed her comment to her husband.

"Ah. I understand now what Kelly meant when she shared her praises for you," Sully remarked to the older woman. They politely smiled at each other.

Everyone continued to become further acquainted while enjoying the appetizers. The Morins arrived with GG in tow and they were shortly followed by Sam, Adam's coworker, who escorted Bo into the clinic. A cacophony of noises broke out from the clients staying at the clinic, instigated by the initial barking of Bo and Davey. Sully and Kelly went about calming their patients while the two dogs were allowed to sniff and get to know each other. Once Kelly returned, she noticed the shirt on Davey with the comment "Bitches love me."

"Cute shirt!" she grinned. "I like it."

"It was a gift," Freida explained. "I wouldn't buy clothing with that wording. Sarah talked me into having Davey wear it today, and at least the lettering matches the color of his yarmulke."

"Oh, Mom! It's adorable! I'm glad I got it," Sarah defended her purchase.

"Well, it *is* the correct term for female dogs," Kelly observed before leaning to whisper in Sarah's ear. "And I happen to be wearing my shiksa panties for tonight, another purchase of yours." The two giggled.

"Are you two laughing at me?" Freida questioned.

"No, Mame," replied Sarah. "Just, uh, some undercover girl talk." She winked at her cohort while Freida shrugged and left to refill her drink. Kelly loved how her relationship with Sarah was developing. It gave her hope for some form of progress with the older Cohens.

Morty, as if reading her mind, stepped closer to the girls. "Kelly, I just want to say I know your start with us has been a bit bumpy, but give us a chance."

"Mr. Cohen, I feel I have been offering chances all along."

"Yes, that you have. But Freida . . . Mrs. Cohen . . . she pours out all her love for her children and doesn't realize that sometimes it drowns them. She was very satisfied with Joel as Sarah's choice, and the fact that he's a rabbi certainly helped. But, you know, she doesn't do well with new ways and changes. So she'll need more chances. Me, I think you're just fine."

"I am trying, but two things will never change. I'll never be born Jewish and I'll never be Golda."

"That's a good thing! Golda is just like my wife, and we can't have two of them in one family. Oh my heart! I mean, I'll survive with the one I have, but it would kill me to know my son would have to go through the same marriage I have. And I'll tell you another thing. In my whole life, I never saw Adam the way he has been this past week. You are definitely his soul match."

"You mean soul mate," Kelly corrected. Morty shook his head.

"No. Soul match. That's more than a soul mate. It's the person, the soul mate, who not only strikes your heart, but lights your very soul on fire and lets your passion burn. You are Adam's soul match, his eternal flame. And now I'm one hundred percent certain of it."

"Wow," Kelly murmured. "That's sweet. Thank you so much for sharing it with me."

"You're welcome. And you happen to beat Golda any day. So there you have it."

Kelly blushed as Freida returned with a refilled wineglass. "What are we discussing?"

"Just matches and fire, dear," Morty replied. "Matches and fire."

"Are you planning to light more than all these candles you have burning tonight, Kelly?" Freida looked around the room. The young vet connected eyes with Mr. Cohen and the two grinned.

"Actually, yes, I plan to light a lot more beginning tonight."

"Okay, everyone!" Sully interrupted the moment with an urgent announcement. "Time for all of us to head out to the side exam room so Kelly can greet Adam alone. Could everyone please hurry and pick up one or two items and carry them out back?"

The group handily removed all clues from the room and headed through the side door. Freida carried Davey out with her hand covering the part of the graphics on his tee that she disliked. Sam and Ashley shared whispers and laughs while helping each other move Bo and Mr. Shrimp. The door closed. Kelly was not surprised by Mrs. Cohen's attempt to cover the word "bitches" on Davey's tee, but she was very curious as to what was going on between Ashley and Sam. Unfortunately she had no time to find out, seeing as Adam was about to arrive momentarily. She opened the camera on her phone and reversed the angle so she could do a last-minute check on her appearance. She heard a car door close and knew Adam had just arrived in the Yafah LX.

That was close! I should have watched the clock a lot closer. Well, here goes nothing, girl! The door opened and Adam appeared. His very presence made her heart race with anticipation as the current of their connection electrified the room.

"Adam . . . I . . ." Words failed her as he walked closer. "I want . . ." He swept her into his arms and their kiss stole her breath away. His confident hold was familiar and she felt drugged by his scent. She urgently wanted to surrender herself fully to him right there at that moment.

He spoke first. "Hi."

"Hi indeed. I missed you so much."

"I was here all along."

"I know. I just got way into my head with wrong assumptions and let it get the best of me. I'm so sorry."

Adam put his finger up to Kelly's lips. "No sorrys. We're together again. That's all that matters." He kissed Kelly again. "I love you and only you."

"*That's not true!* What about us?" Kelly and Adam turned to see his mother barging through the side door. "Don't you love your family?"

"Freida! She didn't say the code word! You're ruining it!" Morty followed his wife, admonishing her for her premature entrance.

"He's my son and he needs to be corrected. He doesn't love just her. What about his family? Doesn't he love us too?"

"Mame? Tate? What are you doing here?" Adam asked, perplexed.

"Adam, you said you only loved her. You don't love us anymore?" Freida was focused on her one worry at the moment.

"It's a phrase, Mame. Of course I love you too. Now could you please tell me what the two of you are doing here? Is Davey okay?"

"Yes, he's fine. Kelly here is—" Freida began.

"Is taking it from here, Mrs. Cohen. Thanks," Kelly jumped in with confidence and took the lead back. Adam maintained a puzzled expression as Kelly smiled and took a deep breath.

"Adam, *IT'S TIME* to pick up where we left off." She gave the code. The rest of the Cohens filtered out into the room, along with the Morins, Davey, Bo, Mr. Shrimp, Sam, Sully, and Kelly's roommates.

Adam looked back and forth between Kelly and the crowd that was now encircling them.

"Honey, I chose the clinic because that's where our story started, and my intention tonight is to do exactly what you suggested—to pick up where we left off. I believe that was New Year's Eve, and you had a question you were asking me. We just happen to have everyone here because, when we start our life together, we also start it with both our families. I want to do it the right way and include all the love that surrounds us." Kelly motioned for Mr. Shrimp and Ashley brought the feline to Adam. Kelly continued, "I believe Mr. Shrimp has something for you to check out." Adam looked at the cat and saw a cute box attached to his collar. He proceeded to open it, only to find a key.

"A key? You changed your mind and want to live together first?" Adam stated.

"That key unlocks the box that our buddy Bo has for you," Kelly explained. She signaled Sam to bring the goldendoodle forward. Adam rubbed Bo's ears and stroked his coat, then used the key to unlock a pocket-sized box fastened to Bo's collar.

"This is becoming quite intriguing," Adam declared as he removed the lock to open the petite case. The group let out a combined gasp and cheer of encouragement. The box contained the very ring he had planned to place on Kelly's finger at the New Year's Eve party.

"And now I think I've definitely figured out what comes next." Adam beamed. He first turned toward his parents. "Tate? Mame? Are we good?"

Morty smiled. "Baruch. L'chaim. With pleasure."

"Mame?"

Adam's mother let out a dramatic sigh. "As those who know me would attest, I've made many sacrifices in my life without an ounce of kvetching. I am just like the mother of Moses, and I always try to find a way to continue on somehow, because your happiness is clearly more important to me than my own. So . . . oy . . . go ahead. We'll figure it all out," she conceded.

"I'll take it!" Adam exclaimed. He placed one knee on the floor and directed his gaze at Kelly. The crowd whooped, but their cheer fell upon the deaf ears of the two who were transfixed by each other. "Kelly, we met in this very room and our story started here. I don't know what life holds for the two of us together, but I do know it'll be beautiful. Even with our different branches of faith, the tree of life we create will be amazing because your God and my Yahweh are one and the same and our beliefs share the same roots. Plus we happen to have the same wicked sense of humor! These last few days I've learned that I just cannot live without you. So, Kelly Marie Leary, will you honor me by saying yes, and marrying me?"

"Yes, yes, yes," Kelly gushed and Adam slid the ring on her finger. The young couple embraced and kissed each other with a celebratory joy amid applause.

"Woof! Woof!" Bo jumped up, insisting on joining the hug.

"Arf!" Davey struggled to jump down from Freida's arms, until she relented and released him. The Maltese lunged back and forth at the trio, finally allowing the newly engaged couple to pat him.

"I guess our fur family has a lot to say about our engagement," Adam joked as the two barkers began to frolic amid the crowd.

"Well, except for Mr. Shrimp, who I'm sure wants no part of the show with these two right now," Kelly declared as people moved forward to offer their congratulations.

"I guess we'll all be seeing a lot of each other now," Freida mentioned.

"That's great, but why is that?" Adam asked.

"Do you not realize the amount of time it's going to take to train Kelly in running a Jewish home?" Freida replied. "And I'm sure it's going to involve lots of repetition and correction. You're actually very lucky I'm a loving mother who has that kind of patience to give." She hugged her son as Kelly watched Adam roll his eyes with a grin. Mr. Cohen hugged Kelly and congratulated her.

"And now you can join our new family business as our official veteran-genarian. So something good for all of us!"

"Tate! She's a veterinarian," Adam corrected.

"Meh. Close enough," Morty asserted. "Mr. Expensive Shoes with his fancy words. Congratulations to the two of you."

Freida chimed in again. "Yes, congratulations. And so I guess we'll pray for puffins."

Morty looked at his wife. "Be happy for yourself, son. It's too late for me."

Freida shot back with a statement directed at Kelly. "First lesson. Always keep your husband in line, or your Adam will become your Morty. Hmmph." She left in search of Davey while Morty headed in the opposite direction in search of appetizers.

"That's quite the pair," Kelly's Uncle Mike observed. He and Aunt Julie congratulated the newly engaged couple, with GG in tow.

"Very nice. Thanks for including us, honey," GG offered her appreciation. "Love is beautiful. It always has been and always will be."

"Aww, thanks GG," Kelly replied with an added tender hug.

"And I'll be sure to tell your other girlfriend at the nursing home that you're taken now," GG nodded to Adam. "She was really hoping to hook up with you too. Yep. She'll be disappointed."

"Who?" Adam asked.

"Um," Kelly helped, "I think that would be One-Eyed Lookum. Remember?"

"Ohhhh, yes. That's right. Adele." Adam recognized the reference. "Thank you for telling her, GG. You do that." He smiled and humored her, then thanked Kelly's family for joining them.

"Well, well, well, if this isn't the best news in the world today, or of the year, I don't know what else could be," Jenn stated.

"Total agreement on that one," Melissa added. "Unless, of course, you said you had a twin brother for me. That would probably be even better."

"Hey! What about me? I'm older than you, so that gives me first dibs," Jenn reacted.

"Dibs, shmibs. I get the twin because I thought of it first," Melissa argued.

Jenn began, "But—"

"Ladies!" Kelly interrupted. "You're arguing over a hypothetical person who doesn't exist!"

Adam added, "*But*, make it triplets and the other two show up, and I'll hook you both up. Okay?"

"Deal. Oh, definitely a deal," the two sisters spoke at the same time. The foursome laughed and enjoyed a group hug filled with happiness.

"Where's Ashley? I know she's here," Kelly asked.

"Oh, she's a little delayed," Melissa replied and Jenn offered more details.

"Yeah. It seems there's been a whole lot of chemistry going on between her and Sam. She gave him her number."

"Really?" Adam and Kelly smiled.

"Mmhmm," Melissa spoke again. "And I believe he won't wait long before giving her a call. Those two are really hitting it off."

"The way things are going already, the year after your wedding, we'll be going to another one. Just saying!" Jenn offered her opinion.

"You think so?" Melissa pondered. "I don't know. You can never tell with these things. Then again . . . well, okay. Maybe. Or maybe not. Oh, I don't know!" She laughed at herself.

"I have a gut feeling," Jenn stated. "As a matter of fact, I read on the internet that—"

"No!" the group protested in unison.

"No more internet urban legends," Kelly added.

Adam interrupted with an announcement. "Everybody! Could we have everyone's attention, please?" The crowd turned toward the couple being celebrated. "Could everyone please grab a glass of champagne? I'd like to make a toast for us, for Kelly, the lady who just made me the happiest man in the universe, and myself."

Glasses of champagne were handed out to everyone and little bowls of treats were placed on the floor for Mr. Shrimp and the two dogs.

"Thank you, everyone, for sharing in this moment with us, a moment I wasn't even aware was going to take place tonight. Kelly, that's what I love so much about you. You know what I need to do to be happy, even when I'm slow to realize it. And vice versa. Thank you for tonight. I am beyond excited for our future together, and no other words can do justice for this moment that I can think of, except one English word and one simple Jewish phrase."

"Jewish is always perfect for any moment," Freida murmured.

"So please lift your glasses," Adam continued. When all were raised, he and Kelly gazed into each other's eyes and declared in unison before the group, "Godspeed. L'chaim."

The two kissed and Kelly whispered, "And then some."

Acknowledgments

We would first like to thank the following people for their generous wisdom and expertise while helping us to write this story:

Dan Linehan, jeweler extraordinaire who "makes women happy for a living."

Dr. Pam Sullivan, excellent veterinarian and pet whisperer.

Our Jewish friends and fact-checkers, Lynn Kaden and Debbie Smith, as well as JewBelong, which is a wonderful online source for understanding the Hebrew community.

Our beta readers, Jan Delmore, Kathy Odell, Donna St.Cyr, and Diane Bolduc, whose feedback helped to polish this story.

The amazingly talented team at Mountain Arbor Press, as well as Jessica Parker, whose phenomenal wisdom and knowledge of all things books guide us like a master sensei. A mention must be made here as well to acknowledge the people in this world who try to build bridges between all faiths, bringing understanding and showing that the greatest gift that binds us, above all, is love.

Of course, we would like to thank our husbands for always saying "yes, dear" and supporting us in our writing endeavors, making books like this one possible. Lastly, and most importantly, we thank God, who makes all things possible.

About the Authors

Mary Becker is a happy wife, a proud mother of seven, a grandma who lavishly loves her grandchildren, and a lifelong fan of Dr. Seuss. She is also a multi-genre author creating fun, educational books for children and lighthearted romantic comedies for their mothers. When Mary is not typing away at her home in Dawsonville, GA, she enjoys baking cakes (except for the inedible one she once served to company), gardening (when the weeds have already been pulled), and frolicking with her two dogs while watching her cat nap.

Diane St.Cyr Janelle grew up in a family of seven in New Hampshire and always dreamed of becoming both an elementary school teacher and an author. She taught for many years at St. Anthony Elementary School in Manchester, New Hampshire, and now she feels blessed to pursue her passion for writing. She dabbles in all things creative, likes to honor her French and Abenaki ancestries, and thoroughly enjoys her time spent living and laughing with family and friends! Diane currently resides in Exeter, New Hampshire, with her husband Marc and their two children Emilie and Mathieu. She continues to chase her dreams and delights in sharing her humor with others for the joy it brings to life's journey.

Mary and Diane first met as neighbors in Georgia, quickly became good friends, and now enjoy writing together. It's better than therapy!